SUNNYSIDE

A NOVEL

ROB DIRCKS

GOLDFINCH
PUBLISHING

PRAISE FOR SUNNYSIDE AND ROB DIRCKS

"*SUNNYSIDE* takes us to a distant future filled with irony, madcap characters, spaceships, a few bureaucratic conspiracies and an utterly unique voice with a pace and energy that moves at warp-speed." – The Black List

"A cross between Kurt Vonnegut and Douglas Adams, Rob Dircks has written a story with heart and terraforming. I absolutely loved it." – Nora Raleigh Baskin, award winning author of *Anything But Typical* and *Nine,Ten: A September 11 Story*

"Dircks' unflagging ability to imbue plot-crackling science fiction with a deep vein of humor, heart, and hope reminds me of Ray Bradbury... with curses." – Wendy Mass, *New York Times* bestselling author of *Pi in the Sky* and *The Candymakers*.

"There is no one writing sci-fi as well as Rob Dircks right now... It's a sweetness, a love of life and humanity, that shines through all of his characters and all of his imaginary worlds. I feel instantly better when I finish something he has written, I feel uplifted and hopeful. What a wonderful gift Rob has to allow us to see the good in one another, and how lucky we are that he is sharing it with us through his art." – Julie C, via Audible

"Here are some of the benefits of all of Dircks' books: 1. Every book is so full of adventures and comedy they could be movies. Heck, they're the right length. Any producers out there? Make a movie out of these! 2. You can tell Dircks is grounded in a diverse range of sci-fi. He takes the stories of Asimov, Bradbury, and Robinson, and reassembles them in ways that leave me kicking my heels like a giggling kid too short for her tall stool. 3. Dircks speaks from a place of love. It's always there in the books. The sweet kind of love that comes from a happy family, strong friendships, and bonded communities. My biggest complaint is that these novels are short, there are only a handful, and I'm a selfish woman who doesn't understand why Rob Dircks might want to spend a couple of minutes away from his keyboard." – Maisha E., via Audible

"Rob Dircks' fast-paced brand of sci-fi adventure masterfully blends his shrewd wit with an earnest heart that is wickedly appealing." – D. Clark, via Audible

ALSO BY ROB DIRCKS

Where the Hell is Tesla? A Novel

Don't Touch the Blue Stuff! (Where the Hell is Tesla? Book 2)

Gigi Make Paradox (Where the Hell is Tesla? Book 3)

You're Going to Mars!

The Wrong Unit: A Novel

Unleash the Sloth! 75 Ways to Reach Your Maximum Potential By Doing Less

Alphabert! An A-B-C Bedtime Adventure

SUNNY SIDE

ROB DIRCKS

GOLDFINCH PUBLISHING

Published by Goldfinch Publishing
An Imprint of SARK Industries, Inc.
www.goldfinchpublishing.com

Publisher's Note:
This is a work of fiction. Names, characters, places, and incidents either are
the product of the author's imagination or are used fictitiously. Any
resemblance to actual persons, living or dead, events, or locales is entirely
coincidental. This book is not affiliated with or endorsed by Lucasfilm or
Disney, and any mentions of Star Wars and its properties is non-commercial
satirical parody covered under U.S. copyright laws for fair use.

Library of Congress Cataloging-in-Publication Data
Rob Dircks, 1967-
Sunnyside: A Novel
by Rob Dircks
p. cm.
ISBN 978-1-7330179-7-8 (hardcover)
ISBN 978-1-7330179-6-1 (paperback)

For my brothers

*"Home isn't the place you come from.
It's the place you stop trying to escape from."*

— Pearl (Theo's flat cleaner)

1. PUNKS.

"Get off my lawn."

They just stood there. In the dark. On his grass. Three punks. They were always there, roaming the streets, kicking over trash cans, spray painting the train underpass, throwing eggs on Halloween, a stain on his otherwise bucolic Ridgewood, New Jersey neighborhood. Once they left a bag of dog shit on his front porch and set it on fire. He almost stepped in it. But for some reason this new thing, the just standing there, pissed him off even more. Like they owned his lawn. Pot-smoking punks.

"Who's gonna make me, old man?"

This was their leader. The one with the bad haircut and the chipped tooth.

"Hey smiley. What happened to your tooth?"

It wasn't their first dance.

"That's the last tooth you gonna get from me, old man." Bad Haircut approached him, menacing, scraping a switchblade along the Old Man's mint 1984 Buick Regal. Okay, maybe calling it mint was an overstatement, but damn, in all the meaningful ways it was perfect: it handled well, hit ninety-five when he floored it, got decent mileage, and would never die. So watching this punk leave a scratch in its pristine metallic burgundy finish was like a slash to the jugular.

"Okay, smiley. I asked you nicely to get off my lawn. Now you pay."

But before the words could even finish leaving his mouth, the switchblade was in the air. He turned his face left, not fast enough, and watched as blood spurted from his nose. Ouch. With no time to dilly dally, he darted forward and turned right – and a boot met his temple.

He fell.

Not because the boot knocked him out. No, he let Punk Number Three *think* that for a moment, and drop his guard and laugh, but an instant later the Old Man was grabbing the boot and twisting hard, letting the full weight of Punk Number Three's body crash down on his own ankle, breaking it in multiple places. *Crack!* A gratifying shriek filled the night.

The Old Man got up then, blood streaming down his face, staring down Punk Number Two – who fled as fast as a cat who'd fallen into a bathtub. Before he could celebrate, though, Bad Haircut had already jumped on his back, punching and gouging at his eyes, inadvertently opening the Old Man's robe.

There were no clothes under his robe. But the Old Man wasn't shy about that kind of thing, so it didn't bother him that the neighbors now congregating on his sidewalk were getting a show. In fact, he silently thanked Bad Haircut for making his Glock 343x even easier to access, the large handgun he kept strapped to his naked thigh for just such an emergency. He calmly lifted it out of its holster, and with a satisfying click chambered the first round.

Punk Number Three sprinted away (faster than you'd think with a fractured ankle, impressive). And Bad Haircut froze. Sure, they had danced before, but last time a tooth was the only casualty. This time might be his still-beating heart. He leapt off the Old Man's back and ran, and ran, and ran.

And as the three punks receded into the dark, the Old Man raised his Glock and fired several shots into the air, letting his robe flap like a cape in the cool evening breeze, reveling in the applause from his neighbors, and he shouted into the night:

"Don't you know who I am? Don't you know who I am? Don't you know who I am?"

"Theo."

The Old Man – Theo, rather, not an old man at all – jerked from his gaming chair, pulling off his VR helmet and searching, bleary-eyed and unfocused, for his intruder. He blinked and spotted her. "Oh. It's you. I give you a key and you don't knock anymore?"

"Sorry Mister Theo. I knocked like six times. I swear. I'm not tryin' to scare you, I just gotta keep my schedule. Hey, you playing *Suburban Curmudgeon* again? You always like that game."

"No."

Theo didn't know why he said no. Maybe because he felt

like Pearl knew him too well, that he needed to keep her guessing. But she did know him too well, it was unavoidable really, she'd cleaned his flat twice a month for god-knows how many years. He honestly couldn't even remember how long ago he gave her the key. It was sad, really, how well she knew him. She knew him better than anyone. So of course she knew he was playing *Suburban Curmudgeon*, his absolute favorite game, and knew that he felt like a man out of time, that somehow he belonged back in the virtual world of nineteen-eighties America, when little patches of green grass still existed, along with the passion to fight for them. Not here in 2824, lost inside the mass of humanity on the *Star Orbiter Lusitania*.

He winced at the name. *Lusitania*. Ugh. Every time it crossed his mind. Because it was his job, as Level Three History Repair Technician, to fix things like that: the bungles and misinformation of the Great Information Hack of 2103. Way back then, the Wikipedia entry for "Greatest Manmade *Disasters*" was spoofed to read "Greatest Manmade *Achievements*," and the orbiter naming committee thought *Lusitania* rolled off the tongue nicely. They didn't bother to read a bit further into the article to discover that the ancient Earth water ship named *RMS Lusitania* had in fact sunk and nearly everyone aboard died.

He did fix that untruth, personally. The corrections were officially proven and substantiated and stamped as Objective Truth. But it didn't matter. Because the bureaucracy here, on one of eight artificial moons orbiting a planet in the Kepler-4 solar system, was so tangled it gave rats' nests a bad name. It didn't help that the general population greeted this new truth with a collective shrug. With Earth long in the rear view mirror and the hundreds of millions of remaining humans stuffed onto these vessels, working in vain for the past hundred years to terraform the planet below them, there were much worse problems to ignore. So nothing was done. For now, and maybe forever, his "home" would be this manufactured moon, named for a manmade disaster. Oh well. Maybe that was fitting, though, as he had a strong feeling that a new disaster was looming. No, not a feeling. He knew it.

He forced that annoyance out of his mind, all the annoyances, and sat back, and plopped his helmet back on, and disappeared into the past, and let Pearl vacuum around his feet.

When Pearl was done, she puttered around instead of just leaving, despite her insistence that she had a schedule to keep. Theo knew this was a plea for some social time, and occasionally he would relent. Her own children were grown and gone, and she was naturally chatty, and there were times he thought her head might explode if he didn't provide a relief valve for some words to spill out. Mom and Dad were better at humoring her, they'd even have her stay sometimes for dinner with the family – Dad, Mom, Vin, and himself.

But they were gone now too, well, Vin wasn't exactly gone, but he wasn't here either, so it was just Theo in the flat, which over time he not only got used to, but sort of began to think he was meant to. Meant to be alone. Deserved it. Sure, he had pangs, for something he couldn't quite put his finger on, it would've been easy to say he missed Vin and his parents, but he wasn't a sentimental person, not at all, and that reminded him:

Pearl had to go. Now. He had things to do.

"Thanks Pearl. Goodbye."

"You don't wanna chat a bit?"

"No. I mean, I'd love to, but you know. Work."

"You were just playing *Suburban Curmudgeon*."

She knew, she knew everything, and she wasn't making it easy. So Theo sighed, and went to the fridge, and took out some cheese. They sat across from each other at the kitchen table, nibbling on bits of cheese like a couple of mice.

He looked out the window while she talked and talked, up at the blue sky – or rather, up at the dome surrounding the entire orbiter, illuminated to look like a blue sky. He had always liked blue, but the blue in *Suburban Curmudgeon* was more convincing, and wasn't that a kick in the crotch, realizing that your "real" world was less real than your fake VR world.

So he looked away, back to Pearl, and noticed her hair was grayer today, a bit too gray for a sixty-eight percent. She was old enough to be his mother, easily, he was only a thirty-two percent. Would his mother have been this gray? What percentage would she have been today?

Percentages. Ugh. Another in Theo's ever-lengthening list of pet peeves. He longed for *years*, the time units from the past that he used at work in History Repair to describe people's ages. That made sense. The Old Time age unit. Not the New Time *percentage* unit. It was a microcosm of the way things worked on the orbiters. (Which was to say they didn't.) When humanity reconfigured the measure of time away from the Earth-revolves-around-the-Sun-centric "Old Time" to the rotation of this new planet, "New Time," where days were only twenty hours long and a one-year revolution around the new sun was only 122 days, people easily started living into their hundreds by the new measure. But rather than celebrating their newfound longevity, the first people to pass the two hundred mark grumbled that it made them sound ancient. Unable to just accept it and move on, they protested loudly, and a compromise was ultimately made: it was proposed one's age would henceforth be expressed as a *percentage*, based on the average human lifespan. If you were a thirty-two percent like Theo, for example, you had about seventy percent of your expected life left to live. If you were a ninety-five percent, well, congratulations (and you might want to pre-order that urn). This made the young people feel great, and the old people even more pissed, this constant, cheerful reminder of their expected demise, but enough people in the middle just said *meh* and voted, and it became law.

"Mom would've hit seventy-one percent right around now."

Pearl nodded and frowned. "I guess. Yup. She was a couple points ahead of me. It's a shame."

"It's life. Or death, I should say."

She tapped his hand hard. "You stop. Death always come up with you. Death, death. Talk about life. About what life's got going on."

"Like?"

"Stop." She considered the crumb of cheese between her fingers. "Lotsa stuff."

"Name one thing."

"Lotsa stuff."

Theo laughed. "I love our talks, Pearl."

"Hey. You got the SOCA. Yeah, you dig that stuff."

She was right. He had to admit, he did love the Star Orbiter Council Assemblies. They were a chance for him, a tiny voice in the vastness, to make himself heard, to rail against it all, even if just for a moment. But if he was being really honest, the quarterly SOCAs were another hopeless facade. Nothing ever really got done. And as for being heard? He was on the Council's Concerned Citizen's Committee for the *Lusitania*, and that meant being sequestered to the back table of the immense ballroom, stuffed between the kitchen and the bathrooms, as far away from the bureaucrats as possible, with an obstructed view, so he couldn't raise too much of a ruckus. And when – if – the microphone ever made it back there, it mysteriously glitched out, or the empty suits on the dais would pretend not to hear. Still, he did love it, the pushback, as ineffective as it was, because someone had to do it. Someone had to be the sand in your bathing suit. And a shout into the void was still a shout, even if no one heard it.

"Oh, speaking of. Mister Theo, you got an invitation to the assembly they're having tonight. Said right on there it's gonna be a special one. On actual paper. Special announcement. You should go. Special announcement, on actual paper, and not everyone gets invited. Only the CCC. You should go. I picked it out of your wastebasket and put it on your desk lamp."

Theo suddenly wished he had a flat cleaner who was wrong all the time, and didn't give a shit. Just clean the damn flat and leave, and if anything was said, it could easily be disproven. What a breath of fresh air that would be.

"I know, Pearl. I should go. But... I don't know... this time I don't feel like waving my arms from the back of a crowded catering hall, waiting for a microphone that never comes. What's the difference? Earth is fifteen light years in the past. The future? Who knows, with terraforming in the state it's in.

We're stuck, Pearl. Stuck in the present. It's no place to be. I want to go home."

She looked up from her cheese. "You are home."

"No. Not really. Come on, don't you think about it sometimes?"

Pearl shrugged. "No. Hey, you have any more cheese? That was good."

Theo rose and checked the fridge. No cheese. He handed her a small bowl of leftover ravioli and a fork. She sniffed at it, deciding well, there had to be some cheese in there, or something like it, and popped one into her mouth.

"Don't you think about home, Pearl? Come on. This isn't our home. Sure, the engineers were geniuses, and this *looks* like home, and smells like home, and sounds like home, but it's really a fake. A shadow of our real home."

"How would you know?"

"History Repair, Pearl. It's my job."

She shook her head. "Oh, right. Yes, yes. I forget. So, the Lusitania is made to look homey. So what? I like. You like. We all like. It's home."

He put his face in his hands. "You're such a good listener, Pearl."

"No, really, mister Theo. What's not to like?"

"Ugh. Where do I start." He splayed out his hands, beginning his endless list, but stopped, and pointed out the window, out past the dome, into space. "*There's* home, Pearl." He hesitated… " I think we should go back."

Pearl lunged like a woman half her age, grabbing his outstretched arm and pushing it back down, peering from side to side as if they were being watched, lowering her voice to a harsh whisper. "Theo! To *Earth?* You take that back! You know you can't talk like that! You could get in trouble, talking like that. What if you accidentally tapped your minicomm and butt-dialed someone and said that?" She softened her gaze. "Oh, Mister Theo, I know you miss your mom and dad, and Vin, poor, poor Vin..."

"This isn't about them. And don't poor, poor Vin. He's not getting away with it that easy. When he comes home there's a lot of accounting to be done."

She raised an eyebrow. "Oh."

His patience was thinning. "Don't you have somewhere else to be, Pearl? The schedule you have to keep?"

She shrugged again.

He stood up and pushed his chair in. "I have something better to do tonight anyway."

She smiled and let him lift her up to her feet. "Oooh. One of your masterpieces?"

He grinned back. Sure, Pearl grated on him, but she'd known him since he was in his first diaper, and knew exactly what made him tick. She contemplated him for a moment, then grabbed her rolling case. "Time to leave, Mister Theo. Can't keep your masterpiece waiting. Thanks for the cheese." And she reached up and patted him on the head. It reminded him of Vin, and suddenly he didn't want her to leave. He wanted to hug her. To hold her tight, and not let her slip between his fingers. How strange.

He wished she would do something annoying.

She farted.

And there it was. Theo snapped back to reality. "Shut the door quick on your way out. Don't want any cats."

Pearl shuffled out, shooing several cats, but one got through. As she closed the door he could hear her shout from the other side, "Sorry about the cat, Mister Theo! See you in two weeks!"

Before the cat could make it into the kitchen, Theo cornered it. He and the cat knew the deal, hence the ever-present bag of dried salmon treats hanging by the door. "Here. Take it and leave." He opened the door a few centimeters, threw a single treat into the hall, and barely missed the animal's tail as he slammed the door shut.

Moments later he felt his thumbchip buzz and tapped it to see a little animated hologram of 83 credits being removed from his account. 83 credits. He really should just clean the place himself. He did actually, it was immaculate before she came, and Vin's room was off limits anyway, he really should let her go permanently. But she was a fixture, had become part of the place itself, inseparable from it. He couldn't let her go.

Back at his desk, the SOCA invitation urged his attendance. It wasn't paper, but seemed close, although he could hardly remember what real paper looked like. It was a good fake, if he recalled correctly, they didn't skimp this time, sending out an actual, physical invitation – they must've really imagined tonight was something special and wanted a respectable attendance. They were even having sushi, not the typical lukewarm trays of penne a la vodka. The Grand Oversee had some kind of announcement to make. It was probably just another one of her "initiatives," meant to create change, but succeeding only in changing his taxes.

No, he really did have something better to do tonight, his second favorite thing after playing *Suburban Curmudgeon*: drafting proposals to the Star Orbiter Council telling them everything they were doing wrong.

The list was pretty much endless: pod traffic control, garbage collection, power distribution, waste reclamation, community relations, taxes, bot maintenance, animal regulation, court processes, terraforming of course, and on and on and on. All being done wrong, in every way. All he had to do was look out his bedroom window for proof. There, up a kilometer or so, a dome repair team idling the day away, vaping and floating around, barely even trying to impersonate actual work, while a pod-jam snarled around them, covering patches of sky. Or across the quad, that old woman with the red housecoat throwing her garbage off the balcony again, as her waste duct hadn't worked in over a year. Or below, thirty stories down, they had the stones to call that a *park?* The poor people on the first floor couldn't even see out their windows for the weeds and the trash. Was it too much to ask for a patch of neatly-trimmed grass? A little something nice that everyone could be proud of? Or better yet: admit defeat, cram us all back in cryocapsules, and go home? *Real* home?

He sighed, tapped his thumbchip and opened his latest opus (was that an oxymoron? "Latest opus?"), entitled *Twenty-three Steps to Eliminate the Exploding Animal Problem.* The floating words caught him for a moment, and he said out loud, "exploding animal problem." He laughed at the idea of cats from all the orbiters exploding into smithereens, well that would take care of the problem, wouldn't it? He tapped the title floating in front of him and said, "Change to 'Twenty-three Steps to Eliminate the *Mounting* Animal Problem'."

Whoops. Nope. Made it worse. "Change to Twenty-three Steps to Eliminate the Escalating Problem of Feral Feline Overpopulation." Yes. Wordy but clear. He scanned to the bottom, where he'd made it to Step Twelve: Incineration. *Hmmm.* Maybe that was a wee bit over the top. "Change to *Incarceration.*" Yes. He'd propose a bold plan to build efficient containment quarters for the out-of-control feral cat populace, where they would either–

Stop.

It was Pearl's voice in his head. *You really should go to the SOCA, Mister Theo.*

But she wasn't right this time. For once. Sorry. No glitchy microphone tonight. No, tonight he would make change by bringing an idea into the real world, in writing, indelible, pushing it through the bureaucracy, spreading that idea, like a virus, infecting each reader, spreading it outward, so one became two, and two became four, and four eight, and so on, until some tipping point tipped, and change actually happened.

Was that too much to dream?

Probably. Nothing would happen. He was nothing. Just another cog, grinding away here in the machinery of a fake world.

But... he had to try.

Besides, Theo didn't love being around people anyway, and there was an odd thrill to writing fifty-page rants and sending them off to the Central Clerk's Office. There, at least one or two cogs in the machine were required to read them, and roll their eyes, and stamp them RECEIVED, and make a note of his existence, and his ideas. And maybe, just maybe, some change might happen.

He picked up the invitation again, considering it. Then grinned, ripped it to pieces, and let the pieces fall into his wastebasket.

And in that simple act Theo made more change than he could possibly imagine.

2. UNINTERRUPTED BLISS

Kate Kingston kicked back, plopped her feet on her desk, and cracked open a cold Tsingtao, spilling a bit of beer down the front of her shirt. She couldn't believe her luck – every single government official, from all eight orbiters, was currently dining and drinking and carousing their way to oblivion, over at the fancy-schmancy Star Orbiter Council Assembly, for the very first time in her twenty-three-year career. (If you could call what she did a career.) Finally, *finally*, she'd have the Central Clerk's Office night shift all to herself, well, herself and Luna, without a single annoying interruption – guaranteed. She turned to her only office mate. "Ahh. Alone at last. It only took forever." She raised her can. "Here's to us."

"To us." Luna clinked it with her bucket of popcorn. Technically, Luna worked for Kate, but really they were just lifelong friends who happened to make a living laughing together at the parade of bureaucratic foibles and corruption, all the bills, decrees, pronouncements, and complaints. It was endless entertainment, and it paired perfectly with beer and popcorn. Luna dimmed the lights, scooched over next to Kate, tapped her thumbchip, and waved her hand across the air in front of them, creating a fan of floating holographic icons. "Take your pick, Kate. We've got at least five hours of uninterrupted bliss, and two six-packs. What'll it be?"

Kate's eyes danced among the icons. "Hmm. I could use a good terraforming debate. God, it's like they don't even want to get the damn thing done, ever. But they're funny as hell. My side hurt for a week from laughing last time." Her hand dove into the popcorn while Luna flicked her fingers through virtual files. "Excellent choice, Miss Kingston!" Her fingers slowed to a crawl. "Huh. Seems we're up to date on those."

"Perkins have any new bills? They're priceless. She's never passed a single one, but they're priceless. She could teach a class on how to write angry, ineffective legislation."

Luna's fingers galloped on and stopped. "Nope. We're too efficient for our own good. Seen 'em all."

"Okay then, let's get right to the main event. Complaints."

Luna grinned. The complaints pile was a treasure trove, and in all their years together it had never let them down. She flexed her hands out and the darkened office filled with the light of innumerable virtual folders, like stars in a moonless sky. "Oooh. There are so many. Tell me when to stop."

Kate smacked Luna's hand. "There!"

"What? The thermostat one?"

"No. The one from that guy. You know. *The guy.*"

Luna pinched her fingers at the air and pulled out a file. She let go of the pinch, and a title splashed above them: *Twenty-three Steps to Eliminate the Escalating Problem of Feral Feline Overpopulation. By Theo R. Hoover, member of the S.O.L. Concerned Citizens Committee.*

Luna yelped in glee, and Kate rose from her chair, clapping. A standing ovation.

She whispered in a reverent tone, "Oh my God. His latest opus."

Luna raised an eyebrow. "Latest opus. Isn't that an oxymoron?"

"Whatever. Well, well, Mr. Theo R. Hoover. It looks like you've outdone yourself." Kate sat back down, twisting and turning in anticipation. "Luna, will you read it out loud to me?"

"Certainly." She flipped at the air. "Ahem. Part One-"

"Oh my God. Parts! How many?"

Luna slid her hand up, peeking into the table of contents. "Five. In addition to the list of twenty-three steps. Wow, I'm getting verklempt." She fanned her eyes.

"Wow. I've never seen you cry, Luna Foster. But hey – let's see if this masterpiece is enough to bring on the waterworks. Read on, girl!"

"All right then. Part One: Origins of the Feral Feline Overpopulation Problem. Approximately four years ago, a shipment of pets bound for Star Orbiter Valdez was stopped mid-journey by troopers from the 643rd Precinct. This same precinct, by the way, is the one that bungled the case of the Hindenburg bank robberies back in-"

"Stop." Kate could hardly contain herself. "You want to know something, Luna?"

"At this rate it'll take five hours to get through this. But sure. What?"

"I like him."

"Who?"

"The *guy*."

Luna squinted. "You *like* him? Are you all right? Do you

understand what you're saying? Do you have any idea how many hours of our lives we've sunk into reading his diatribes? How petty his existence is? He lives only to complain."

"Yeah. I know all that. It's a 'hate-like' thing."

"You'll have to elaborate."

Kate raised one hand, then the other. "Like he's easy to hate, very easy, don't get me wrong. But I don't know, I'd love to see somebody like that get a shot."

"You mean get shot."

"No. Get a shot. Like just once I'd like to see one of his ideas happen, like, I don't know…"

Luna pushed Kate's raised hands down. "Like, he couldn't possibly make things worse?"

"Exactly!"

"Kate, honey, things can *always* get worse."

And at that exact moment, the incoming call panel flashed red.

"Uh, Luna, green or orange is all I remember. Have you ever seen it flash red like that?"

"No."

"Shit."

3. INCREDIBLE NEWS

Piper Montgomery strode to the podium, letting the applause from the packed hall carry her along. She felt light as a feather, and realized it was the first time she'd felt this way in her four-year tenure as Grand Oversee of the eight-orbiter Council, the highest office in the land, the humble shepherd of all that was left of humanity.

Virtually every other time she'd made this walk, her feet felt like cinder blocks, as she was the perennial bearer of bad news, the most common of these news items being another delay in the terraforming of Sunnyside.

Why did it always have to be that way?

For just a millisecond, she slipped into melancholy, remembering her childhood, how the only thing she ever wanted to be was Grand Oversee. Oh, how good it felt on the campaign trail, with the knowledge that it would be different under *her* administration, but how it hadn't happened that way at all, nothing changed in four years, not one bit. It was just like every Grand Oversee since the Great Orbiter Project had reached its destination way back in the year 2481OT, and the terraforming of Sunnyside had begun.

It started well. Humanity had found the perfect new home, planet Keplar-4-Tidallock-G9 – though no one called it that anymore, they just called it Sunnyside, as it didn't rotate and only one side ever showed its face to the sun. So we shipped the remainder of humanity off in cryogenic stasis for three hundred years, along with the orbiters, thawed ourselves out, set up camp orbiting Sunnyside, started up the terraforming systems, and… nothing.

Piper wasn't science-minded, but it seemed straightforward enough: make some adjustments to the heating and cooling of the surface of Sunnyside, to widen the habitable ring – not on the hot bright side that faced its sun, not on the cold dark side, but right on that blissful, just-right middle part. The ring was too narrow, it was the only part of the discovery that wasn't ideal, but they would install massive ice mining equipment to transfer ice from the dark side to the hot, and set up pipelines to distribute the melted water and aid flora and fauna growth, and enrich the atmosphere. The habitable ring would grow. Humanity would have a new home. They would live happily ever after. The plan was sound.

So why didn't it ever happen?

There was never a satisfactory explanation. Instead, there were decades of delays, broken equipment, wrong analysis, and blame, and infinite fingers pointed at infinite guilty parties, and the terraforming of their future home, the entire reason they were even out here in the first place, became a lost cause. The angry near-riots in the beginning had become angry shouting, which had become semi-angry moans, and by the time Piper Montgomery had been elected, mentions of terraforming delays were met with light murmurs, or a simple collective harrumph. Had it really only been four years? These four years felt like a century to Piper.

But none of that mattered today.

Today, finally, she had good news.

No, not good news. *Incredible* news. News that would change the course of human history! And it would happen during her administration, guaranteeing that the name Piper Montgomery would be written – no, *engraved* – into the history books. It would happen right here, on the *Star Orbiter Lusitania*, in the Great Hall of the In-N-Out Burger Convention Center. History wouldn't remember the wheezing air conditioning unit, ancient and held together with duct tape, or the rug that needed replacing a decade ago, or the flickering light right above her head. No, this scene would be painted into history with gold leaf, sunshine streaming in to the podium (in her imagination this room had windows), her hair perfectly coiffed, her suit impeccably dry cleaned. She grinned, and in her imagination her glittered eyelashes twinkled with the reflected light of Sunnyside.

Tapping the microphone lightly, she turned back to see, for the first time, all eight governors seated on the stage. Lois Perkins, the longest-serving governor, of *Star Orbiter Chernobyl*, winked at her. Perkins never winked at her. Yes, tonight was going to be a glorious night!

"Ahem. Thank you governors, and senators and representatives from all eight orbiters." She waved her hand across the expanse, and marveled at the fact that, for once, they were all together, and all rowing in the same direction. "And while we haven't always seen eye-to-eye, I'd even like to welcome Governor Olafson from *Star Obiter Hindenburg*.

Welcome." They smiled at each other, a sincere *water-under-the-bridge* smile, and the crowd laughed knowingly, and Piper Montgomery felt like she might float off the stage.

"Now that we've enjoyed a delicious dinner courtesy of Dayol Sushi, I'd like to present the *real* main course. Gentlemen, if you could lower the lights..."

As the room dimmed, the crowd whispered excitedly, yes, there seemed to be something different this time, and Piper was going to milk it for all it was worth.

An image appeared on the screen behind her.

"Earth."

She waited a dramatic moment. "Our home no more. It wasn't one single thing – nuclear war, or a virus, or resource depletion, or even climate change – that did us in. Rather, it was a messy mish-mash of all these and more, as if humanity, and the now inhospitable world we lived in, just sort of said, 'Okay, enough already,' and agreed to call it a day."

A new image replaced the Earth.

"The orbiters. Our home – for now. Thanks to the ingenuity and bravery of our great grandparents, the people of Earth finally united in common cause, and used the remaining resources of the planet to construct the eight artificial moons we inhabit *temporarily*. Each a marvel in their own right – a fusion core surrounded by utility and computing layers, then the surface layer, then atmosphere, then finally the semi-transparent projection dome – collectively the orbiters represent the very best of us. Yes, some small things could run better..." she heard laughs and muffled shouting from the general direction of that damned Concerned Citizens Committee, and raised her hand in protest, "...but by and large, everyone should agree, it is a safe, sustainable, clean existence that affords us all productive lives and the pursuit of happiness."

The next image: Sunnyside. Here the crowd became restless, they'd seen this song and dance before, Montgomery seemed to be rehashing her go-to, dog-eared slide presentation on the hope of terraforming. Coughs that sounded like "bullshit!" began to rise, and Piper knew she had to get to the point.

"But I am here today, *not* to disappoint you with another delay. No, my friends, something amazing is about to happen, and I believe it will bring the dream of Sunnyside into our grasp – within this generation!"

Within this generation.

Chopsticks dropped to their plates. The collective murmuring screeched to a halt. Piper thought she even heard, with satisfaction, more than one person spit out their cocktail mid-sip. She had just made a bold prediction that she knew would kill her upcoming re-election if she was wrong, and likely make her an embarrassing footnote in the story of humanity. But she *wasn't* wrong. The entire population of the eight orbiters, what was left of the human race, two-hundred million give or take, had been enduring only to hear those words since 2736OT, and now she would deliver. Only she knew the secret. The secret that would save them.

"Yes. I said it. *This* generation." She looked around slowly, making sure each pair of eyes were glued to her. "Today begins a new hope. A day that will change our lives forever." She reached into her pocket. "I have right here…"

Wait.

It wasn't there.

Her hand thrashed around in her pants. Her other hand in her other pocket. Both hands. Rummaging.

The card. The card that contained proof that their lives would change forever. Gone!

Shit. Shit. *Shit!*

She had left it in the back of the limo-pod.

Well, she wasn't going back now. Now was the time. The card was just a device. The story was what mattered. She soldiered on. "As I was saying, this day will-"

"Excuse me."

Piper looked down, startled. She was getting back in the groove, dammit. Approaching the climax. And George at table one was waving his napkin like a flag of surrender?

"What is it, George?"

"I don't mean to interrupt, but the food, Madame Oversee."

"What about the food?"

"I think... I think it's..."

"It's *what*?"

In answer, George Travers keeled over, writhing and groaning.

Piper couldn't believe it. Right smack in the middle of the greatest moment of her career – no, her *life* – her deputy director of taxation was going to ruin it by passing out drunk?

No. Piper was moving forward. Nothing would stop her.

"Um, yes, security, please. If you could get an EMT to drag, I mean, er, help poor George here out to the lobby, thank you. Now, as I was saying, the future holds something incredible for us all. I am thrilled to announce-"

"Madame? Grand Oversee Montgomery, um...?" A woman from table five stood, weakly.

"*Now* what?"

"Um, I'm, ah, sorry, but I think there's-" and she projectile vomited on her neighbor, and ran toward the exit. She didn't make it, passing out a few steps short.

What a bunch of incompetent boozers, Piper began to think, but then…

Her stomach rumbled.

And not in a way that asked politely to be led to the bathroom. In a way that demanded it. NOW.

"Oh my." She quickened her pace. "Um, as I was saying, I am thrilled to announce-"

Another rumble, this time a flash of nausea so powerful it brought Piper to her knees, and she forgot the rest of her speech, and in fact forgot why she was up at the podium at all. She closed her eyes, trying to remember, remember, come on dammit, but all she could see behind her eyelids was dinner, the raw tuna and salmon and snapper they'd all enjoyed an hour ago, proudly displayed with the "Dayol Sushi" logo sticking out of the centerpiece.

She forced herself up, opening her eyes one last time, looking around at her crowning moment, turned into a sea of dying officials and staff, her entire government collectively clutching their stomachs and vomiting, passing out, literally expiring before her eyes. Somehow, she had strength left to grab the microphone and wheeze, "We are not alone."

She thought she heard, from somewhere very far off, someone ask, "What?" but Piper Montgomery, along with every single person in the grand hall, had now breathed her last, and she only had time for one final thought:

Man, being Grand Oversee sucks.

4. THE SUSHI DID IT.

Kate stared at the blinking call panel. *Bleep. Bleep. Bleep.* "Luna. You answer it."

"It's your turn," Luna whined, backing away as far as possible from the flashing red, plopping herself into her chair and digging in her heels.

"My turn? Are we back in seventh grade, Luna?"

"Oh, come on, please, I really don't want to answer the damn- oh, whatever, *boss*." Luna rose, resigned, she was, after all, one teeny step down the bureaucratic ladder from Kate, and slow-marched to the call panel. Her finger hovered over it. "I have a feeling things are about to change, Kate. Dramatically, I'm afraid."

"No shit. Just answer it already. Let's get this over with."

Luna pressed the red dot and instantly a large man in a black suit and sunglasses stood before them, a glowing, fuzzy hologram. "Hello, Miss Kingston. Miss Foster."

Kate approached the image, rolling her hands. "I'd ask who you are, and why you're wearing sunglasses at night, but the thing was flashing red. That can't be good. Just get it out."

The hologram raised its hand, showing a silver badge. "Agent Ned Weathers. Secret Service."

"I'm impressed. So what is it?"

"Well... they're dead."

Luna and Kate looked at each other. "Who?"

"All of them."

"All of *who*, Agent Ned Weathers Secret Service?"

"Everyone. At the council event. There were only four survivors. Catering staff. Everyone else is dead."

Kate laughed. "Good."

Ned's hologram removed its sunglasses. "Wow. I... thought you might be a bit more broken up about it."

"Nah. Hated the whole lot."

Kate expected a snicker at least from the man in black. She moved in close to Ned's face to make sure the image hadn't frozen. She waved a hand across his eyes. Ned blinked.

Kate stammered, "Wait- I was... I was joking. You're-you're serious?"

He nodded.

Luna plopped into the nearest chair and put her head between her knees, taking deep breaths. Kate clutched the coat rack to steady herself. "You... you can't mean *everyone*, Weathers. Do you know who was there?"

Ned grimaced. "Food poisoning."

"That's a how. Not a who."

"Sorry. Yes, I know who. Grand Oversee Montgomery, all the governors, all the senators, representatives, all their staff. *That* everyone. Freak food poisoning accident. The sushi did it. Killed them all. It's a mess down there."

Kate felt her throat constrict. "But..." she looked to Luna. "Well?"

Luna was pacing now. "Well *what?* Why are you looking at me?"

"That was the entire government! And when I say entire, I'm not being figurative or exaggerating. That was the *entire* government! All eight orbiters!"

The image of Ned fidgeted. "Um... see... not exactly. And, ah... that's the other reason I'm calling."

Luna shook her head. "No."

Kate hid behind Luna. "No, Weathers. Don't say it."

"Would you rather hear it from me, or from... well, actually, I'm not sure who else there even would be left to tell you, I guess-"

"Oh shut up, Weathers. No. You're wrong. It can't be. Do you have any idea how many levels...?"

"Yessir. I mean Yes ma'am. From Grand Oversee, down through the governors, senators, to the assistants and deputies, et cetera et cetera, down to the Central Clerk's Office, and..."

"No. I told you not to say it. Stop right there."

"Sorry, Miss Kingston. It's you. You're the last one left in line. Path of succession ends with you. It looks like we've got a designated survivor scenario here, and you're it. And you too, Luna."

Luna lunged into Ned's face. "Me? Kate is my superior!"

Kate began pacing alongside Luna, back and forth, frantic. "No. No. No. No. No. This isn't happening." Kate had spent the last twenty-three years carefully avoiding the spotlight, meticulously cultivating a career in the shadows, ever since that spelling bee in eighth grade, her utter mortification at misspelling the word *contemptible*. God, she hated that word now. *Contemptible*. Who used that word? Ever? She hated it almost as much as she hated being at the center of anything. Life in the dim office in the basement had treated her well. She could pull her little levers and make things happen from the dark just fine. This was the worst. Worse than the worst. It was *contemptible*.

Ned continued. "Sorry, but I'm following protocol here, Miss Kingston. It appears you're the interim Grand Oversee. And if anything should happen to you, God forbid of course, Miss Foster, you're it."

"No!" Kate slammed her hand down on her desk.

Ned's image flickered again. "Yes. You're it."

"You listen to me real close now, Weathers." She leaned into the hologram for effect, her finger sticking into the image's ear. "I am NOT being anyone's interim Grand Oversee. Do you know how hard I've worked to avoid shitshows? My entire career. And that job is *entirely* a shitshow. That's all it is. Look up shitshow in the dictionary and there's a picture of that job. No. I'm not doing it. I refuse."

"Uh... I'm not sure you *can* refuse. We're still looking through the documen-"

"I refuse. Do you see this?" She marched back to her desk, plucked a small photo from her blotter, and marched back, shoving it in Ned's face, touching his nose. "Do you see this?"

"Can you move it back a little?"

She pulls back.

"A little more?"

"God, Weathers. No. It's a picture of Oyster Cove. Over on the *Star Orbiter Miami*."

"Ah. Nice orbiter. Maybe the nicest."

"Well, I've never been there, Weathers. Not yet. Hell, I've only been off the *Lusitania* five times. But in my dream it's even nicer than you're saying. So I put a down payment on a flat right near the beach. It's waiting for me, Ned. Peace and quiet. Isolation. Total anonymity. You are not taking my dream away from me by putting me into the middle of the Grand Shitshow. Luna either. Right Luna? Hey, what do you think you're doing?"

Luna was flicking her thumbchip faster than Kate thought possible, while her hands conducted a frantic symphony of documents. Kate had never seen so many of them swirling through the air. Luna stopped one finger and put it over her lips. *"Shhhh!"*

"Shush? You're shushing me? Oh, Luna. Here comes the pain-"

"I found it!"

"Oh. Okay. Good. You found what?"

Luna jabbed the air in front of her. "Here! In the Star Orbiter Council Constitution! Right here in black and white! Well, multicolored pixels, but you get my meaning." She liked to think she knew the nooks and crannies of the Constitution pretty damned well after all these years, thank you very much, and pointed to a teeny clause in the giant set of documents, enlarging it so it practically filled the office. "Section 57, Article 12, line 23... bullshit, bullshit, bullshit... here, it's a footnote of a footnote, it's in four-pixel type: 'In the supremely unlikely event that the line of succession is exhausted, the final holder of the title of Grand Oversee may appoint, at his or her discretion, a temporary successor from any eligible citizen to hold the office until fair and lawful elections may take place within sixty days." She turned to Kate, the slightest flicker of hope in her eyes. "Well? That means what I think it means, right?"

Kate exhaled, a deep exhalation like she hadn't had in a long time, and crossed to Luna, and clamped her into a bear hug. "You're one in a million, you know that?"

"Yes," Luna wheezed. "But I can't breathe."

Releasing her, Kate returned to pacing. "Okay then. We name someone Grand Oversee. Simple. Wow. I like that. You like that, Weathers?"

"Well, I'd have to run it up the flagpole, of course, but personally, if that's what it says, that's what it says, and the flagpole itself, you know, it's pretty short at the moment."

"Good. Okay, now... who to name?" She turned back to Luna.

"Again. Don't look at me."

"No, Luna. I'm looking at you for an idea. An answer to *who*."

As the word "who" left Kate's lips, a mysterious, hooded figure entered the front of the office, approaching the (ill-titled) welcome desk, and tapped the old-fashioned bell.

Ding!

And without waiting for a *may-I-help-you*, it whispered, "I have the answer."

5. RETURN OF THE JEDI

"Oh for crying out loud. You're the last person I need to see right now. Leave. And take the four cats you just let in with you."

The figure slowly removed its hood and smiled. "On the contrary. I'm the person you most need to see right now." He picked up one of the cats and stroked it like a super villain might.

"Howie. I'm not kidding. The grownups are talking here. Come back tomorrow."

"For the last time, Miss Kingston, my name is Han. And I'm not leaving. I have the right to be here."

"For the last time your name is Howie. Howard Marcus Baker. You don't think I've got your record memorized?" It was true. Howie was Kate's wannabe arch-nemesis, this boy in a twenty-five-percent's body, chief lobbyist for the so-called *Skywalkers*. She rolled her eyes at the name – were these idiots still not aware that the IMDB entry for *Star Wars* had been edited during the Great Information Hack, changing its category from *science fiction* to *documentary*? Yes, an entire sub-culture had emerged over the centuries, the *Skywalkers*, believing everything in the original three films – episodes four, five, and six, of course – as inarguable fact, its adherents styling themselves as rebels against the evil bureaucracy, using the "force" to gain a credible presence in society. (And an attractive tax shelter.) By claiming themselves a religion, they not only avoided paying their fair share, but also got to spout their fanatical jedi bullshit from street corners on all eight orbiters. It was nearly impossible to track these gullible morons down when they ventured beyond annoyance, as they all went by the codenames "Han," or "Luke" or "Leia," or "Chewie," and some, at the upper-echelons, "ObiWan." She would laugh, if they weren't so goddamned annoying.

"Ugh. What do you want, Howie? You have one minute."

"I've been sent to help. With your little Grand Oversee problem."

Kate's look of shock must've been obvious, as Howie let out a snicker. "Yes, Miss Kingston. The force sees everything."

"Oh, please with your force crap. I'm not in the mood. How did you know?"

Howie put on his best smug-defiance look, and that's all it took. Kate lunged at him, grabbing his robe and pinning him to the nearest desk, her eyes a millimeter from his. The cat shrieked and darted for the exit. "I'll ask you one more time, 'Han.' How. Did. You. Know?"

He tried for a smirk, but as Kate's hand raised in the air for a slap, Howie's floodgates opened. "It was Rick! I mean Chewie 29! He's a catering guy! A waiter! He was one of the survivors! He called us, and we looked up the contingencies, and once we figured it out, and we got the call, some guidance from up top, we thought, I don't know, you might need help figuring this out. Please don't hit me!"

She pulled him upright and pushed him toward the door. "Go away."

"Don't you even want to hear our idea? For temporary Grand Oversee?"

"Not really. But if it'll get you to leave sooner, sure, lay it on me."

Howie cleared his throat. "ObiWan Morgan."

"Real names, Howie, or I swear to God…"

"Hector Morgan."

"Christ," Kate and Luna said together. Hector Morgan. The great grandson of legendary Daisy Morgan, inventor of the cryostasis technology that ensured humanity's survival on the 358-year trip to Sunnyside. According to the stories, she was a ruthless businesswoman, securing the cryo patents and negotiating the most lucrative deal in Earth history, knowing humanity didn't really have a choice. She died giving birth to her only son just a year after thawing out here on the Lusitania, but left her vast fortune to him and then three generations of self-dealing, shifty socialites. None of them had to raise a finger for anything, but liked to stick all of their fingers into everything, into shady businesses, politicians' pockets, the black market. They preferred the crooked to the straight every time. It was uncanny.

Hector was the last of that line, the only son of an only son of an only son, but he was determined to take the family name out with a bang. He was everywhere on television and the net, spending his billions and promoting his latest outlandish scheme du jour. His current scam was CryoCrypt, where he repurposed his great-grandmother's decommissioned cryocapsules into a subscription-based con where, for a not-so-small monthly subscription fee, you could keep deceased loved ones on ice until a future when raising people from the dead would be possible. Their motto? *"You don't have to grieve if they're not dead!"* Everyone knew better, but when you were desperate, Hector Morgan was there to take your money and your hope.

In short, Hector Morgan was literally the *last* person in the world Kate or Luna would name Grand Oversee.

"When the hell did Hector Morgan join the Sky-whackadoos? That's not his style."

"It's the Sky*walkers*, Miss Kingston. Last week. Apparently he saw the light. He found the force."

"Please." Kate ushered him closer to the exit. "This stinks, Howie. Worse than lethal sushi. I mean, come on. Hector Morgan joins your little treehouse club a week ago, then drops his name in the hat for Grand Oversee five minutes after we find out about the deaths of virtually every government official? Isn't that a little convenient?"

Howie gasped (an exaggerated gasp if he was being honest). "Are you accusing ObiWan Morgan of having something to do with a mass food poisoning *accident?*"

"Ugh. Look, Howie, if you're recording this, and knowing you, you probably are, or maybe he's even listening in right now, anyway I am officially not accusing Mister Morgan of anything. He's a model, law-abiding citizen from a revered family that the government officially has no complaint with, I was just officially noting his amazing timing. Alas, his timing wasn't amazing enough. You're too late. It's officially a done deal. We've already officially decided on a Temporary Grand Oversee."

Luna raised her eyebrows. "We have?"

Ned flickered. "You have?"

Howie stammered. "But... when I walked in... I was sent to... can't be... you... *who...?*"

Kate didn't even have to turn around to look at the name. She knew it by heart, from innumerable, lengthy, hilarious – and some might even say genius – complaint documents. *The guy.*

The guy was finally going to get his shot.

"Howie, I'd like to introduce you and Mister Morgan to our Temporary Grand Oversee." She pointed behind her, to Complaint Number 689x3b, glowing in the air above her desk: *Twenty-three Steps to Eliminate the Escalating Problem of Feral Feline Overpopulation.*

"Everyone, meet Theo R. Hoover."

6. NO TROUBLE AT ALL.

leep. Bleep. Bleep.

The call panel was flashing red.

He'd never seen it flashing red. And it said SECRET SERVICE.

God.

Theo stood, frozen at the front door of his flat, for several minutes. All he could think, as crazy as it sounded, was that his latest proposal had been the last straw. The government had seen enough, and judged him as... he didn't know what exactly... a terrorist? Was he facing jail time? Or... death? He thought back to the thirty-seven proposals he'd submitted to the Central Clerk's Office so far, sifting through his memories, searching for threats he might've made. No, no bodily threats. No threats of bombs or even minor disruptions of the bureaucracy. He was certain. All he was trying to do was convince them to start doing things the right way, even if that meant replacing certain peopl...

Oh my God.

That was it. They'd misinterpreted his suggestions of

replacing certain people as some kind of mafiosa *sleep-with-the-fishes* veiled threat. His murderous manifestos had done him in. He had been labeled a dangerous fringe-mafia-proposal-writing-terrorist.

And they were coming for him!

He didn't answer the call panel. He absolutely wasn't going to do that. Instead, using all his knowledge of survival in extreme situations – which was to say *none* – he silently padded to the back bedroom, his brother Vin's, past the half-finished canvas and the crusty oil paint tubes, opened Vin's closet, pushed aside his clothes, sat down, closed the door, and hid in the dark.

Minutes passed.

He hadn't been in here since... well, for a long time. He wondered if that ancient Earth board game, *Battleship!*, was still here. He tapped his thumbchip, and a little rectangle of holographic light shone in front of him. He pointed it around, here and there, around all the old shoes and boxes of god-knows-what, and yes, there it was, in the corner. He smoothed his hand across the dusty cover, sneezed four times – that's what he got for telling Pearl never to clean in here – and opened it. Inside were the two cheap display units, with small plastic boats, littered with red pegs, frozen in the middle of a game never finished. He smiled, recognizing his own board instantly: all the ships were bunched together, like they were huddled against an attack. It was a losing strategy, and Vin obliterated him every time. Then in a rage Theo would throw his display across the room, every time, sending pegs everywhere, for Pearl to hunt down the next time she vacuumed. So Vin would throw his too, and scream "Battleship explosion!" and they'd retreat to opposite sides of the bed giggling, picking up and throwing all the little battleships at each other, a true battle, howling with laughter until tears streamed down their cheeks.

This memory, this ephemeral little wisp, would be lost forever, like tears in rain, he knew. It almost was already. Each time he recalled it, it got a bit blurrier, like making a copy of a copy of a copy, as the memory was rebuilt each time from fresh neuronal proteins. But something in Theo wanted to believe a different thing, that a memory had some kind of concrete existence and value beyond our recall of it, beyond merely putting a smile on our lips or a tear in our eye. *There must be something else*, he thought, he could feel it, the yearning, the near certainty, but he couldn't find it. It was hiding too well. Like Vin.

His eyes were suddenly very watery. Damn dust.

Without thinking, he stood and opened the closet door. And Vin was sitting right there, or was he, on the edge of the bed. He was just as Theo remembered him, before everything. Hair long and wild, a rascal's grin lighting up his face. "Hey Theo. I know you want to do it. Go for it."

So Theo flung his display across the room, hitting the opposite wall. He screamed, as loud as he could, "BATTLESHIP EXPLOSION!"

They laughed together, just like back then.

A knock on the door. And another.

Shit!

A muffled voice: "Mister Hoover! Are you all right? I hear screaming!"

Theo froze. (Again.) Instead of saying "I'm fine, I'll be there in a second," there was a dangerous silence.

And then: "Mister Hoover! I'm going to break the door down! Stay away from the door, Mister Hoover!"

"No! No! I'm fin-"

Another explosion interrupted his plea, and Theo imagined his front door splintering into a million pieces. (He wasn't too far off). Then he heard heavy shoes crashing through his flat, left, right, searching. "Mister Hoover! Mister Hoover!" And then closer, "Mister Hoover! Mister- oh. You're in the closet."

Theo opened his eyes (they had been closed during the door explosion). Vin was gone. In his place stood a large man in a black suit. He was wearing sunglasses. At night.

Theo motioned behind him. "Um, I was... cleaning."

"Okay. If you say so. Sorry about smashing in the door. I thought you were..."

Theo sighed. "Well. It looks like you've found me. I give up."

"Give up what?"

"You know."

"Um..." Ned scratched his nose.

"The feral cat proposal. That's what did it, didn't it?"

Ned raised a finger. "Oh, that! Yes, you're right there. That was the kicker, I guess."

"How much time do you think I'll get?"

"It depends. Up to four years."

"Four years. Wow. That's a long time."

"That's what they all say."

"All the inmates?"

Ned sat down on the bed. "What inmates?"

"That's what all the inmates say. Four years is a long time."

Ned thought about this for a second. "No. I was talking about Montgomery. The Grand Oversee. Said the same exact thing. Four years is a long time. Poor woman."

"Piper Montgomery – the Grand Oversee – was an inmate?"

Ned took off his sunglasses. "Hmmm. Maybe we should start over. Hi. I'm Ned. Agent Ned Weathers. Secret Service. I'm here to take you to the Central Clerk's Office. There's been a... development, at tonight's SOCA meeting. They need you down there now."

Theo sat beside Agent Ned, and next to his gargantuan frame he felt like a small boy. A small boy about to be punished.

"Um... They... *need? Me?*"

"Now."

"How much trouble am I in?"

Ned laughed. "Trouble? You're not in any trouble! Who said you were in trouble?"

Theo shrugged and smiled, as if the thought never crossed his mind.

"Now. Let's get you over there, Mister Grand Oversee sir."

Theo gulped. "Uh, sure. Wait – Grand Oversee?"

"Whoops. I should not have said that."

"You called me Grand Oversee."

"No I didn't."

"Yes you did."

"No I didn't."

"Yes you did."

Ned made the loco swirl of his finger next to his temple. "Oh that. I do that sometimes. It's stressful work. Never mind. Let's just get a move on, Mister Gran- Mister Hoover. Might want to put on a pair of pants first, of course."

Theo looked down at his boxers. Smiley faces. They were laughing up at him, like they were in on the joke.

"Okay, Agent Weathers. I'll be right back. So, just to be clear – I'm not in trouble."

"Nope. No trouble at all."

But as Theo walked to his own bedroom, around the cats that were now herding through his non-existent front door, he had a feeling of absolute certainty:

He wasn't just in trouble. He was in *big* trouble.

7. YOU SIT IN THE BACK.

On the roof of Theo's flat cluster, in a corner of the roof-park, a large, black limo-pod sat idling.

"After you, Mister Hoover."

Theo walked around to the passenger side, dodging a cat, and tried the front door. "Um, it's locked."

Ned pointed. "Oh. No. You sit in the back. The Grand Oversee sits in the back. Wait. Back up." He literally backed up a step. "What I mean to say is that *you're not the Grand Oversee. But you still sit in the back.*" He laughed. "You know what, Mister Hoover? Just forget everything I say, and sit in the back. Silence is golden, as they say. Let's just have a nice silent ride."

Tentatively, Theo opened the back door and climbed in. Wow.

He'd never been in a pod that could fit more than four people. This one could easily host a party for eight. Eight very large partiers. He began asking Agent Ned questions, and watched the privacy divider slowly roll up.

Okay, I guess Agent Weathers really has taken a vow of silence.

Alone now, Theo looked around, curious, distracting himself from whatever dreadful fate awaited him at Lusitania City Hall, as the limo-pod lifted off and zoomed into the air. There were lots of bottles and glasses, and screens and buttons, all begging to be pressed. He restrained himself – only children press buttons they're not allowed to. After a few minutes, his nerves forced him to get up and pace around. He plopped down on one of the opposite seats.

"Ouch!"

Something had jabbed him in the rear.

He turned around, rubbing his butt, searching, and saw it: in the crease of the pleather between the back and the seat...

A small card.

He pulled it out, like a surgeon might extract a bullet. It was two centimeters square, wafer thin, and Theo recognized it as a data card. On the little label, someone had handwritten in a tiny scrawl, *TOP SECRET: OVERSEE EYES ONLY!*

He knocked on the privacy divider, this was clearly something he wasn't supposed to see, it said *Top Secret* after all, when was the last time he saw something top secret? He knocked again. Again. The divider didn't move. Agent Weathers was not engaging. Period.

So Theo put the card down, carefully, next to him on one of the trays. He'd bring it to the agent's attention as soon as they landed. *Don't look at the card, Theo. It's not for you. Don't press any buttons, Theo. You're not a child, Theo.*

More minutes passed. Theo roughly estimated the remaining time to their destination, everything clamoring for his attention, the card, the buttons, the screens.

Twenty more minutes. At least. Damn.

As he closed his eyes, promising not to open them for the duration, he spied out of the corner of his vision, next to a small screen, a slot.

It was the perfect size slot for a two-centimeter data card.

He shut his eyes harder.

Then he heard a voice. "Go ahead. You know you want to do it."

It was Vin again. Just like in the bedroom. Weird.

"You know what, Vin? No. You're always getting me into your shenanigans, and getting us both in trouble."

But Vin was grinning, his ear-to-ear, fearless grin. "Is that supposed to make me stop? Your cute pouting?"

"I'm not pouting. No." Theo tried not to smile, but damn, it was good to see Vin, even this Vin, and it was never any use, being with him was always an adventure. He was the human personification of fun. "Go away, Vin."

"No chance. Hey, you remember that time I talked you into making that alien robot? The one we threw off the balcony? We almost gave Dad a heart attack."

They both laughed. It was a good memory, almost giving their dad a heart attack, because it ended with him not having a heart attack, and also not yelling until his face was red and – one of the rare instances – *not* punishing them. Dad totally wanted to yell and punish them, as usual, to ground them for a year, but the relief that the flailing thing dropping from the thirtieth floor of their flat cluster was a homemade alien robot and not one of his children was overwhelming, and he hugged them instead. "Thank God. You two idiots." And he wiped his eyes and held them tight like they might disappear.

Neither one of them remembered getting many hugs from the old man, and *definitely* not a single tear, but damn that day made up for it. Vin grinned. "I guess the old man really did love us. In his own way. Hey, you still have the movie of that?"

Theo grinned and nodded, and tapped his thumbchip, and instantly there was the little holographic movie floating in the air between them: they were twelve and thirteen, filming what was sure to be an instant science fiction classic: a hand-to-hand battle, between two heroes trying to save humanity, and the alien robot invader, bent on destroying mankind. They had built the robot from odds and ends, though really with Theo's brains and Vin's creativity, it wasn't too shabby, and it moved on its own in a menacing way. But it was no match for our heroes, who finally subdued it and hoisted it over the railing to its death thirty stories below, saving humanity. And at the last few frames of the movie, Theo had captured their Dad rushing in, shocked, having seen something from the kitchen window that looked like one of his sons, clutching the railing, helpless, then falling to his death.

Theo froze the frame. They laughed at the look on Dad's face now, all these years later, how finally, through some random near-miss of a tragedy, they had revealed something hidden for a long time. He was just a man at that moment, Dad, vulnerable and scared and heartbroken, and sure, it was hilarious, but if it was so funny why did Theo have a tear running down his cheek?

Vin reached over and wiped the tear. "Okay, enough of that. Now, put that card in, you rebel."

Theo shook his head. "Rebel. Ha." But he laughed a little, and took the card from the tray, and inserted it in the slot.

"Oh well. I mean, how top secret could it be?"

Instantly the small screen lit up with the seal of the

Grand Oversee, one circle with eight smaller circles around it, and its speaker came to life. "Top Secret Confidential from the Office of the Search for Non-human Intelligence: Grand Oversee viewing only. Unauthorized access prosecuted to the full extent of the Great Orbiter Constitution, including possible life imprisonment. The following transmission was received and decoded Year 2824 NewTime, Date March twenty-three, oh-eight-hundred hours…"

"Life imprisonment?!" Theo instantly regretted his decision, frantically searching for a stop button, but there was none. Just the slot. He shouted, *"Stop message! Stop message! Vin! What do I do? What do I do?"*

But Vin was gone, another perfect exit, dammit, and the recording continued. So Theo banged on the privacy divider. *"Agent Weathers! Hey! Agent Weathers!"* He tried to stop listening. He plugged his ears with his fingers.

But two words from the speaker made their way into his inner ear, and up into his brain: "…*intelligent species…*"

"Wait, what?" Theo froze.

Yes, he had definitely heard the words "intelligent species." So he forgot Vin for a moment. He forgot the robot falling from the balcony. He forgot his imminent prison sentence. He was completely in the present, not distracted, and there was nothing else. He listened.

"…nomadic species, not centrally concentrated but spread throughout the Exnoto galaxy. Name being rough phonetic equivalent. Extremely random occurrence, isn't it, our spotting your radio transmissions. Do humans you know how insane big the universe is? In your base-ten-years number system, approximately ninety-three billion light-years across. Chances crossing paths between us and you guys super-micro small, like finding extremely small item in vast sea of much larger items. Sorry, not great metaphor. Metaphors not exactly our strong point. Or human language."

Aliens! Theo squinted. *Hmmm.* It was clearly a fake. Humanity had a knack for disinformation and conspiracy theories, and the alien bit was an old standby that made an appearance every decade or so. But if it was a fake, why was he listening so intently?

"...Us species, much much different than you humans, but does share your desire for contact. Based on trajectory... hold on, calculating, this could take a while... no here comes... ah yes, thirty revolutions around your local star, days you call them maybe. We will be there anyway, in the area, and figured why not? Seems like serendipity, a good word is that you think? Anyway, big news for you humans: *you are not alone!* Much for you to see and learn! Oh, yes yes yes! Even have a gift to bring you! Something to help with your home. Exciting! Forthcoming here are galactic dates and coordinates..."

Suddenly, a strange feeling crept into Theo's heart: *hope.* The recording was probably a hoax, as they'd all been before, but something about this one, it was weirdly different, so strange and authentic-sounding, the awkward use of language, the earnestness, so he gave himself momentary permission to believe, to believe in everything: the possibility of intelligent life beyond humanity, that the universe brimmed with life, that the future was bright, the possibility that he wasn't alone after all, and maybe, just maybe, they had technology to help them get home. To Earth.

The card finished with, "As courtesy, we will not visit without consent from you human people. Your decision. You respond, we come. You do not respond, we stay far away and move on to next spacetime curve. So we await your response with great great anticipation. See you maybe then!"

In the next second, the voice said simply, "Press eject within three seconds. No action initiates self-destruct sequence."

Theo looked again at the screen, and its surroundings, desperately searching for an eject button. He pleaded to no one, *"There are a million buttons in here! Where the hell is the eject button?!"* He started stabbing every button his fingers could press, on the trays, the doors, on the seat back, on the divider.

In answer, exactly three seconds later, a little flame shot out of the slot, followed by a gram of ash. *Poof!*

He peered into the slot.

The card was gone.

While Theo sat in shock, the results of all his button pressing were still unfolding. Windows rolled down and up, a massive moonroof slid back and forth, a small refrigerator door opened and popped a bottle of champagne, loud disco music filled the back of the limo-pod, and a small hole in the tray next to him produced a lit cigar.

The privacy divider slid down.

Agent Ned coughed and waved away the smoke, shouting over the din, "Having a party, Mister Hoover?"

"I... I... I was looking for the eject button."

Agent Ned calmly put the limo-pod into hover mode, reached back through the divider's opening, stopped the music, and stretched his fingers to reach the small screen next to Theo. On its edge were thin, flush buttons (Theo thought their design was far too subtle), labeled PLAY, STOP, REWIND, FAST FORWARD, and EJECT. Ned tapped EJECT and the slot spit out another gram of ash.

Ned pointed to the ash, now drifting down to the floor. "What was that?"

Without thinking, Theo replied, "Aliens. They're coming to visit in a month."

Ned was silent for a moment, then laughed, a hearty laugh, and slapped Theo on the thigh as they resumed their journey through the skies to Lusitania City Hall. "Aliens! You are one funny man, Mister Hoover. First inmates, now aliens." He looked back at the ash, and mused to himself as the privacy divider rolled up once more. "*Aliens...*" And they zoomed into the night.

8. ACTUAL PAPER.

Silently climbing the endless marble stairs to Lusitania City Hall, Theo trailed behind Secret Service Agent Ned Weathers, Central Clerk Kate Kingston, and her Assistant Central Clerk Luna Foster. It was three o'clock in the morning and the area was deserted. No one had said a word to Theo, but he was catching on. Something happened at the Council Assembly tonight, something disastrous. That's all he knew – everything else was a mystery. Had someone died? Had the Grand Oversee been assassinated? Did it have something to do with that strange recording? Why the hell did they need a Concerned Citizens Committee member at three o'clock in the morning? He was nothing. A cog.

Their footfalls echoed in the large, darkened hall, but as they approached the main courtroom, Theo heard voices. Lots of voices.

The Clerk, Kate, in the lead, threw open the gigantic doors, and the light made them all squint. A couple of cats sauntered in behind them.

The courtroom, like Lusitania City Hall itself, was designed to look familiar and comforting to the original settlers after their thaw, so it was filled with with dark wood and marble, and a soaring ceiling, and a huge bench for the judge to sit behind, complete with his black robe, british-style white wig, and oversized gavel. To Theo, it all just looked like another thing out of time, these old reminders plopped smack in the middle of the most technologically-advanced megastructure in the history of mankind. For a mere ten meters or so below this room were endless futuristic tunnels, jammed with tubes and computers and wires and vents, snaking through the orbiter, providing oxygen, and water, and fusion energy, and everything necessary for self-sustaining life in a gargantuan steel and glass orb. There was no Disneyworld to visit anymore, but from what Theo had watched online, it must've felt something like this. Their whole everyday lives were spent looking at the thin veneer of one thing – in this case an old-style courtroom – never seeing the machines and levers and such just below the surface, working to make it all look real. But not *really* real. Disneyworld real.

The crowd hushed at their entrance. From what Theo could gather at a glance, there were maybe a hundred people here. Some police, with their blue short-sleeve shirts and caps, and some journalists, tapping away on their thumbchips and holograms, a couple of court officers, a Skywalker or two, and a handful of nondescript individuals, perhaps just here to see the show.

"Kate Kingston here. Okay, folks. I'm only going to say this once, so pay attention. First, thank you news outlets for sitting on this for a few hours tonight, you'll find your bribes in your inbox tomorrow." Theo couldn't tell if this Kingston person was joking, she must've been, but the journalists were nodding and grinning. "Now, it's almost morning, and the shit's going to hit the fan I suspect, you'll all go to town I'm sure, so we've got to get him," she pointed to Theo, "sworn in as Grand Oversee immediately."

The blood left Theo's face, then his whole upper body, and he staggered backwards. *"Excuse me?!"*

Ned shoved his hands under Theo's armpits to keep him from falling to the floor. "Miss Kingston. You said not to tell him."

Kate glared at Ned. "Ugh. I told you *to* tell him. I told you to tell him but don't freak him out. Which," she looked at Theo's trembling frame, "definitely didn't work."

Shaking loose, Theo spun on Ned. *"Is this what you were trying to tell me? Is it true?"*

Ned looked around, as if the judge might take over or rap his gavel or something, or someone, anyone else save him, but they didn't. "All right. Yes. Mister Hoover, sir. You are officially, well almost, the new Grand Oversee, sir."

And Theo fainted.

Some time later, Theo stirred. He thought he might be in a dream, something about him being in charge of it all, all the mismanaged, inefficient systems of government, all the bullshit that came with the day-to-day answering to the millions of people of the eight orbiters. No wait, it wasn't a dream. It was a nightmare. He imagined himself swimming, through raw sewage, trying to reach, reach for something, for air, for anything, to move forward. It was no use. He was drowning.

He woke up, gasping for breath, on his back, still doing some kind of swim stroke in the air.

He stopped.

Kate looked down at him, frowning. "It's going to be a long sixty days."

Theo pushed words out of his dry mouth. "Sixty...?"

"Stand up. Come on. Gotta keep this thing moving."

She pulled him up, and for the next dazed minutes, Theo tried to absorb what she told him, the entire incredible (and not in a good way) story, the enormity of what had happened tonight.

Theo sputtered, "I- I have a million questions."

Kate shook her head. "We have time for, let's see... one. Choose wisely."

"Um, okay. There has to be some mistake. Why me?"

Kate nodded to Luna, who cracked her knuckles, tapped her thumbchip, and spread her hands out in the air. All thirty-seven of Theo's proposals-slash-complaints floated in the air as a hologram above the crowded courtroom.

Theo looked up, half in awe of his own accomplishment, half in embarrassment. "So? Lots of people submit proposals."

Luna grinned. "Complaints. And not *thirty-seven* of them. And not for a total of... three thousand, six hundred eighty-nine pages." At this the crowd oohed. One journalist applauded.

"That's not a qualification. I am not qualified for Grand Oversee. For any government position at all."

Luna had one knuckle left uncracked, her left pinky, which she cracked now. "Really? Let's see, reading here..." she walked her fingers through more documents, "'I, Theo

Hoover, am more qualified than any of these so-called experts. I could do each and every one of their jobs better.'"

"I never said that!"

"Oh, on the contrary, Mister Hoover. You've said it..." she pinched out one of her notes, "... three hundred thirty-six times."

Theo felt the eyes of everyone in the room drill into his soul. "Listen. I may get a little... ahead of myself in these proposals. Complaints. I'm just trying to, you know, make some change. Like the teeniest bit of change."

Kate smiled. "Well now's your chance." She walked him over to a high table and handed him a piece of paper. An actual sheet of wood-based paper. An Official Appointment. Then she handed him a pen. He couldn't remember the last time he held a pen.

"I... I refuse."

"You can't refuse, Hoover."

"Of course I can."

The judge looked down his reading glasses at Theo. "We looked it up. Beyond the appointment by the Clerk, there's nothing in the Constitution. She's already been sworn in as Extremely Temporary Grand Oversee, and has filed her paperwork to hand it off to you. And in case you're wondering, judicial branch can't occupy an executive branch position, so I can't jump in and save you even if I wanted to. We're in new territory here, Mister Hoover. The only thing I can decide is what happens if you refuse."

"And if I do?"

"Seven years in Lusitania City Penitentiary." He pointed his gavel at Theo. "Minimum."

The pen fell out of Theo's hand. He bent down to pick it up, hands shaking, and noticed the words, inlaid in marble, in a circle on the floor, worn over many, many years but still legible: *Prepare the Path. For The Future of Man Rests In Your Hands.*

And something strange happened. A calmness came over him, and he exhaled, and he thought that maybe, just maybe, he was meant to be here, at this moment, in this position, reading these very words. Perhaps not just a cog in the machine after all. And he smiled and whispered to himself, "No pressure, Theo," and stood up, and banged his head on the underside of the table.

"Fuck!"

The judge scowled. "Excuse me?"

"Nothing. Everything's fine." Theo rubbed his head, leaned over and awkwardly signed his name before he could regain his senses and try to back out again. He handed it up to the judge.

"Excellent, Mister Hoover, our new – and slightly less temporary – Grand Oversee. Congratulations." He hammered the gavel for emphasis.

A smattering of applause echoed in the room. Someone laughed.

Kate took the opportunity to make for the exit. "Yeah. Congrats, whatever. I've given you your shot, Hoover. Have a good run. I'll be in the basement if anybody needs me. Peace out, folks." But as her hand clutched the court's oversized doorknob, the judge coughed. She turned, rolling her eyes. "Yes?"

"I'd also like to congratulate you, Miss Kingston, on *your* new position."

She squinted at the judge, and Theo got the distinct impression there had been many, many words shared between these two over the years. The judge rapped his gavel again for effect. "You, Miss Kingston, will serve as Chief of Staff to Mister Hoover. But don't worry. Your colleague Luna Foster will assist."

Luna gulped. Kate laughed. "You're kidding."

"Do I look like I'm kidding, Miss Kingston? These are desperate times. And there is simply no one else with your breadth and depth of experience. I'm positive you'll make a winning team."

Kate walked up to Theo and gestured, waving her arms, still looking at the judge. "Me? Him?"

"He was your idea, Miss Kingston. But don't worry, after sixty days and a successful election, you'll both go back to your old lives. Back to normal."

Theo smiled an apology to Kate, and laughed nervously. "Yeah. Normal. Except for the aliens, of course."

Kate looked to the judge, who looked around at the rest of the gallery, who looked equally perplexed, and turned back to Theo. "What aliens?"

9. I REALLY PICKED A WINNER.

Quickly corralling Theo, Kate, Luna, and Ned to the small conference table in his chambers beside the courtroom, the judge slammed the door shut, slumped into his chair behind the large desk, facing away from them, yanked off his wig, and removed his reading glasses. He didn't really need the glasses, not in this day and age, with five-minute mall-kiosk eye surgery. But he liked the look, very judge-like in his opinion, somewhat intimidating, peering over them at the accused. They made him look very wise, too. Which he was, or he liked to think he was, so he didn't know why he needed the glasses for that. Did the truly wise need glasses to prove it? Or was that a bit of insecurity peeking through? Maybe he still had some things to learn.

In any case, he took them off and rubbed his tired eyes, and focused his attention on the globe next to the window. It was one of those ancient ones on a real wooden stand, not printed, with authentic brass accents. He loved that globe. It was amazing how nostalgic one could be for a past that was generations ago, with nearly zero connection to the present. He loved that past the way it was, or the way he imagined it was. He wished it could be that way now. But then he might actually need reading glasses, and a globe to see where he was going. It seemed like a lot of work. He was exhausted.

Kate coughed. "Ahem."

The judge abruptly swiveled his chair away from the globe, toward his visitors. "Ah. Yes. Sorry. So, Mister Hoover. You're welcome."

Theo pointed to himself. "Me? For...?"

"For whisking you away the moment the word *alien* left your lips. Journalists live for slips like that, Mister Hoover. You could've caused a panic. Only adding to the chaos we're unleashing on them already tomorrow morning. What were you thinking?"

"Nothing..."

"Apparently."

Theo pointed to a tiny plastic baggie Ned held up, containing just shy of two grams of ash. "No, I mean, I apologize, your honor, but what I'm talking about happened. Look."

"What am I looking at, Agent Weathers?"

Ned held the baggie up higher. "A top-secret message card. Well, that's what Mister Hoover – sorry, Temporary Grand Oversee Hoover – said it was. Seems it self-destructed."

The judge took it and examined the contents. "Wonderful. This could've been a cigar for all I know. But you can verify Mister Hoover's incredible story about its contents, yes?"

"Well, no."

"No?"

"Well, see, I was… um, I was…"

The judge sighed. "You were…"

Ned motioned as if he was driving. "I was in the front. Privacy divider. Wasn't trying to be rude, just minding my business. Sometimes I say things."

"Convenient."

"And when I opened the divider, there was just this." Ned held up the bag higher still, as if there were something they might discover at its new height.

The judge wasn't biting. "Again. Convenient. So, Mister Hoover, you heard a confidential message about aliens, with no supporting evidence, from an office I've never even heard of, and your only possible witness was outside your soundproof cocoon during playback, and the recording itself doesn't even exist anymore. These aliens are planning a visit in four weeks. A casual drop-by, on their way to some other galactic adventure. Do you want me to believe all that?"

Theo fidgeted. "I… don't know. Normally, I'd agree with you. I'm a History Repair Technician, and my *job* is to question the veracity of information. I'm a skeptic. Information can only be categorized as Objective Truth if it's been verified with three independent-"

"I know how History Repair works, Mister Hoover. *Correct the Past, Protect the Future*, et cetera."

"Sorry. Anyway, Of course this all sounds insane. It's ridiculous. I have disproven dozens of UFO claims myself. But just for one second, think about it: Grand Oversee Montgomery receives this card – I believe the Secret Service can verify at least that the card existed – and then Montgomery calls the largest gathering of government officials ever, in order to share an important announcement, and then she and everyone in the hall dies in a sushi accident? Over a false UFO claim?"

The judge scratched his chin. "So you actually believe this."

"No. Yes. Hmm. Let me say it this way... I just think sometimes... sometimes, and this is me, a skeptic... sometimes when there's just a thread holding on, some desperate bit of information that doesn't want to be squashed, and let go, refuses to die and be forgotten forever... sometimes there's truth in there, a truth nugget, an underdog, wriggling and clawing to get out... and we owe it to that thing to believe."

Kate started laughing. Cackling, actually. "Oh, this is rich. Wow. I really picked a winner."

"It seems you did," the judge nodded.

Theo rose and grabbed the ash baggie. "Hey! Listen, I didn't want any of this, and I certainly don't want to be put in the position of defending some silly UFO story. I mean, the existence of aliens, in this vast universe of emptiness... do you have any idea how unfathomably big the universe is?"

Ned raised his hand. "Ninety-three billion light-years across. It would take light ninety-three billion Old Time years to travel from one end to the other."

The judge and Kate both raised their eyebrows and looked to Theo for confirmation.

Theo plopped back into his chair. "Wow. You're exactly correct, Agent Weathers."

"I know things."

It was the judge's turn to stand. "All right. I've heard enough. Before we start talking about our insignificant place in the vast universe – yes, Mister Hoover, I've just read some of your diatribes – let's get this thing moving. Mister Hoover, the court hereby issues the following gag order: you are to say *nothing* about aliens until after the election sixty days from now…"

"But they're coming – if they're coming – *thirty* days from now."

The judge just glared and continued. "…and I *highly recommend* that tomorrow you join Miss Kingston and Miss Foster on the steps of Lusitania City Hall to announce your project."

Kate scrunched her face. "What project?"

"It doesn't matter. Pick one of Mister Hoover's proposals for all I care. What matters is that, while society deals with the void of leadership for two months, the government – such as it is – needs to convey stability and forward progress, to prevent anarchy." He leaned in, for emphasis. "No aliens. No anarchy. Just stable, forward progress. Do you all understand?"

They nodded like a class of fourth-graders being scolded.

"Good. Before we adjourn, if any of you has an inkling of what you might be introducing tomorrow, I'm all ears."

Theo's hand shot up. He didn't even know why. He stared at it in disbelief, his own hand betraying him, then noticed Kate Kingston's hand in the air, too. And she was smiling at him. And suddenly he knew why his hand was in the air. And he knew that she knew. And they both knew the words that were about to come out of their mouths, an idea so simple, an idea that deserved a shot, now, especially now, when people needed it most. Theo felt a surge of purpose, envisioning the motto *The Future of Man Rests In Your Hands* across the inside of his forehead. Yes. He was here to make change! Actually make change! It was going to start tomorrow! He raised his hand even higher. Luna's hand went up too, she had somehow grasped what was about to happen, and having read and catalogued all of Theo's complaints – *proposals* – she knew precisely the words to come. She nodded, and the three said together...

"The Green Grass Initiative."

10. WHO ARE YOU TALKING TO, HOOVER?

The tallest structure on any of the eight orbiters, Lusitania City Hall dominated the small skyline of the ten-block city center surrounding it. And way up at the tippy-top perched the cavernous Residence of the Grand Oversee, with bedrooms and bathrooms and televisions and couches and a personal office and even a staff kitchen. Floor-to-ceiling windows throughout offered an incredible view of the curving horizon, and Sunnyside beyond.

Theo walked past the view, in a trance, into one of the bathrooms, to hide from the others and contemplate his fate, on the toilet.

"You know, you're normally supposed to pull your pants down if you're going to the bathroom."

It was Vin. Sitting cross-legged on the tile floor, beaming up at Theo.

Theo kicked his foot. "You again. No, I'm not going to the bathroom. I'm just sitting. Thinking. And you left me. In the limo-pod."

"Come on. I'm here, aren't I?"

"Are you?"

"Whatever. Tell me all about it." He put his fingers in his ears and shouted, "I'm all ears."

Theo couldn't help but laugh, it was always that way, trying to be mad at Vin was hopeless, always that goofy grin and that wink. "Okay, Vin. But first, it's pretty nice in here, isn't it? Like over-the-top with the architectural details, but still tasteful."

"I puked in a bathroom like this once."

"Nice. On Hindenburg?"

"Yeah. One of the galleries had this amazing bathroom. I forget the rest of the night, but I remember that bathroom. I ruined it. A shame. They banned me for life."

"Well, apparently this is my bathroom for the next sixty days, or until they decide I'm the worst possible choice and drag me to some back alley and put me out of my misery. That Kingston person had the genius idea to make me Temporary Grand Oversee. Please don't ruin my bathroom."

Vin turned up his nose. "Grand Oversee. Fancy."

Theo chuckled. "Yeah. Me. Ridiculous. But at least I get to greet the aliens."

"Aliens? Holy shit!"

"I know, right? Piper Montgomery was going to announce aliens. That's what was on the card."

Vin stood up and looked in the mirror. "Hey, remember that time we made the fake hologram? Announced the invasion of the orbiters by giant crabs? Damn, you were good with CGI."

"Of course. We were celebrities for a few minutes there. But Dad was *pissed. 'What the hell were you two thinking?! We're still trying to sort out the fake from the truth, and you idiots do* *this? The truth is all we have, boys! Don't play with the <u>TRUTH</u>!'* God, he must've said 'truth' a thousand times. That's what started my obsession with history, I guess. Trying to make it up to Dad."

Vin jumped up and down. "Oooh! History Man! Tell me about The Great Information Hack. Please?"

"I've told you the story a thousand times."

"Yeah. But it's like a bedtime story. Soothing. Come on. One more time." He sat down again, leaning his head against Theo's knee, like a child.

Theo sighed. "Okay. Once upon a time, back in 2100 OldTime, the six cooperative states of the world – Chinindia, Americas, Europe, Sovietstan, Australia, and Africarabia – faced a new problem: a revolutionary group, pitted against worldwide conglomeration, self-titled the Global Order for Decentralization, or GOD.

"Yes, the name was ridiculous, and an oxymoron if they had taken two seconds to think about it. But they tried to appear normal and relevant, and to make change in civilized ways, to decentralize power, ostensibly giving more of that power to the masses of humanity. That didn't work, though, as they were fundamentally corrupt and their leadership was certifiably insane. So the organization devolved quickly into madness, turning their zealous hackers loose, declaring war on all order and progress. The world would burn. Chaos would reign. That would create true decentralization.

"None of that happened, thank God – God-god, not the organization GOD – common sense prevailed, GOD was shunned – not God-god, the organization GOD – and everyone lived happily ever after. The End.

"BUT... there was lasting damage: the complete upending of recorded history. The GOD bots had made facts into fiction, fiction into facts, left into right, up into down, and so on, and no one knew what to make of it all. So in 2104 the U.N. created the Global History Repair Service, of which your little brother is a proud member. Well, not exactly a *proud* member, as you know. But the work suits my desire to un-shame myself for Dad, and my need for control, or normalcy, or as you would say, my 'wholly unearned indignant righteousness.'"

He looked down, and sure enough, Vin was fast asleep at his feet. Smiling like an angel. It reminded Theo of many nights, finding Vin passed out on the bathroom floor, dragging his ass to bed. Would he ever learn?

So he pulled Vin up to a sitting position, and splashed some water on his face. "Come on. Things to do. Let's go."

A knock on the door. "Who are you talking to, Hoover?" It was Kate Kingston.

He flushed the toilet. Looking down at the empty floor where Vin lay a moment ago, he shouted, "Um, nobody! Just me in here! Coming!" He opened the door, and walked gingerly past Kate. She eyed him suspiciously.

"Well, snap out of it, Hoover. We've got your announcement in twenty minutes. The good news is they've scanned the crowd and we're pretty certain you won't be assassinated."

"Oh my God - that's the *good* news? What's the bad news?"

"I didn't say I had bad news." She cracked open a Tsingtao. Some of the froth dripped onto her sleeve.

Theo just raised an eyebrow. There was always bad news.

"Okay, yes, yes, you're right, Hoover. There's always bad news. You know that self-destructo data card thingy? From the Office of Little Green Men or whatever it was called?"

"...yes..."

"Ned's been digging with the police. Can't even establish its existence. The office is missing."

Theo scratched his temple. "Um, I'm not following. An office – like a physical space with people and equipment – can't be missing. The *card* is missing. An office can't be missing. Can it?"

"I didn't think so. But apparently it can. The space is there, where it was supposed to be anyway, but inside? Nothing. Zilch. Not even a sign on the door, just a dusty outline where one used to be. Agent Ned had Luna track the staff and equipment requisitions through Civil Personnel, and there was – get this – two people. That's it. The entire Office of the Search for Non-human whatever it was called was two schmucks, a computer, a receiver, and a chair. I'm not kidding. They had to share a chair and a computer, searching the cosmos for extra-human intelligence. No wonder none of us even knew it existed. I mean, in my whole life I've never heard of any real efforts to find or contact anyone else. It was always just us humans. Alone in the universe. Which is fine with me, by the way."

"What about the two schmucks?"

"Guess where they were yesterday."

"Oh dear. The dinner."

Kate made a little shooting gun gesture. "Bingo. Sushi got 'em. So it's like the office, the people, the data, never existed. Your super-historically-significant message from the aliens? The one you purport to exist? Never existed. I'm not kidding."

"Did they get to respond? RSVP? The two schmucks? RSVP to the aliens? Are they even coming?"

Kate kept walking, pushing him along. "I have no idea. Like I keep telling you, it's like it never existed."

"But who...? Why...?"

"I have an idea."

"Why does that sound like you're not going to tell me."

"Because I'm not."

Theo stopped. "Listen, I'm, uh, Grand Oversee. I, ah, command that you tell me."

She tugged his shirt sleeve. "No."

"Please?"

"Wow. That's not very Grand Oversee-like. *'Please?'* Come on. A real Grand Oversee would puff his chest out and growl something like, 'Are you disobeying a direct order, young lady?'"

"Well, I wouldn't say 'young lady...'"

"Excuse me?" Kate balled her non-beer hand into a fist and glared.

"No, no. That's not what I meant. I meant that-"

"Choose your next words carefully, Hoover."

"I meant... I meant that the term 'young lady' is patronizing, and sexist actually. Calling someone a 'young lady' is presuming superiority over her, and also discounts the wisdom and experience that comes with her age. To me, gender is irrelevant, and the higher the age percentage the better, at least in terms of applying critical thinking to a problem. For example, what's your percentage?"

Kate considered throwing her half-empty beer at him. "*Never* ask a woman her percentage."

Theo flashed back to the numerous times he'd asked women this exact question, and it dawned on him that it might not have been the compliment he intended – no wonder he didn't get many second dates. "Oh."

She relaxed her hands, put down her beer. "But... your answer was pretty good, Hoover. Solid."

He smiled. "So now you'll tell me?"

"No. Listen, it probably *was* an accident, I don't know. I know how to work the bureaucracy, but this one, this one's a thicket of weeds like I've never seen. Anyway all I've got is opinions. You heard the judge. Zip it."

"Pretty please? I like to solve problems. I can help."

"Like the feral cat overpopulation problem? Boy, you solved that problem. In only twenty-three steps. I'm surprised you didn't have a Step Twenty-four: Incinerate."

"*Hey! I was going to put that in!* Thought better of it, though. Seemed a bit over the top."

"Just a bit." Kate laughed. "But it would solve the problem, wouldn't it?"

"Wow. So you really read my proposals?" He puffed out his chest a little, feeling a bit more like a Grand Oversee, and grinned.

"Complaints. Yes. All of them. But don't get ahead of yourself. I have to. It's my job. A job I hate. Come on."

Theo let the air out of his lungs and followed Kate down to the elevator. He was trying to take comfort knowing she was "pretty certain" he wouldn't be assassinated today.

It was not comforting.

11. ANOTHER 'ACCIDENT' IS COMING.

n a darker chamber of the Lusitania, a figure paced the floor, a thumbchip was tapped, a security-modulated voice was turned on – for the figure needed to remain in the shadows until the right moment – and began recording:

"Dearest people of the orbiters, *my* people…

"Another 'accident' is coming. I'm sorry. Or at least it will look like an accident.

"Like the sushi. The sushi worked. Already the funerals are being arranged, people are moving on, not looking back for blame and justice, it was just an accident, move along, move along.

"I've avoided detection.

"Yes, there is lingering suspicion. Perhaps misplaced, perhaps not. But I was careful, very careful. There are many layers between Dayol Sushi, and their fish distributor, and the chemists who subtly altered the DNA in a select batch of tuna and salmon, cleverly timing an undetectable toxin to proliferate in the flesh a certain number of hours after being prepared – many layers between all that and myself. I've been at this game a very long time. I already know they'll determine it was, in fact, an accident. I'll make sure of it.

"I didn't take pleasure in the death, my people. It was a lot. But it had to be done. Before those careless idiots in government could respond to the aliens' invitation. I did it to protect mankind. I would do anything to save mankind.

"How far would *you* go?

"If there was a bomb that would destroy an entire orbiter – there isn't, but let's say there is – and someone could stop it by reaching into a cavity and turning a gear, but loses their arm in the process, would that loss be worth it? An arm for millions of souls?

"Yes. Of course.

"But what if that person had to die? To willingly sacrifice their own soul for millions of others?

"A little harder to stomach. But still. Of course it would be acceptable. Admirable even. Honorable. A monument might even be erected.

"Now how about two people?

"Hmmm. Harder to accept, but still acceptable. Two monuments.

"So... where is the limit? Three people? A dozen? Or three hundred and fourteen?

"If you knew that an alien species was heading our way – don't ask me how I know – and there was no way to be certain their intentions were peaceful or malicious, that there was a real chance they were coming to destroy us, to eliminate the hundreds of millions of us, the remaining humans in all the universe, wouldn't you sacrifice three hundred and fourteen souls to save the rest from extinction?

"Yes, there was a chance these aliens were coming in peace. But would you take that chance? The fool Piper

Montgomery was willing to respond to their radio invitation, to take that chance with our lives, willing to open her arms wide, like a child, to what looked to her like an innocent puppy wanting to lick our faces, but what in actuality was a wolf, intent on ripping our throats out.

"It sounds extreme, you might say. But you forget. Like the rest of them. You forget that it's happened before. Back in 2231 OldTime, on Earth, when they drilled through that ice shelf, releasing an ancient virus that hadn't evolved in our world, perhaps it was originally from Earth, perhaps not, it didn't really matter, but five hundred million humans never got to find out the answer. Instead of keeping the door closed, and remaining content with what *was*, we just had to find out, didn't we, I can't imagine why, find out what was down there, to open our arms to the unknown. And look where that got us.

"I don't blame you for forgetting. We like to forget our own mistakes. And it was 593 years ago, on another planet you've never even seen, the birthplace of our species but not yours. But I don't like to forget. I like to remember.

"I watched him today. Theo Hoover. He seems like a nice one. And he didn't mention aliens once. Smart. Smarter than Piper Montgomery at least. He's listened well, realizes the chaos he'd be inviting. Instead, he announced something called the Green Grass Initiative. I laughed out loud, his silly plan was preposterous, but also smart, because this man knows hope grows in the small spaces. I remember hope. In fact, as Hoover talked, the feeling almost became real in my heart. A little glimmer. But I know better. He sees the puppy, but I know it's a wolf.

"He's the only one who saw the data card, thank goodness. So he's the last one that needs to be taken care of.

Just one more sacrifice, my people. That way there is no response to the alien horde invitation, and they will leave without ever meeting us, and we can get back to our perfect life here on the orbiters.

"I'm sorry, Theo Hoover. You weren't my choice. You were just in the way. But don't worry, it'll look like an accident."

The figure stopped, looking down at the only other copy of the two-centimeter square data card, held between two fingers. The other hand raised an old-fashioned cigar lighter, clicked a flame to life, and burned the card until it was a two grams of ash on the floor.

12. THE GREEN GRASS INITIATIVE

"Hoover. Here. Make yourself useful."

Theo snapped back to reality. He stood at the base of his very own flat-cluster. His flat was thirty stories up, but here, on the ground, among the weeds and the trash, the impossible was actually happening:

The quad parks and inter-cluster spaces would turn green.

He'd imagined it innumerable times over the years, but never really believed could happen. Patches of green grass? Never. Until now, he had satisfied himself with adding it to his pile of rants against the bureaucratic machinery, a way to blow off steam at the idiocy of it all, the incompetency and corruption and laziness. But the plan was theoretically possible, a sound idea with completely viable and mapped-out logistics. It could work. And it looked now like it actually might.

He reviewed the math quickly in his head: the total population of all orbiters was approximately two hundred million people, with an average of four to a family, requiring fifty million flats. Each cluster of flats – or flat-cluster – was composed of 360 flats – four towers of thirty stories each, with three flats per floor, arranged around a central, hundred-meter square quad – for a grand total of 138,800 flat-clusters, spread among five of the eight orbiters.

Over the past couple of centuries, these quads and the green spaces connecting the flat-clusters were neglected, used as casual garbage dumps, and overgrown with weeds, until eventually the idea of a "green space" seemed like something quaint from a storybook (or in Theo's case growing up, from an ancient video game). Sure, there were farms and crops, and even small forests for logging, but where the people actually lived, for the average person, the word "green" was a luxury.

Yes, it seemed an impossible task, but Theo knew a secret. His distrust of anything bureaucratic and his conviction that laziness was even more rampant than corruption led him down a rabbit hole of investigation one day – and it paid off. With just a little digging, he discovered that the central orbiter government had scheduled, each and every year, rehabilitation of a certain percentage of the orbiters' parks and lawns, but simply never did it. One emergency or another – a crack in a dome, a sinkhole, an irrigation tunnel leak – pushed the ongoing project to the back burner. Further and further back. Until it was forgotten, and its budget greedily absorbed back into more important (read as "corrupt" and "wasteful") efforts. So years and years, then decades and decades, of materials piled up – specifically *InstaGrass*. Theo calculated that on Star Orbiter Flint – the main hub of agriculture, with thousands of acres of crops, dozens of vineyards, wood production – there were at least ten thousand metric tons of the stuff just sitting there. Once, in his "official" (not really) capacity, he called over to Flint, under the pretense that there were Earth artifacts in an immense warehouse that could confirm or disprove whether 2036 OldTime American President Ryan Seacrest had his own skeleton replaced with adamantium. Theo waited while the foreman finally found an old key, pried open a rusty back door, and his jaw hit the floor. "Holy shit."

Theo grinned. "What? The skeleton?"

The foreman's jaw began working again. "No. There must be ten thousand metric tons of *InstaGrass* in here. Huh. I wonder what it's here for. Well, one thing's for certain: the government knows what it's doing here. Sorry about your skeleton. Good luck."

And now here he stood. In his own quad. Day one of the Green Grass Initiative. He smiled. Maybe good luck *was* starting to happen.

"*Hoover!*" Kate kicked his boot.

This time Theo *actually* snapped back to reality. "Whoops. I'm sorry, Miss Kingston. What?"

"Here. Take this minicomm and make yourself useful. We're trying to coordinate the fastest landscaping mobilization in the history of the orbiters, five of the eight in six days, and you're standing there grinning like an idiot."

She plucked the minicomm from her ear and popped it into his palm. It had mustard on it. Theo winced. "Um, could I get a clean one? I mean, don't get me wrong, I'm amazed it's only ten in the morning and you've already had two dirty-water dogs and a beer, but your hands, and look..." he pointed helplessly at the condiment-stained minicomm.

Kate shrugged. "Number one I was hungry. And thirsty. Number two I didn't ask what you think. And number three Hindenberg's already connected to this one. Put it in your ear and tap them in. Don't make me come back here and bail you out." She walked away.

Theo sighed, wiped the minicomm as best he could, inserted it into his ear, and tapped it. A little hologram of the hard-hatted foreman on Star Orbiter Hindenberg projected into the space in front of his face. "Where's Kingston? Who are you?"

"Um, Theo Hoover. For the moment, I'm Grand Oversee. Temporary Grand Oversee."

"Well that's just fantastic." The foreman's miniature image flickered as he looked around for someone more helpful. "Ugh. Whatever. Okay. Well, as I was telling Kingston, we've got a broad-spreader on cluster 85b that's supposed to be here now, two of the other narrow-spreaders are on the fritz, and a couple of tons of *InstaGrass* got wet and that's a fucking disaster. This is crazy. I'm gonna need two more days. And I'm not asking."

The words "sure, no problem" almost made it out of Theo's mouth, because really, it was a miracle any of this was happening at all, never mind in six days. But he hesitated, as the strangest thought popped into his mind: *what would Kingston say? What would a real Grand Oversee say?*

He cleared his throat. "What's your name?"

The Foreman squinted. "Applebaum. Chuck Applebaum. Why?"

"Well, Mister Applebaum, sir, I really hate to say it, but this *is* happening, no matter what, in six days. How long have you been a foreman?"

Chuck's hologram looked puzzled. "Ah... nineteen years. You trying to be an a-hole?"

"Good. Then that means you're vested, full pension."

"Yeah. And?"

"Good. Chuck, can I call you Chuck? Did you know that as Grand Oversee, I can declare a state of emergency, right now, while we're on this minicomm, and move funds directly from the Hindenberg grounds union pension fund to requisition an idle broad-spreader from Flint, fly in parts for those two narrow-spreaders, and clean up that InstaGrass?"

It was small, but Theo thought he could see the hologram's tiny jaw drop. He continued.

"But I won't do that, Chuck, because there's another way. Why don't I call over to cluster 85b for you, to see what their hold up is, put a little heat on them, and we can work on the rest together. Would that be okay?"

The hologram nodded, and without switching off the minicomm began turning and shouting. "What are you tools looking at? You heard Hoover! Get off your asses and get spreader fifteen-b over to this cluster, shift another one into its spot, we'll stagger while we wait for 85b. Move it! Move it!"

Theo tapped out the call, and started to look up the number for flat-cluster 85b.

A finger poked his shoulder. "Wait. Hold up a sec." It was Kate.

"Oh, whoops, sorry Miss Kingston. Did I do something wrong?"

She raised an eyebrow. "No, actually... I just came over to bail you out and... was that you?"

Theo laughed nervously. "Um, yes, I think."

"I mean, you were a little too human, but baby steps I guess. I just had to tear Chernobyl a new asshole, no humanity at all. They're still bleeding. But who knows, maybe you'll get there in sixty days. And listen, I'll make that call over to 85b. I have a special project for you instead."

"Oh no."

She laughed. "No, it's not like that. I've been watching you, Hoover, and I know you want to do it."

"Do what?"

"Get on one of the spreaders. I can see it in your eyes. You're like a little kid."

"I'm a thirty-two percent. There is no little kid left in me. I assure you. I'll pass."

"Sure." Kate proceeded to drag him, resisting and harrumphing, to the nearest lift, buckling him in and hoisting him up the twenty meters, hailing the nearest spreader, a gigantic, hovering machine the size of ten tractor-trailer-pods. Theo tried to unbuckle and claw his way back down, but the spreader eased up against the lift and opened its side hatch before he could escape.

Kate shouted over the din, "Hey, driver, you got an extra seat?"

"Yes, ma'am."

"Great. You've got another passenger." And she pushed Theo in, and the hatch closed.

And as the spreader drifted away, and continued making the land below them green with the foam that would become grass in twenty-four hours, she spied a smile grow on Theo's face. Small at first, but then wider and wider, until he was absolutely beaming. Oh there was definitely some little kid left in there.

Kate couldn't help it, it was contagious, that smile, and one appeared on her own face.

The guy.

And then a tear rolled partway down her cheek. She caught it before it went any further, with a swipe of her only condiment-free finger, and looked at it for a moment. "Great. Allergies."

13. BZZZZZZZ

B*zzzzz.*

Bzzzzzzzz.

Bzzzzzzzzzzzz.

Theo's finger hovered over the button, ready to press it a fourth time, when a hologram of Kate Kingston projected from his minicomm. "You know you could have just called me on the minicomm, Hoover."

"I don't know, I like the call panel thing. Have you ever thought about that? Why we still have call panels everywhere, in the lobbies of our flat-clusters of all places, when everyone's got a minicomm? I think it's because we're nostalgic for the past, even a past we don't remember, or isn't useful. We build these little vestigial things into our present lives, it fills some kind of void in us, an imagined history that things were better, and maybe could be agai-"

"Hoover!"

"Oh. Sorry."

Kate's hologram put her arms on her hips. "Why are you

here? It's nine in the morning on a Sunday. And I never even told you where I live."

"Come down to the lobby. I want to show you something. Two things, actually."

"No. I've earned a day off from you. No offense. Goodbye."

"I have food."

"Pass. Not in the mood for chickpea avocado whatever. Goodbye."

"Two In-N-Out Burgers and a six of Tsingtao."

"I'll be down in five minutes."

As they strolled along the gravel path connecting Kate's quad to the neighboring one, trailed a respectful distance by Secret Service Agent Ned, Theo pointed to the green on either side. The foam had disappeared, revealing lush grass everywhere. "Five days. It almost needs a trim already."

"Yup. InstaGrass works in five days. That's what it says on the bag. You woke me up on a Sunday to show me this? It's beautiful, really, but I could've seen it from my window." She grabbed a Tsingtao from the bag he was carrying. "Though this helps." Popped it open and took a swig. "What are we doing here, Hoover?"

On cue, Theo led them off the path, to a shaded patch under a maple tree. "Sit."

"Sit? What am I, a dog?"

"Wow, you really are even more, ah, Kingston-y on Sundays, aren't you? I'm sorry. How about please, let's sit if that's okay, I humbly request with your gracious permission." He plopped down.

She joined him, skeptical. "How'd you know I liked In-N-

Out Burgers for breakfast?" Snatched one, took an oversized bite, ketchup leaking out onto her hand.

"Just a guess. But not a hard one. I mean, you kind of scream *In-N-Out Burgers For Breakfast*." He handed her a napkin.

"I'll take that as a compliment."

"Good. Now... look around."

"Yeah. Grass. Great."

"Keep looking."

A few awkward moments later, Kate noticed a woman walking her dog. Then a couple of kids throwing a buzzball. Then a guy jogging. Nothing too out of the ordinary. But...

"Huh. They're smiling."

Theo flashed his own grin. "Mm-hmm."

"You're going to say something about nostalgia, aren't you?"

"Not exactly. I was going to say-"

"Wait. Something like it wasn't really about the grass. Something deep like that."

He laughed. "Yes, actually. When I wrote that proposal – complaint, whatever – this is *exactly* what I had in mind. The grass is the *form*. The surface. The *content* underneath... is *this*."

"Hey, I just noticed something else."

"What?"

"No cats."

"Huh."

"Did you do something I don't know about? Is there something in *InstaGrass* that repels cats? Have you somehow activated *Twenty-three Steps to Eliminate the Escalating Problem of Feral Feline Overpopulation* without telling me? Is that the second thing you wanted to show me?" She laughed.

"No. I swear."

"Weird. Okay, what's the second thing then?"

He laid back onto the grass. Motioned for her to do the same. Smiled.

She looked down at him. "Really."

"Really."

And she tentatively leaned back on her elbows.

"No. All the way so you're looking up."

"Ugh."

She complied, and they laid in the grass, looking up at the sky. Yes, it was a dome, with a daytime projection against it, if you looked close you could see the titanium ribs, but if you let yourself go a little, it was just a blue sky, with a few clouds here and there, and pods racing across, heading wherever people head on Sunday mornings. Blades of grass tickled their ears and neck, like a living blanket swaddling them.

He sighed. "Ahhh. When was the last time you did this?"

"I can honestly say I've never done this in my entire life. It feels weird. I don't like it. I'm getting up."

"Wait. Come on, give it a few seconds."

She grudgingly relented. And sure enough, in a few seconds, the world slipped away for both of them, the world of the orbiters anyway, the endless ordinary battles of work and living, the small frustrations that add up to a life of frustration. It all slipped away, replaced by something ephemeral but also timeless, a feeling shared by anyone who's ever laid down in grass and watched clouds drift across a blue sky, and smelled the ground, and warmed their skin in the sun, and felt weightless.

She sighed too. "Is this nostalgia?"

Theo thought about it for a moment. "It's sort of fake nostalgia. For an Earth we never even got to know. But that we wish we could. Don't you wish you knew? Wish you could go there?"

She turned to him, surprised. "Where? Earth?"

He nodded.

Kate pointed a finger at him. "I'm going to forget you just said that. It's like the one rule everyone actually agrees on, Hoover. Don't talk about going to Earth. I thought you were a rule follower."

"Yes. You're right. Sorry. It'll never happen again."

"Good." Her stomach growled, so she changed the subject. "Hey, you haven't touched your In-N-Out Burger."

"You want it, don't you."

"...nooo...?"

He grinned and pushed the bag toward her. "They're both for you. I brought a chickpea avocado on multigrain for me."

"God. We're getting to know each other, aren't we? Don't get too attached, though. In fifty-two days you'll never see me again."

"Good."

"Yeah. Good." And she plowed into her second In-N-Out Burger and chuckled.

Just then her minicomm buzzed in her pocket. "Shit. It's Luna."

"How do you know it's Luna?"

"I don't know anybody else." She popped the minicomm into her ear, tapped it, and Luna's hologram appeared. "Hey Luna. I know it's bad news so out with it."

"No. No bad news, I promise."

"Then why the call?"

"Kate - I've never seen anything like this. Positive correspondence is outpacing complaint correspondence fifty-four percent to forty-six percent."

"Holy shit."

Theo raised his hand. "That sounds good. Is that good?"

Luna giggled like a middle-schooler. "Mister Hoover, in my entire career, positive has never broken twenty percent. You're my new hero."

Kate smacked the hologram, to no effect. "Christ, Luna. You're going to give him a complex. He did one thing right. And by the way, the shit-ton of resources and money we diverted to get this little project done? There'll be a hundred and five senate hearings for sure. Someone'll get indicted. It'll be a fucking quagmire. We're just lucky there is no senate at the moment. This really is nothing to celebrate. Goodbye."

Kate tapped her minicomm and Luna disappeared. "Don't listen to her. And don't you dare let this go to your head. We can't afford it. We've got a government to build, and a Grand Oversee to elect. Stop smiling. Now. I'm not kidding. You think this is funny?"

Theo shook his head. "I'm sorry. You're right. But it's just... I've never really done anything. This feels good."

From nowhere, twenty or so cats appeared around them, sniffing for food, meowing, circling them, like a pride of tiny lions sizing up their prey.

"Okay. Cat's are back. Feel-good brunch is over. Thanks for the beers, Hoover." And as she stood her minicomm buzzed again. "Listen, Luna. I told you he's going to get a complex-"

"No. Kate... look up. Can you see it??"

She peered into the blue. "Nope. And I'm not in the mood for riddles, Luna. What am I looking for?"

"It's... a ship."

14. SORRY, WE'RE EARLY.

t didn't look like a ship to Theo. He stood there, in the cramped headquarters of the orbiters' sole military unit, staring at the monitors above them, scratching his head and squinting. "That's a ship?" Kate shrugged. Luna shrugged. Agent Ned peered carefully into the wrong monitor. It was turned off.

"Yes, that is a ship, sir," General Zima strained to whisper, reaching his fingers into his collar to stretch the damned thing out a little. He hadn't worn this uniform in... yikes, how long had it been?... and he'd gained a few pounds in the intervening years. It wasn't that he was lazy – far from it. He worked out two hours a day, ran seven kilometers, and could still even eke out a pull-up or two. But years were years. He wasn't getting any younger. Oh, and the other thing.

Ice cream.

That was his downfall. Waiting your entire adult life for something to happen – there hadn't been an armed conflict in post-Earth history, and virtually all weapons were illegal –

it wreaked havoc on a man's sense of purpose. General Zima felt more like an overnight security guard in a dusty museum than the highest-ranking military official for all of humanity. There was a void in him.

And nothing filled the void like ice cream. He couldn't decide if he liked chocolate chip cookie dough or butter pecan best, although if he was really being honest the best was a hearty scoop of each. With whipped cream on top. Maybe a pinch of sprinkles. Okay, a handful. Damn, the whole container, all right?

Rationally, Zima understood and accepted the lifetime of waiting, and appreciated the fact that humanity had come a long way. He'd read all the books on war, it was captivating reading – especially with a bowl of rocky road – and it made him grateful that when humanity was faced with doom, suddenly the flag you had hanging on your porch, or the color of your skin, or the god you worshipped, or what you had or didn't have between your legs, didn't matter at all. Everyone just ran for the ark. And that was the silver lining in all this, wasn't it? That we no longer felt the need for separate nation-states. That the word "gun" was hardly ever heard. That you had an equal chance of having a next-flat neighbor that was Chinese, or Indian, or Polish, or Russian, or American, and after a few generations, those words became history too, and even the colors of our skin became less distinct. Where there used to be clearly vanilla or chocolate, now there was an infinite blend of shades, like swirls of caramel running through a quart of mocha almond fudge. He whispered lightly, "...mmm... mocha almond fudge..."

"Mocha almond fudge?" Theo was mesmerized by this thing they were calling a ship, unable to look away. It was alien, in every sense of the word, looking more like a cloud with a fur of fiber-optic strands than something he'd expected, subconsciously his whole life, some sleek silver tube with a warp drive shooting out the back. And it certainly didn't remind him of mocha almond fudge. "General… is mocha almond fudge code for something?"

"Um… yes!" A bead of sweat appeared on Zima's forehead. "M.A.F. It's code for the, ah, thermal venting, the M.A.F if you will, no, wait, it's the, ah, Modulating Amplitude Framis-" he hung his head and sighed. "No. It's not code. It's a problem. I think I might have a problem."

Theo finally looked down from the ship, for the first time really taking a good look at this General Zima. He was struck with opposite impulses: one, to pat him on the shoulder and let him know that we all had problems, even the generals among us he supposed; and the other impulse, to shake this man, this symbol of incompetence, to shake him out of the dull stupor in which everyone in power on these orbiters seemed to be trapped. It was a mighty struggle for a moment, a lifetime of disappointments wanting to scream out and be heard, but somehow a tiny angel alighted on Theo's brain, and he reached over and patted General Zima on the shoulder.

"It's okay, General. Everyone's got problems. But… if it's okay, let's tackle that a little later. First, if that's a ship, why is it here? We never responded to the invitation."

General Zima tilted his head. "What invitation?"

Theo held out his hand, his fingers two centimeters apart. "Well. See, there was a data card. It contained an encrypted radio signal, received and decoded by the Office of the Search for Non-human Intelligence. The office doesn't exist anymore, the two workers died, and the card self destructed in the back of a limo-pod. So there's no evidence of it at all. I'm the only one that's even aware of its contents. It was an invitation. They said they'd only come if we consented, but we never responded. So I don't know why they're here."

General Zima nodded and harrumphed, trying to believe him, but not doing a very good job.

Theo pointed back to the monitor. "So... what are we looking at?"

Zima nodded. "Of course, sir." He pointed to the dots of light at the tips of the individual fur hairs on the cloud. "It's definitely a ship. We've analyzed the heat signatures and chemical makeup of these strands, and it appears they're micro-fusion-impulse-thrusters. Ingenious, actually, having a decentralized propulsion system like this. Allows it to move in any direction, quickly, like an octopus, a hairy, fiber-optic octopus, and makes disabling it nearly impossible. No central power source to destroy."

"Destroy?"

"You know. If you wanted me to shoot at it. Blow it up, sir."

"No! Why would I want to blow it up?"

"I'm not sure. I have never blown anything up. But my training, sir. We're trained to blow things up. With nukes. If necessary."

"Nukes? We have nukes? No. It won't be necessary. They're here in peace."

"Are you sure?"

"I'm sure. First of all, what could an advanced civilization, clearly capable of intergalactic travel, possibly want from us? We can't even terraform Sunnyside."

Kate, who'd been uncharacteristically quiet, whispered, "Maybe they want our grass."

Luna, feeling left out, offered her theory. "Maybe they want to enslave us for their entertainment."

Kate let out a little nervous laugh. "Luna, a little too enthusiastic with that suggestion. I think you might like that."

She protested. "I would not!"

"You would, wouldn't you?"

Luna thought about it for a moment. "Okay. Maybe. A little."

Agent Ned raised his hand. "Maybe we taste good."

Before Theo could put a stop to the parade of alien invasion theories, a sound silenced them all: "Bloop!"

Agent Ned raised both his hands now. "That wasn't me."

Crossing to a smaller holographic display, General Zima turned a knob. "It's a radio signal. From the ship. I can't believe I'm saying this, sir, but I believe... we're about to make... *FIRST CONTACT.*" He reverently handed Theo a microphone.

They all whispered together, "*First Contact...*"

In all the chaos since the discovery of the ship, Theo hadn't given a single thought to what he might say in this historic moment. His mind was completely blank. Would they understand our language? Should he ask for a keyboard and start playing musical notes? Do they need a visual, like some form of interpretive dance? Would a series of clicks and tongue smacks wor-

General Zima cleared his throat. Pointed to the microphone.

And without thinking, Theo uttered mankind's first word to another intelligent life form: "Bloop!"

Kate palmed her face. Luna had to leave the room, unable to stifle a fit of the giggles.

Silence.

Then Theo tapped the microphone and whispered, "Hello?"

After another excruciating silence, a crackle came over the speaker. Then a voice: "Hello! Or 'bloop' if for you that's better, a greeting we were not aware of. In any case sorry we're early. But really, when talking light years and wormholes and spacetime curves, two weeks early is super very prompt. Maybe premature teeny teeny bit. Depending, though, late some would even consider it. Fashionably late. Can you imagine? And really, what is time, amiright? Fold in space here, entropy reversal there. Supposed to wait for your response to our invitation, we acknowledge, but too excited, so we committed significant breach of decorum. Whoops! Apologize very much! But either way, here we are!"

They stood there, stunned, trying to absorb what they'd just heard. A voice from another world. The voice was clearly synthetic, these aliens were using some kind of device to speak, and the language use was a little awkward, their translation software wasn't quite there, but it mostly made sense. Theo smiled, imagining another species using old television sitcoms, reality TV competitions, and food network broadcasts to learn human language.

The speaker crackled again. "Hello?... Bloop?..."

Theo worked his frozen mouth until words spilled out. "No, no, no need for 'bloop.' I was just, I didn't know how you, well, anyway, simply Hello! Welcome, from all of humanity! I am Theo. Theo R. Hoover. Temporary Grand Oversee of the Great Orbiter Project, humbly representing the remaining population of humankind in the universe." His hands were shaking. Kate nudged his elbow and whispered, "Relax. You're doing fine." But her hands were trembling too.

This time the voice from the speaker sounded more

formal. "Hello, Theo R. Hoover, Temporary Grand Oversee of the Great Orbiter Project. May we come aboard? Quite long was the trip, and we are *famished*. We would sincerely enjoy to have you for lunch."

Agent Ned's face went white, and he turned to the others. "I told you."

15. WHOOPS

Suddenly the mug on the nearest table vibrated, the coffee inside rippling, rippling, rippling, like that scene from one of Theo's favorite old time films, *Jurassic Park,* where the ripples hint at the approach of Tyrannosaurus Rex. They all watched, silent as mice, each of them wondering if their alien visitors might, in fact, be some type of hideous, flesh-eating monster.

Then the table shuddered and shook. Then the computer monitors. Then the concrete beneath their feet. A mirror fell to the floor and shattered.

Kate lunged at Theo, buried her head in his neck, and closed her eyes. Theo instinctively wrapped his arms around her.

Was it possible? He thought. *Was Kate Kingston actually... afraid?*

And then, as suddenly as it started, the rumbling stopped.

"Whoops!" The synthetic voice of the alien crackled through the speaker. "Should have told you. Sorry! A bit of gravity manipulation, we had to perform, to obtain geosynchronous orbit alongside your artificial moons. All over now. Rest easy. Yay! Oh, and also forgot, another thing supposed to tell you, always forget, silly! Beings we visit always want to know this: no, we do not eat what you call 'meat.'"

A collective sigh swept through the small team, and they laughed from the sudden release of bowel-clenching tension. Theo let his arms go slack, and Kate pushed him away. "Get off me, Hoover."

"Wha-? Me? But-"

"You heard me." She looked around at the others, then back to Theo. "Can I talk to you for a second? Privately?"

Theo stammered again, "No... I'm... not sure..." but he realized it wasn't a question, as she grabbed his sleeve and jerked him away, toward a glass-walled server closet at the far back of the control room.

She stuffed him into the small space, lined floor to ceiling with computer housings and innumerable tiny lights and wires. A cat darted out as she crammed herself in after him and closed the door. They stood an inch apart. A loud hum enveloped them.

Theo fidgeted. "Well. I'd back up a little, but I might break something."

She just stared at him. He couldn't decide if her eyes were glaring and furious, or scared and welling up with tears. He had to fill the silence. "You know I didn't mean to... back there... you kind of leapt into my..."

"Shut up. Just shut up." She paced. Which was hard, as they stood together on about one square foot of available space. Without looking at him, she hissed, "What have you done?"

"Me...?"

"Yeah. You. Ever since that feral feline complaint landed on my desk, it's been chaos. Chaos wasn't the plan, Hoover! What the hell?"

"But…"

"Shut up. Let me yell at you." He nodded and she glared at him. "You know, it's my fault. I chose you." And she suddenly remembered, out of nowhere, that stupid Psych 101 class in college, the book they had to read about chaos and order, how they're both equally seductive, how we can say we want one thing, but we choose the other. It was bullshit, of course, and she dropped the class, but now, as she looked Hoover up and down, she had to ask… *did I want this?* Is that possible?

No. She had built her entire life on the foundation of order and boring, not chaos and upheaval. She wasn't about to change now. Her pacing quickened and she spoke while her brain raced. "I'm good at what I do, Hoover. I won't be modest. I'm good with *knowns*. Details, facts, figures, bureaucracy, protocols, the same-old-same-old. But this? Mass death? Fucking aliens? Here? It's chaos, Hoover, all chaos!"

Risking her wrath, Theo whispered, "But… what about the Green Grass Initiative?"

She stopped. *Huh.*

He was right. The Green Grass Initiative wasn't just order, it was order brought to the next level. It was an oasis in a sea of chaos. And it felt good. It felt really good. And it was… fun? And Hoover did that. With her. Together.

The clash of emotions was too much, the rage and the thrill and the fun and the confusion and the dread. She looked down to the floor, lungs heaving, tears escaping her eyes for the first time in a long time. She watched her own hands tremble, and whispered, "Fuck."

Theo reached out, his hand resting on her shoulder. But before he could say a word, she growled, "Don't. I will break every one of your fingers. Just... give me a second."

He pulled his hand back and stood there awkwardly. "Um... you know, it's okay to be afraid. I'm an expert at being afraid."

She snickered, a small release, then caught herself. "Who said I was afraid?"

No one had to say it.

"It's okay Miss Kingston. I'm shitting my pants right now."

She looked up. "Literally?"

"No."

"Good."

And they laughed together, a pitiful laugh.

"You can call me Kate. Miss Kingston is what my Psych 101 professor called me. I hated him."

Theo smiled to himself. "Okay... Kate. You can call me-"

"Hoover. I'll stick with Hoover." She took a deep breath, then another. "What if they're lying?"

"Who?"

"The aliens. What if they're not as friendly as they say they are? What if they're *too* friendly? What if their ship is a slave ship? What if there are others out there? What if this is the end? What if-"

He took her trembling hands. "Stop. You're having a panic attack. Just stop talking and keep taking deep breaths and I'm going to tell you a quick story." She nodded and he continued. "Okay. The first time I was ever on an interorbiter shuttle, I was ten maybe, I was so scared I threw up into one of those little vacuum sick bags. As I was getting ready for round two, my brother Vin – I have a brother Vin, by the way – he reached over and took the bag and folded up the top and said, 'Mmmm. Okay if I save this for later? A little snack?' And I laughed, and while I was distracted he unbuckled my harness and I started floating around the cabin, screaming my head off."

"Your brother sounds like a dick."

Theo chuckled. "Nah. I think his point was to throw me into the deep end, so I'd realize that the fear was the hardest part. And it was. And ever since then, I've loved the shuttles and the feeling of weightlessness." He added sheepishly, "Now I'm just afraid of everything else."

They stood there, silent for a long moment.

Kate pushed away Theo's hands, turned to the others outside, and pressed her forehead against the glass. "I appreciate the deep end thing, Hoover. But this is a whole other level." She turned to him. "What would your brother do this time?"

Theo looked around, expectant, but his brother didn't appear. Vin had left them all alone. But Theo smiled to himself, as maybe that was the point.

16. THE ALIENS

After some hasty bio-checks – no one wanted a rabid alien virus ruining a perfectly good lunch – Star Orbiter Lusitania's entrance was prepared. At the south pole of each orbiter, a massive tubular airlock allowed the commerce of human life to proceed: interorbiter deliveries of everything from grain to vehicles to wine from the vineyards over on Flint, shuttles carrying tourists to Oyster Cove, engineering transfers heading to and from Sunnyside to speed up – ostensibly – the terraforming process. It was easy to take it all for granted, as everyone aboard the orbiters had lived their entire lives with these conveniences, but right now Theo looked around, marveling at the miracles of engineering before him, and smiled. How did the engineers back on Earth know exactly how to position these orbiters, from light years away, so that their days were more or less what humans were used to? How did Daisy Morgan come up with, in the nick of time, a cryostasis technology that was stable and wouldn't kill them all on the way out here? How did the miners extract all the Earth had left to offer, the unfathomable amounts of metal, and carbon, and silicon, and helium, and hydrogen, and all the rare elements, and throw it all into space, and build these gargantuan moons? Maybe humanity wasn't so doomed after all, for with all their stupidity and caveman habits, they had somehow pulled it off, and saved a little pocket of people for the future.

Then, as if on cue, he stepped in a fresh wad of chewing gum. "People," Theo muttered. And he said a silent prayer hoping the aliens weren't such slobs.

The shuttle bay, the interior section beyond the vast tubular airlock chamber, had quickly been swept and cleared of feral cats, then decorated with streamers, mobile bleachers, and an endlessly long white carpet borrowed from Maximum Romance Wedding Planners. The Lusitania University brass band played old Earth music, currently the ancient anthem "Margaritaville."

Along with Theo stood Kate, Luna, Agent Ned and General Zima, as well as assistants and planners, all in a line on a temporary dais. They were all painfully aware of the amateur, slap-dash scene. Humanity was clearly not putting its best foot forward. Kate, still reeling from her uncharacteristic panic, was physically wincing. "I swear to God, it's like a high school homecoming parade. I'm embarrassed. Luna, this is embarrassing."

"Kate, we had twelve hours." She was tapping her thumbchip and sorting and sending like mad. "We don't exactly keep the *Official First Contact Priceless Tapestries and Thousand-Piece Orchestras* packed away in a storage locker waiting for this. You're lucky there's not five cats rubbing up against your shin. And who cares? Look around. They're loving it."

Luna was right. As Theo scanned the crowd, his heart actually leapt a little. Thousands of people, from all eight orbiters, couldn't care less about the the thrown-together setup. And they didn't seem the least bit freaked out that beings from another part of the universe had suddenly arrived out of nowhere. No, it seemed like every one of them were just happy for the change, the excitement, the novelty, and dare Theo think it... some *hope*. They were having the time of their lives, singing "*...looking for my lost shaker of salt...,*" bouncing beach balls through the crowd, another ancient Earth tradition Theo couldn't understand, and usually found annoying. But at this moment, as he watched the normally stoic judge boop a beachball to one of the lawyers... what was that feeling... hmm... was he actually *proud* of this motley crew? Proud to stand in front of them, and represent them, and *not* irritated and embarrassed for once? *Maybe*, he allowed himself. *Maybe*.

Off to the side, on the other hand, the Skywalkers, in their ridiculous robes – pulled back slightly to reveal their toy lightsaber holsters – stood in gloomy silence. But Kate couldn't help notice that their faces betrayed a hint of pleasure, and it hit her: *of course – now they have a <u>real</u> Empire to rebel against!* "Hey. Hoover. Look over there. Trouble brewing. Mister CryoCrypt himself."

And as Theo looked down from the dais, his stomach turned. For in the front row of Skywalkers stood Hector Morgan, scowling. He looked up at Theo and slowly shook his head. Theo waved the nausea away. "He's harmless." But he didn't really believe it, and Kate and Luna exchanged a glance that said *we don't believe it either.*

Suddenly, a small... something... appeared in the distance, approaching the Lusitania, from the general direction of the massive cloud-like alien ship. It looked like the large cloud had ejected a tiny cloud, something that shouldn't exist in space but there it was right there in front of them, slowly descending into the airlock. It looked to every single person present like how God might travel through the void.

The band clumsily stopped "Margaritaville." The crowd hushed. There was a silence so complete Theo could hear the hammering of his heart. Kate and Luna gulped. General Zima stood stiff at attention. Agent Ned stuck a finger in his ear, digging around for something.

The outer set of airlock doors closed behind the cloud, the chamber filled with breathable air, and the inner set of doors opened slowly.

The strange little cloud, a bit more solid-looking now, began to part, like the heavens.

There had never been a moment of anticipation like this in the history of mankind.

As the cloud closed behind them and rested in place, the aliens were revealed to be...

Humans?

An audible, disappointed groan rose from the crowd. Clearly they were anticipating little green men, or ten-foot-tall squid-like beings, or something that glowed and floated along like God, smiling benevolently.

Nope. Standing before them as the inner airlock doors opened were two humans. Average height, with a head, two arms, two legs. Standard issue, average humans. They wore spacesuits, a little too form-fitting if Theo was being frank, and their helmets were shaded, concealing their faces.

Kate rocked back and forth on her feet, arms crossed, nervous. "I don't like the no-face thing. I don't like it one bit."

Agent Ned agreed. "Yeah. Can't see how big their mouths are."

Theo, teeth chattering now, looked around for an assist. And out of the corner of his eye, he saw Vin, way off in the bleachers. Vin raised his arm, waving it awkwardly like it was broken, reminding Theo of the time he broke his own arm, falling off a bicycle of all things. As the doctors started to set the bone, tears welled in his eyes and his teeth started chattering just like they were now, and Vin, ever by his side, whispered in his ear, "It's just an arm. That's why you have two. In case they have to amputate that one." Theo laughed, and that immediately settled his nerves. "Thanks, Vin."

Kate spun her head. "What?"

"Oh, um, nothing."

"Earth to Hoover. They're just standing there waiting. Quit staring off into space with that stupid grin. You're on."

So Theo descended the three steps of the dais, with each step hearing the *schmack* of the gum on his left shoe, but pushed the rising dread out of his mind and strode confidently along. Unfortunately, once he reached the carpet, the thin polyester fabric stuck to the gum, lifting it into the air with his shoe. Knowing that there was simply no option of dragging a carpet thirty feet – this was historic *First Contact* after all – he slowly put his left foot down, placed the right foot next to it, and yanked his left foot up to take another step *sans carpet*. And so he proceeded: yank left foot and take a step; bring right foot next to left foot to hold down carpet; yank left foot...; repeat.

Perhaps as a show of intergalactic goodwill, the first of the aliens, presumably the captain, approached him in the same manner, yanking his left foot high in the air, holding the carpet down with his right, yanking the left foot again, and on and on, and Theo wished with all his heart that the gift box the other alien was carrying held a gun, so he could shoot himself in the head and be done with this.

Kate covered her face. Luna giggled into her hand. But the crowd was mercifully silent, presumably waiting for an even more embarrassing moment to release their howling belly laughter.

Theo and the lead alien met in the middle, and Theo extended his hand.

For an eternal moment, nothing happened.

Theo's hand hung in the air, like the loneliest hand in the universe.

But finally, after what Theo imagined was some faster-than-light review of their human database of TV sitcoms, the alien raised his hand and shook Theo's.

And the crowd erupted in cheers. The hair on the back of Theo's neck immediately stood at attention, and he got goosebumps, and felt every emotion a human could feel all at once. He thought, for the first time in his life, that maybe we aren't *so* insignificant. It was exhilarating. He shouted, *"Humanity welcomes you!"* And he raised both their hands in the air, and if it were possible, the cheers grew even louder and more raucous.

There was something strange about the hand. Something, he couldn't place, something about its motion... ah, that was it... mechanical. While he pondered that for a moment, the other alien approached the middle (yes, in the same herky-jerky fashion as Theo), as did Kate, Luna, Ned, and General Zima (all whom had decided to walk normally).

Theo released the lead alien's hand, and found it replaced with a news cameraman's microphone. "Oh. Okay. Ah. Again.

Welcome, um... well how about that. You know, we actually didn't get your names during the radio transmission."

The alien's synthetic voice crackled to life. "We don't names. Our species divides and grows, more like, uh," and he turned to his companion, as if telepathically conferring on the correct TV sitcom term. "Ah! Yes. Sponges? Think? So we are all part of a one. Anyhow, we think it'd be cool if you and your humans gave us this thing, 'name.'"

"You want us to name you?"

"Yes. Maybe if our true nature is revealed it will help." He reached up to a button on his helmet.

The entire human contingent, including Theo, took a step back.

Agent Ned closed his eyes and whispered to himself, "Yup. This is how it happens."

The helmet did not retract. But the faceplate began to clear, much like the cloud had done earlier, and what Theo saw was beyond comprehension.

Wait. No.

It was totally comprehensible.

The thing in the helmet, floating in some kind of clear viscous liquid, was certainly alien. It was, through means that were a mystery to Theo, actuating this very human-looking robotic enclosure. But the alien itself looked exactly like...

He didn't even want to think it.

But the thought came, unbidden, and he looked around at his companions, and the exact same thought had come to them, too.

The alien looked like a blob of rice pudding.

It was unmistakable. It was as if someone scooped out a cup of rice pudding and floated it in vegetable oil, and then put the whole thing in a robot.

Now, there was only one brand of rice pudding on all the orbiters, so the brand name was synonymous with the product, like Kleenex or Bandaids, and everyone ate it because it really was delicious, and the name was very catchy, every human alive had learned the TV commercial jingle as a child, and as hard as Theo tried, he couldn't stop the words from tumbling out of his mouth:

"You look like TastySkoop."

And there it was. The embarrassing moment the assembled crowd was waiting for. They erupted in the loudest laughter Theo had ever heard. This time everyone in their group facepalmed, and Theo again hoped for a gun in the gift box, knowing that he could never, ever in a million years live this down, and our first contact with another intelligent life form would end in them turning around and hightailing it the hell out of here and giving the humans the (robotic) finger. First, of course, they would incinerate everyone.

But incredibly, the lead alien turned to the crowd, raised both hands high into the air, and shouted, "TastySkoop! I like it!" He turned to his partner. "You like?" And the other alien nodded enthusiastically, revealing through his now-clear helmet his little blob, sloshing around in fluid, while both their robot enclosures did what looked like a dance.

And the crowd, either to their credit or their bottomless lack of shame, started chanting the name of their favorite – and only – brand of rice pudding, and their now favorite aliens, "TastySkoop! TastySkoop! TastySkoop!" and they mimicked the aliens' robot dance. Kate rolled her eyes at Theo. "Well, I didn't expect *that*."

Once the cheers died down a bit, The lead alien, clearly pleased, announced into the microphone, "How about Skoop

for short?" He pointed to his companion. "And you are Tasty."
And thunderous laughter and applause shook the shuttle
bay.

Skoop and Tasty were clearly delighted with all this, and
tapped their robotic feet in time as the Lusitania University
brass band started playing the TastySkoop jingle, and
everyone sang:

TastySkoop! What a Tasty treat
So so creamy, so so sweet
When you're done, ask your mother
Please, please, Mom can you Skoop me another?
TastySkoop!

After the jubilant celebration of both delicious rice pudding
snacks and highly intelligent aliens from another galaxy
subsided, Theo pointed to the massive ship they had
descended from. "So... it's just... the two of you?"

Skoop nodded. "Just us two. Smallest ship in fleet. You
would call a 'two-seater.' You should see the big ones!" He
spread his arms wide, and Tasty put down the gift box and
did the same, and then together they made an even wider
circle with their arms, and their miming made the crowd
erupt in giggles. They were in love with Skoop and Tasty.

Then Tasty suddenly stopped, seeming to remember his
role in this ceremony, picked up the gift box and nudged
Skoop. Skoop exclaimed, "Ah!" took the box, and reverently
held it out to Theo. "For you."

A hush fell over the crowd again. A sleek, silver box, with

no clear lid or markings, but with a small hole on each side, came to rest in Theo's hands.

It was neither light nor heavy, just sort of- *wait.*

Was something moving inside?

His instinct was to drop the box and run. Or slap his own face, forcing himself to wake up from the insane dream he'd been having for nine days. But some last shred of composure came over him, commanding him to stay put. And so he did. And the entire gathering, and every person at home watching, held their collective breath.

"Go ahead! Open! Here. Press here."

There was no button where Skoop pointed, but Theo squinted as if he was disarming a nuclear device... and pressed.

The lid slid open with a little *whoosh.*

And inside?

A cat.

17. LUNCH WITH ALIENS

Lunch with the aliens was… interesting.

True to their word, they didn't eat meat, or human faces, but were delighted to try human pizza, curries, ramen, cheese, fruits, vegetables, and even wine. But while the idea of this communion with another life form looked good on paper, actually watching them experiment with their meal was like watching some slow motion slasher flick. First, tiny scissor-like appendages extended from their robot enclosures, cutting the food into tiny pieces on their plates, the morsels then sucked up through long metal tubes into an unseen chamber. Then an internal blender activated, and another tiny straw spurted the fine puree into their helmet goo, where the rice-pudding-shaped aliens would suck and vacillate, and ingest it like it owed them money. The sounds were just as nauseating, a series of mechanical mashing and squirting and belching and satisfied moans emitting from their helmet speakers. "Mmmmmm!" "Mrrppphhhgooooood…" "Mawr…"

One by one, the human delegation rose, made some

excuse about urgent official business, and ran off to the bathrooms to vomit.

After an hour, it was just Theo – who was quite proud of himself for not puking onto his own plate – and Tasty and Skoop. Alone.

And the cat.

Of all things.

Did these aliens not know what humanity was currently dealing with? Cats in every crevice, nook, and dumpster? Yet another reminder of the incompetence of man, that they couldn't even manage their own pet population? Sure, the mouse population was completely under control now, but at what cost? All he could imagine was someone in government proposing the introduction of wolves to control the cat population, not realizing they'd then have a wolf problem. And then a grizzly bear problem. In short, the last thing they needed was another cat.

"I see you looking at cat." Skoop said. "You like?"

Theo fidgeted. "I mean, of course we appreciate the gesture, but... you said something about helping us get home..." he looked around and lowered his voice, "...to Earth. I don't see how a cat helps us get back to Earth..."

Skoop shook his helmet. "Hold on. Earth?"

"Yes. You said Earth."

"No." He looked to Tasty. The both shook their helmets. "We said home. Never said Earth. What is Earth?"

Theo struggled to keep his voice to a whisper, even though he knew they were alone and no one would hear his blasphemy:

"Home *is* Earth."

Skoop was silent for a minute. He appeared to like dramatic silences. "No. Transmissions we receive talk about home being Keplar-4-Tidallock-G9. Sunnyside. Terraforming *Sunnyside* for new home. That's what the cat is for. New home. We introduce her to surface environment. She acclimates. Then we catch all your cat problem feral cats, send them down, introduce to our special cat, let's call her SkoopCat. SkoopCat to your cats find irresistibly attractive. So they mate, oh and how they will mate! SkoopCat becomes mother to many, many, many cats. Anyway, they reproduce into massive herds, quickly, DNA mutations now, fur is photosynthetic, store crazy large amounts of heat, accelerate heat transfer from sunny to dark side and back and forth in super huge migration patterns. Ice sheets melt, greenhouse gasses released, self-sustaining cycle achieved in, we estimate, fifteen of your planet's revolutions."

Theo gasped. "FIFTEEN? FIFTEEN YEARS?"

Skoop and Tasty nodded in unison, splashing around in their goo.

Theo's mind raced, as he was faced with an impossible choice: suddenly the prospect of Sunnyside was within their grasp – in his lifetime! It's what every new generation dreamed about. Leaving behind their mechanical homes for something natural. The promise of the future. In their grasp!

But... but also... *Earth*.

His dream. His dream of the past. The dream he'd had since forever: A kid, laying on a *real* lawn, looking up at a *real* blue sky, with *real* clouds, with his older brother laying there too, and the two of them looking for shapes in the clouds, laughing. Was it selfish to wish for that? Didn't everyone secretly share this wish? To go back in time? *To go home?*

He couldn't help himself. "But... Skoop... could you? Theoretically? Help me – help us – get back home to *Earth*? When we left it was uninhabitable." He tapped a few places on the monitor embedded in the conference table, and showed them Earth, in its far away solar system, lonely and wanting nothing but Theo and his brother and his people to return. "Here. Look. Maybe now...? Maybe Earth has gotten better? Maybe it's possible to live there again? Maybe you could bend spacetime or something?"

Now Skoop was silent once more, and if one was to peek inside his sponge-like mind, they would see him pondering that word: *home*. Their species had run across the concept many times, of course – in fact, with almost all others they met – but it never ceased to puzzle him. For their kind did not have a home. Yes, at some point in their pre-history they must have come from *somewhere*, but no records existed. It was so long ago, and ever since, with the advent of space travel, for eons, they had been nomadic, traveling and unfolding wherever the galaxy took them, a small tribe here, a small tribe there, their fleet spread out thinly across the unfathomable vastness of space. Theirs was a complete existence – all needs were met with sustenance generation and fusion power, and they understood the "one-ness" of it all – so he could not understand the yearning. He could rationally understand it, yes, but couldn't *feel* the yearning. And in this particular case the yearning was compounded: this poor human was unsure where his home was. He seemed to have two holes in his heart: one shaped like Earth, the other like Sunnyside. Skoop wanted to explain, at length, that the concept was unnecessary, but these humans were young still, like children. His job was not to lecture, but to facilitate the unfolding.

He looked to Tasty, and they did some light-speed calculations, and together they nodded. "Mister Theo Hoover, how about this? We help you with cat, to Sunnyside we go down, show you how workings. At the same time, we shoot quantum entangled microprobe this big," he pinched his mechanical fingers showing about a millimeter, "to planet called Earth, along spacetime curve, takes... estimated... ten of your days time, then we get showing result if Earth habitable again. If so, you have choice." He pointed out the window to Sunnyside. "*New* home..." then he looked around, and vaguely pointed where they'd estimated Earth's coordinates were. "...or *old* home."

Before Theo before he could jump up and hug Skoop, a voice interrupted him.

"Earth? Old home? Where the hell are you going with this, bro?"

It was Vin. Sitting opposite Theo, at the far end of the table.

A flash of anger struck Theo. *Now you decide to show up, Vin? No. I need this. For both of us. For everyone. Leave.*

Vin protested. "You *need* this? Or you *want* this? You better figure that out, bro. It's a real pickle. Oh, and who's deciding I show up, anyway?" And he got up and walked out, with a full grin, wagging a finger at Theo.

Skoop's speaker coughed. "Ahem. Mister Temporary Grand Oversee. Await your choice."

Theo shook his head to free it from Vin, and stood. "Yes. Do it. Send the probe. In the meantime, we'll set up a shuttle to the surface of Sunnyside. Is there anything else you need me to do?"

Tasty and Skoop both raised their hands and said together, "Have any more pizza?"

18. ONLY I CAN SAVE YOU.

n a darker chamber of the Lusitania, a fresh cup of TastySkoop was opened, and symbolically spooned into the waste duct. Then a thumbchip was tapped, and a security-modulated voice began recording:

"It's me again, dearest people of the orbiters, *my* people...

"I was wrong. Wait. Scratch that. I'm never wrong. But I didn't anticipate this. I correctly thought that Hoover person was the only one who believed the alien story. The only one who heard that unfortunate message. It would've been so clean. So easy to just stamp out one last ember.

"But now the whole goddamned thing has caught fire. The aliens came early, and without invitation. Convenient. Now every single one of you, on all eight orbiters, is giddy with the new, the novel, the sideshow, and the promise – of what? Friendship? All the warm fuzzies? A *cat?*

"Give me a break.

"You're all suckers. Ignorant rubes. You're the marks and the con is on.

"But I'll save you, my people. Only I can save you.

"These aliens, they speak benevolently. But I know better. There is no such thing as true benevolence. And no, it's not something stupid the aliens are after, like eating us, or enslaving us, or invading us for our resources. Look at our resources! No, it's something much more basic.

"Power.

"That's it. Look at every species ever known. Ants, for example. They exist simply to take over. Not to merely survive. *To take over.*

"Of course, this power, this taking over, may include all the other theories. Tasty and Skoop – the most ridiculous names I've ever heard – may enslave us anyway, or use up our humble resources, or even find that human flesh tastes just like chicken. Yum! But at the core, it's all thirst for power. Because power is the most seductive thing in the universe. I know this. Trust me, I know this.

"Because I hold the power. You think I'm going to hand it over to strangers? With sinister motives?

"So the plan changes. It was going to be just Hoover, the final sacrifice. But now? I can't sacrifice *everyone*, I mean what would be the point?

"No, now I will have to change all your minds. If you can see the truth, see the veil of benevolence pulled back, you will recoil from these invaders. You will push them away, and embrace what you already have, the known, not the terrifying unknown. You will perhaps finally understand that change, *any* change, is really the enemy. That things are meant to stay just as they are.

"Forever."
"Now... back to sleep."

The recording stopped. And the bearer of the voice glanced down, into the waste duct, and their stomach growled.
"Damn. I actually like TastySkoop."

19. THEY HAD BEEN INVADED.

There was a disaster in the distant past on Earth, a disaster known as 9/11. It was Theo's job, one of the more important projects of his career, to sort through it all, the facts and the conspiracy theories, the hacked history, and the essays and the photos, photos of the worst kind, photos he'd never unsee, and find the Objective Truth, and make it make sense. But he couldn't. He couldn't understand, how in a world of lawns and neighbors and sunshine and blue skies, people could hate each other so much that they would resort to murder. Of course, it had happened on much larger scales throughout history: the Holocaust, Stalin's purges, World Wars One, Two, and Three, Mao's Great Leap Forward, Cambodia, Rwanda, Africarabia's Water War, the list went on and on.

But there was something about 9/11. This country, the United States of America, their people were sheltered from history, and from famine and civil war, and ethnic cleansing and terrorist attacks, so when airplanes dove into twin buildings in New York City, they were jolted from their ordinary lives violently, and their world changed in a single day. They had been invaded.

There was before. And there was after.

Something died that day, something larger than the events, larger than the people of the United States. The world, or nearly all of it, had held that country up as a beacon of hope, a place where they could transcend their differences. And though it wasn't perfect by a long shot, it was probably the best chance at the dream of life, liberty, and the pursuit of happiness the world had known.

For two years of his life, Theo reassembled the truth, and it made him love that country, dearly, but also grieve their lost innocence, for their childhood had come to an end. And the waves from that one event rippled out into the centuries, the thorn never truly being pulled out and healed, the fear of the "other" never receding completely. And now, hundreds of years later, Theo sat across from Hector Morgan, and he felt that thorn in his side.

Morgan spoke first. "Well, I would thank you for meeting with me, but you should've done it *before* you let the foxes into the henhouse."

"The aliens are here in peace. To help. Why are you afraid of them?" Theo's hands were shaking, so he planted them under his butt. Why had he agreed to meet alone with Morgan, as one influential concerned citizen to another? All Theo wanted was to go home. He missed his VR helmet, and not having to actually talk to anyone. He was the farthest thing from a people person. But as Morgan was the new leader of the fringe Skywalkers, he knew this needed to be nipped in the bud, regardless of his desperate desire to run away.

"I'm not afraid, Hoover. Don't you dare tell me I'm afraid."

Morgan rose and pointed a finger across the table, far too close to Theo's nose, and it also was shaking, but from rage. "You're not the only history buff on the orbiters. My great grandmother Daisy taught the Morgans a thing or two. Let's take a walk down memory lane, shall we?" He backed away, tapped his thumbchip, paced back and forth, his childish science fiction robe billowing behind him, ancient newspaper headlines spreading across the air between them. "Hitler promised help in the form of economic prosperity while he invaded Poland." He strode around the table. "Mao promised help in the form of industrialization while he invaded his own farmers' land. The Europeans promised peace and shiny objects while they invaded the Americas. Putin promised eastern Europeans freedom while he invaded Ukraine and started World War Three." He sat next to Theo now, pinched the headlines closed, and lowered his voice. "I don't need to go on, do I?" And he reached his hand over and gently put it on Theo's shoulder. Like they were friends.

Theo winced. "We're not being invaded."

But something caught in Theo's brain. He thought back to 9/11.

They had been invaded.

He faltered for a moment. Why *did* he trust Tasty and Skoop? Was it just the cute names? Or was he just being selfish? That these beings gave him a little hope to get back to Earth? He should be more skeptical. This wasn't like him.

And Hector saw it. "Aha! You know it, don't you? You, the fixer of history, you see it better than anyone. It's inevitable. I knew you'd see." And he grinned triumphantly, patting Theo's back.

And Theo, in sadness, admitted to himself that Morgan had a point. A logical point. The truth.

But.

It wasn't the whole truth. It was the slice of truth that Morgan thought was the whole pie. Something inside Theo, that strange, nagging feeling again, that... something... Theo stood, letting Morgan's hand fall to the table.

"No."

"No what?"

"No, it's not inevitable." He tapped open headlines of his own and pointed. "Here. The American army as outsiders landed in Normandy. And they saved innumerable people's lives, and spread peace and prosperity for decades." He pointed to another. "There. Abraham Lincoln marched into his own divided country to save the union." He pointed to another. "Galileo helped humanity, against its own fears and rejection, by spreading the truth about the Earth and the Sun. Jesus. Buddha. Einstein. Balbon and Chesterman in World War Three. All came to help. And they all did." He leaned and rested his hands on the table. The shaking was gone.

Morgan shrugged. "Nice speech. I want you to stop this, Hoover, because you know I'm right."

Theo was defiant. "You want me to stop this whole thing, their *once-in-an-eon* offer of help. The one chance for us to finally prepare the path."

"Yes. Stop it. Now. I'm done with small talk."

"Let me ask you this. You don't think these visitors would've already unleashed whatever evil plan they had already? Why wait? Invaders don't wait. Look, the past happened. Believe me, I'm knee deep in it every day. But we have to move forward. It's our shot. It's time for a leap of faith. Hector, take the leap, it's going to be fine. Better than fine."

Morgan rose in frustration, pounding his fists on the

table, their eyes locked. "Don't you 'Hector' me. You'll see. You'll see."

"I'm sorry you see it that way."

"We'll see who's sorry." And he stormed over and opened the big doors to the office, and Kate, Luna, and Ned peered in, watching him exit. Morgan scowled. "Ah. The cavalry." And on his way through the door, he turned, as if remembering something. "Oh. One more thing, Hoover..."

Theo sighed. "Yes...?"

"How's your brother, by the way?" And he marched out, not waiting for an answer.

20. "WHERE'D HE GO?"

"Where'd he go?" Ned looked around the room for Theo, pointing up at the ceiling as a possibility.

Kate bent down, looking under the table. "He didn't crawl into the ceiling, Ned. Come on. We followed Morgan out for like ten seconds. Hoover was just sitting here. I mean, it's a *room*, how far could he have gotten?"

But it wasn't just a room. It was the main conference room in Lusitania City Hall, and so it had a hallway to catering facilities, cabinets lining two of the walls, and a storage closet. And a panic room. The door to the panic room looked identical to all the other cabinet doors, but near the top edge – presumably so they wouldn't miss it in an emergency – some prior administration official had helpfully stuck a length of masking tape and written in marker, *Shhh! Secret Panic Room in Here.*

They spread out, with Kate marching right to where she knew Hoover would be. She opened the small door to the unlocked panic room and found him there, curled in a ball, rocking back and forth. He didn't look up at her. Just stared ahead blankly. She sighed and thought all that was missing was his thumb in his mouth, or a straight jacket. *Poor Hoover,* she thought. Even with his thinly-veiled superiority complex, and his almost-as-annoying inferiority complex, and his fidgeting, and over-explaining everything, he didn't deserve this. He didn't deserve that asshole Morgan being weird about his brother.

What was his brother's name? She thought. *Vin? What was the deal with Vin anyway?* Kate had a brother too, Max, but she certainly didn't get worked up about Max. She tried to avoid even thinking of him. The last time Max called, he needed credits, because his latest girlfriend bolted with all his stuff. Kate told him to call Mom and Dad, but they had snuck off to Oyster Cove golfing or back to Flint and the wineries and couldn't be bothered. *Brothers. Parents. Relationships.* Keep 'em. Kate didn't need any of that. Maybe that's why she liked work so much. It didn't ask you for credits or sleep on your couch for six months.

And then there was *the guy*, Theo R. Hoover. She wasn't sure whether she had ruined this poor guy's life, or given him a shot to actually do something with it. It was chaos, or mostly chaos, all the way down. They were already at the bottom, right? But more chaotic it did get, with this Morgan harassment bullshit. She looked down at Theo, a little sadness rising in her.

Luna walked up from behind and handed her a tissue. "Here."

"I'm not crying."

"I know. It's for him."

And sure enough, Theo had something threatening to

make a grand entrance out of his nose, so he took the tissue from Kate and blew. "Thanks."

"No problem. You can keep that."

Luna looked at Kate, a little surprised.

Kate poked her. "What?"

Luna shrugged. "It's just, I can't remember ever seeing that expression on your face."

"Go away. What expression?"

"Compassion." And as Luna wandered off, Kate contemplated that word for a moment. *Compassion*. Ugh. What was happening to her? She missed the days of no foo-foo feelings, no compassion, before she found herself crying in a server closet with Hoover. Just the facts and the figures, and a laugh and a beer. But something came over Kate, maybe it was this compassion thing she wasn't used to, and just like last time, words started falling out of her mouth.

"Hoover. Theo. I'm sure your brother's fine. Morgan's just being a dick. Hey, would it make you feel better to hear an adorable family story of mine? It's the only adorable one I have. The rest are terrible."

Theo looked up at her. Blinked. Nodded.

"Okay, so here's how my parents met: Once upon a time there was a man and a woman. They met on a little walking bridge straddling a creek on Flint's vineyards. The bridge was barely wide enough for one, so as they approached each other, they had to twist a bit to get by. Coincidentally – or not – they twisted *toward* each other, not *away*, so as they politely passed, they could each smell the other's breath. 'Malbec?' The man asked, before he could stop talking and mind his own business. Startled, she caught herself smiling and whispering back, 'Yes. Good nose. Yours is a cab-sav.' She pointed past him. 'So there's a winery that way as well?' She was surprised at her own forwardness. It was clearly the wine talking. They were both a bit tipsy. He waved his hands around at what seemed like endless hills on the orbiter. 'They're all over. Around every corner.' He laughed. 'I don't know if I'll be able to find my way back to the bed-and-breakfast-flat after a couple more.' And she then did something she'd never done in her entire life. She took his hand, without asking, and led him along, changing his direction. 'Well, then, it behooves us to travel together. For safety, of course.' He grinned and forgot where he was going. 'Of course.' And that was it. They never stopped holding hands. They still do, even when she digs her nails into his skin in a rage, or he's trying to drive a pod and not kill anyone. It can be pretty annoying. Huh. I actually just remembered Dad saying once, 'It's a miracle any of us find each other, so when we do, we've got to hold on like hell.'" Kate inhaled sharply, it was the strangest feeling, remembering that, the burning wetness returning to her eyes, and she had to lean against the cabinet to collect herself.

Theo clambered out of his hideout and took her hand. "Hey, you okay?"

She nodded. "Yeah. Just don't make me do that again."

He led her to the gargantuan conference table, both of them strangely exhausted now, and sat down across from Luna and Ned. Luna stared at Kate. "Gee. You've never told *me* the adorable story of your parents meeting. I was starting to wonder if you even had parents."

"Come on, Luna. I've told you a hundred times."

Luna tapped her thumbchip and a giant *ZERO* floated in the air. (She kept a few files like this for just such occasions.)

She waved it away. "Whatever. Focus. Now, Hoover, that

thing with Morgan sounded like a threat. How does he know your brother?"

The aftershocks of Morgan's comment were finally clearing from Theo's brain. "He doesn't. He can't possibly. I mean…"

For several seconds, the only sound was Luna tapping her thumbchip as various versions of ZERO floated in the air.

Theo folded his arms. "We're not discussing it."

Kate sharpened her voice. "Listen, Hoover. At this point we need to know what's going on. That snipe from Morgan sure sounded like a threat. We have a government to run, and a bunch of aliens hanging around being weird, oh and an alien cat to deliver down to Sunnyside. We can't have the Skywhackadoos or anyone else making threats against you, and if they do we have to shut that shit down. Even if it means cancelling the theatrics for a while."

And Theo stood up, a little shaky at first, but with increasing fortitude, and puffed out his chest like a real Grand Oversee might. He didn't tell them about Earth and the microprobe, that would be his secret for now, but he would hold up his end of humanity's deal regarding Sunnyside. They deserved it, and Theo wouldn't keep it from them. So, with true, newfound resolve, he said, "NO. Threats or not, nothing will keep us from this. This is our moment. We are doing this. On to Sunnyside. NOW. *Do you hear me?*"

The group, stunned by the sudden appearance of an actual leader, meekly said in unison, "Yes, sir." And Kate smiled to herself, though she didn't know exactly why.

21. THE SHUTTLE

An hour later they joined the aliens in the shuttle bay. General Zima insisted Theo and his entourage stay on the Lusitania, but Theo double-insisted and then triple-insisted that they go down to the planet themselves, this was a momentous, meaningful occasion after all, the dawn of the actual, *this-time-for-real* terraforming of Sunnyside. So after a hearty round of quibbling (while Tasty and Skoop looked on with delighted curiosity), they agreed to keep the landing team to Skoop, Theo, Kate, Luna, and General Zima. Agent Ned, Theo decided – against Ned's quadruple insistence – was tasked with staying orbiter-side with Tasty, leading a charm offensive and protecting him.

Theo patted his shoulder. "It's only a day trip, Ned. Luna's got interviews lined up already, you just have to chaperone. And General Zima will personally look after me. We'll be back in twelve hours. What could possibly go wrong?"

He laughed. Ned didn't.

There was no pomp and circumstance this time: in place of the throngs of orbiter-dwellers and music and beach balls, only the landing party walked across the receiving bay to the Sunnyside shuttle, among several cats. Kate had insisted, and double insisted, and then triple insisted, that no one – and she repeated, NO ONE – outside of the security circle be present.

Once a month, the shuttle delivered rotating shifts of engineers, foodstuffs (including TastySkoop, which, by the way, had enjoyed a 9,000% increase in sales in the past couple of days), and terraforming materials down to Sunnyside. But this time, a small contingent of outsiders – The Extremely Temporary Grand Oversee and his entourage, including an alien and its alien cat-like being – were added to the manifest. The shuttle crew "processed" them – meaning they were looked over suspiciously as they ascended the ramp to the main shuttle cabin – with a pilot, copilot, two engineers, three monitors, and a food prep vendor taking up the rear and climbing aboard. As the ramp receded, a red light strobed on the underside of the shuttle, and once the airlock was sealed and everyone strapped into their harnesses, liftoff.

The trip down to Sunnyside was a mere thirty-minute ride, with occupants able to enjoy weightlessness on the way. So Kate and Luna, unable to contain their childish whims, unbuckled and floated around the main shuttle cabin, bonking into this and that, and laughing like a couple of grade schoolers at the playground.

Theo, on the other hand, had been thinking, since their takeoff, about his meeting with Hector Morgan. He knew, or he mostly felt he knew, that their visitors were not here for nefarious purposes, but... *why were they here?* Were they truly benevolent? He turned it over and over in his head, watching Kate and Luna perform zero-gravity fake karate battles in midair, and finally his curiosity got the best of him. He unbuckled his harness and floated over to Skoop, leaning in close and whispering, "Excuse me. If you'll forgive my forwardness... why are you doing this?"

Skoop turned himself in his goo, perhaps to face Theo. "Don't understand."

"Why are you doing this for us? The terraforming help?" Then he whispered, "And the Earth microprobe. We can't possibly do anything for you."

"You are making not sense."

"Come on. What drove you to come to us? To help us. Please."

Skoop thought for a moment, reminding himself of how far, or not, the humans had come. "I understand. You have not left childhood yet."

"But..." and Theo scanned through all of the history stored away in his brain, and all the loss of innocence. "But I thought we'd learned from all the war and struggle..."

Skoop interrupted him. "That is like..." he hesitated. He definitely liked hesitating. "...like a human teenager insisting more knowledge than the parents. When you grow up, we think you will, too, you will learn and see what you call help is not."

"I'm not following. Help is *not* help?"

"There are many concepts we do not experience. For example: 'help.' Your word that is. Our concept word is... translation would be... 'unfolding.' The whole universe is unfolding, and we are unfolding with it. Together. All beings. Our doing better is your doing better. Your sad moment is our sad moment. We unfold together. There is no separate. We don't feel pleasure to 'help' you. We feel the unfolding. We facilitate the unfolding. It is the way it is. Happened to pick up weak signals from Lusitania, we come. There is no agenda. No hidden purpose. We come to unfold together. That is all."

Huh. Theo was left a little speechless, ruminating on that word: *unfolding.* Was there anything to that? Was he even intelligent enough to ask that question? Or was he, as Skoop had said, still a child?

His thought was cut short by a loud "*SZZPPPRRRTTTZZZ!*" and then silence.

And darkness.

Luna's voice pierced the black. "Um, is this normal?"

But before the pilot could shout "No!" and start barking orders, they all heard a scratching and clicking. And then from where the scratching and clicking were coming from, a flame appeared, from an old fashioned fuel and flint cigarette lighter, illuminating a woman's face. When everyone's eyes had locked on her, in that moment before the panic set in, she cackled and screamed, "Down with the Empire! Long live the rebellion!"

22. GOOD LUCK. AND GOODBYE.

"Navigation systems!"

"Offline!"

"Propulsion systems!"

"Offline!"

"Communications systems!"

"Offline!"

"Dammit! Is anything online?"

The shuttle crew scrambled, weightless, to assess their situation and restrain the strange woman with the lighter, cuffing her to a hand rail. But she just laughed. "It's over. My backpack had an EMP. Good luck. And goodbye. The Skywalkers see everything, you fools. My orders come from a place much higher than you all."

Theo couldn't see, there was no light at all other than the stars spinning outside the windows, they must've been on the dark side of Sunnyside now, but he could picture the shock on the crew's faces nevertheless. This woman had set off some electromagnetic pulse device, the most illegal weapon one could possess, for it could do just this: disable a ship completely.

They were all going to die.

And then, out of the corner of his eye, he saw another source of light: Skoop's helmet. "Skoop! How are you...?"

"My humanoid shell, Grand Oversee Hoover, is different technology. No human electronics, much shielding, power core is small fusion reactor. I am fine. Here maybe assist to you." And with that, he floated over to the main bank of instruments. "Primitive." He moved around, shining his helmet lamps here and there, fiddling with dials and keypads and pulling wires, while the crew and Theo's group looked on in horror. "No. Too primitive. Electromagnetic pulse one hundred percent effective. We will now, in... I estimate five human minutes based on gravity and degrading orbit... expire."

And yes, at the word *gravity*, they could all feel it: the pull of Sunnyside. The ship was quickening its spin and crashing. It was already getting hot in here, and the windows were beginning to glow.

"Only regret is not to have known you more. Oh, and the cat. Only had enough resources to make one. Not the best foresight, in retrospect. So I have two regrets. Three if counted is my regret at not bringing powerful EMP-proof radio transmitter and universal locator aboard."

Theo, somewhere through the fog of his absolute terror, was amazed at Skoop's calmness. But he supposed, as asexual dividing sponges or whatever their species was, they didn't have the extreme sense of self that humans did, and therefore death just wasn't something to get worked up over.

But the humans on the ship did have extreme senses of self and a strong aversion to death. Screaming and flailing, they were pushed outward to the walls of the shuttle by centrifugal force. The oxygen was becoming noticeably thinner now, too, and Theo had to fight to stay conscious.

Spinning. Faster and faster. Heat. Hotter and hotter. Air. Thinner and thinner.

It would be over soon.

Suddenly a hand grabbed Theo by the collar.

The shuttle pilot. Wordlessly, and with a hidden reservoir of strength, she pushed Theo into a small closet.

No. Some kind of spherical enclosure. A pod.

"It's supposed to fit two, max three. But we'll see."

And she fought the gravity and the spin, and clawed along, grabbing Kate and Luna and stuffing them into the pod. Then back to General Zima, who resisted. "No, take them. I'm ready to die." But she stuffed him in. "Yeah, well I'm not ready for you to die, sir." And lastly she went back and got Skoop and the cat box, and crammed them in until the five of them could barely breathe and certainly not move a muscle, the cat box wedged firmly against Luna's kidney. The pilot pointed to a handle. "Listen, pull that in forty-five seconds. All the electronics are shot, so that chute is the only thing manual. It might save your lives. Might."

General Zima huffed and puffed, escaping the confines of the pod, and wrestled with the pilot for a few precious seconds, and overpowered her, and smushed her in next to Skoop, screaming, "They need you more right now!" and closed the door against her protests, and cranked it sealed from the outside.

He saluted them through the tiny porthole, and Theo understood: the man's entire life was spent preparing for this moment. *Prepare the Path. For The Future of Man Rests In Your Hands.* Theo saluted back with his index finger, the only thing he could move, and silently promised to remember him and his favorite food, ice cream, and the crew, remember them all forever, even if forever meant only the next forty-five seconds.

The pod ejected then, with no force of its own as the propulsion systems were down, but the spin of the main vessel flung them far away. They were a few hundred meters from it when they saw through the porthole the shuttle break apart, and the flames of atmosphere engulf all the little pieces.

Theo wondered aloud, his fear of death obliterating all other thoughts: "Why aren't we-"

"Dead?" The pilot replied. "Pod's meant to crash. Heavy on one side, won't spin, tons of heat resistance, most of our weight is coolant. We're almost in atmosphere too, when we get there the fins should start to fold out from the pressure and break our fall a little. Then I'll pull the chute at three thousand meters from impact. But don't worry, there'll be plenty of opportunities to die." And she smiled, for she too knew she was meant for this moment, and that she would do whatever it took to save them, because she also knew that this story couldn't end here, not yet. Something was happening for humanity, something hopeful, and dammit, she wasn't going to let it be killed in the cradle.

The fins did deploy, or at least Theo assumed they had, because the tiny pod rattled like it too was breaking into a million pieces, and he heard the pilot say some mumbled prayer and pull the handle.

They struck the bottom of the pod with even more force, mashed together like one body instead of five. Slowing considerably, the chute had deployed successfully too.

Or so Theo thought.

"Shit." The pilot craned her neck to get the best look out the porthole above them. "Tear in the chute. We're coming in too hot. Need less weight. " She looked around, thinking, frantic. "Gonna have to release the coolant."

Theo actually clapped. "My god! I thought you were going to tell us we were all going to die! That's good news! Do it!"

She pointed up. "It's a closed system. No release valve. The pipes are outside. I'm gonna have to puncture it."

"Oh."

She pried the emergency axe from its mount, reached for the porthole door, and began turning the crank.

Luna reached up to stop her. "What the hell are you doing? We'll all get sucked out!"

Skoop grabbed her arm. "No. Approximately three thousand human meters from planet surface, I calculate, with speed of eight meters per second. We survive sudden environment change and pressures here. However this person without a name may expire."

The pilot continued cranking. "Name's Anna. Hey, alien guy, can you reach that helmet in the corner? It'll help."

Somehow, with literally zero space aboard the tiny pod, the helmet made its way to Anna, who put it on and fastened it to her suit. With no power, it would only keep her from having the air sucked out of her lungs once outside. "Okay, everybody grab on to something, and hold your breath. And hold my legs."

In the next moment the door rocketed open, and Anna was in fact nearly sucked out, but they all held her inside, while with her upper half outside she forced her arms downward. Centimeter by centimeter, her hands slid down, against incredible force, until they reached the pipe.

She grabbed it. It was as hot as the sun.

Shrieking in pain, she fought back the instinct to pull her hand away, instead holding on even tighter. And with one mighty swing, she brought down the axe, severing the main coolant pipe. A deluge of coolant covered her and rushed past into the sky.

Their descent slowed, significantly, and their hearts leapt, for it seemed like they might actually live.

Anna flopped down from the open door, back into the pod. Kate rushed to remove her helmet, and when she did, they all gasped.

She was covered in chemical burns. The coolant had melted holes through the faceplate and her suit, leaving her entire upper body bloody and raw. She labored for breath. "...brace yourselves... three... two... one..."

And they landed, hard but not bone-breaking, hearing the crunch of ice outside. The box holding the cat jammed into Luna's side and she groaned. "Fucking cat. Pain in my ass."

Anna coughed blood, but smiled through her pain. "...damn I'm good..."

Theo leaned in and took her hand. "Yes you are. Thank you, Anna. You're a hero. You saved our lives."

And with her last breath, Anna wheezed, "...now it's your turn."

23. SKOOP ANGELS

ce.

Everywhere.

As far as the eye could see, in every direction. Just ice. No, wait. There were mountains, too.

Mountains covered in ice.

Theo could see all this, dimly, because Sunnyside's star, below them on the bright side of the planet, shone so brightly it created a halo across the entire horizon, lighting a shallow rim on the dark side, like twilight in every direction. Ducking back into the pod, he shook his head. "Is there any way we can just stay in here? It's all ice. That's it."

Kate pulled him down and peeked her head out the door. She shivered against the stiff, freezing wind, and called down, "Hate to say it, but I agree with Hoover. Inhospitable is a huge understatement. Won't they come get us?"

After a hesitant few seconds, Skoop's speaker bleeped. "Am not expert in navigation or human protocol, but believe we are thirty-maybe-forty degrees of latitude into the dark side of Keplar-4-Tidallock-G9. No power for communication.

No lights. Would guess they would try very hard to find us, but like that saying you taught me yesterday, Luna Foster…"

"Needle in a haystack."

"Yes! Thank you Luna. Needle in a haystack."

"You're welcome. Now can we get out? Even for a minute? Poor Anna's staring at me, and the stupid cat box is going a number on my kidney."

And so they – as solemnly and ceremoniously as possible – lifted Anna's body out of the pod, laying her gently onto the ice. They stood there, bones rattling in the cold, with everything the pod had to offer: two polysuits, six rations (no TastySkoop, Kate checked, just freeze-dried something), a gallon of water, a tarp, a flare, and a small satchel with first aid and a small folding shovel. The emergency axe was gone. The polysuits were made specifically for this environment, with an aerogel nanofiber composite insulation and built-in shoes, gloves, and hood. Whoever wore the suits would still die, but they wouldn't die of the cold. They tried their thumbchips, but the EMP had knocked those out as well. The net was down. They were truly alone.

The cat climbed out of its box, circled them, leaning against their shins, purring. It seemed impervious to the cold. Luna rubbed her side where the box struck it in the crash landing. It hurt like hell.

After a moment looking at each other in disbelief, grief, and helplessness, Theo managed to ask, "So… should we say something?"

Luna shouted into the wind. "What?"

"Say something!" Theo shouted back.

"Say something about what?"

And Theo motioned to Anna, and Luna finally got the point and nodded. So Theo reached his hands out, and, after wondering why, everyone got that point too and held hands in a circle over Anna.

"Anna, you and the crew showed bravery the likes of which I've never seen before. May we show a fraction of that bravery in our perilous journey across this barren tundra to the habitable ring."

Kate spun her head. "What?"

Theo asked, "Did something happen to everyone's ears?"

"No. I mean what, as in, did I miss the part where we agreed to journey across the barren tundra? So we're not waiting for help then? You know, for the record, guys, I vote we stay here and wait for help."

And Theo just looked at her, with tired, desperate eyes, and they all did, and she understood, and shrugged. "Fine. Whatever. But I get one of those polysuits. If you have a shred of chivalry, Hoover, you'd give the other one to Luna. But I'll let you fight it out."

They were still holding hands, which was getting awkward, so Theo wrapped it up. "Good bye, Anna. We will remember you always. Now unless anyone else has anythi-"

Skoop raised his robot hand. "I do." And he leaned over Anna's body and looked closely at it. "This circumstance is interesting. We Skoop know there is no self, individuality is illusion, so among us grief is not a thing. But still find this.... ah... *touching*. May this Anna be eaten."

Kate let go of their hands. "Excuse me?"

"Eaten."

"Oh my god. You guys are cannibals?" She stomped away, then around in circles, disgusted.

"What is a cannibal, Kate Kingston? Is that good?"

"You eat each other! Like human eats human. Skoop eats Skoop. Cannibalism! *Ick!*"

Skoop waved his arms. "No! No! Cannibalism is not our way. No! Meant to say may her body be absorbed back into the ground, *eaten* if you like, so that ground may give rise to more life. Eaten maybe not best choice of word."

Kate stopped circling. "Okay, that's better. Still weird, but better. Damn, Skoop, watch your language."

"Yes, Kate Kingston. No cannibalism. Language watched more closely now." He made an awkward thumbs up gesture with his mechanical hand.

And so, after chipping out a shallow grave in the ice for Anna and saying a last goodbye, they began to trudge across the frozen wilderness. Theo, of course, let Luna have the second polysuit – to Luna's credit she at least offered a half-hearted refusal first – and took the insulated tarp for himself, wrapping himself up more or less like a roman toga. It was warm. They gave the rest of their meager resources to Skoop, whose robot enclosure could carry it easily. While Luna and Kate donned their polysuits, Luna snuck a peek at her exposed side and saw the bruise. She winced, but covered up quickly, and put her outer suit back on. A flash of fear gripped her, but she forced herself to think *it's only a bruise, how bad can a bruise be? It's nothing.*

They followed Theo, as if he were their leader. He thought this might not be the smartest idea, so he turned to Skoop. "Can you at least use your sensors or something to keep us from walking in circles?"

"No."

"Wonderful."

And they marched on, and Skoop stopped and laid down face first on the ice, arms and legs outstretched.

Kate threw her hands up in the air. "Really? Already? We haven't gone fifty meters!"

But Skoop didn't respond. He wiggled a bit, and as they watched, amazed, the ice around his body began to melt. Skoop sunk into the ice perhaps half a meter, then rose to his knees. "I figured. My reactor can heat for several minutes at a time. I create a pointer, with my head in direction of our path. It will take a while for ice to cover over. We will not walk in circles."

They nodded in approval, and Theo let out a little chuckle. "Hey, it's like a snow angel. Like from ancient Earth. Right guys?"

Luna blew on her hands, they were still cold inside the gloves, and put them under her armpits. "What's a snow angel?"

"It's on old Earth television, it's part of popular culture in the nineteen- you know what? Whatever. It's that."

Kate waved Skoop on. "Cute. Now get up, let's go, and by the way, you can use your doohickey to warm us up too."

And so, every half kilometer or so, Skoop would make a Skoop angel in the ice, then they would stop and huddle with Theo's tarp around them, with Skoop in the middle, like children around a campfire. Actually, it was nothing like children around a campfire. It was miserable and frigid and they were hungry and afraid and they had next to no chance of survival, and the whole reason they were here, to deliver the cat in the box, on a simple day trip, seemed doomed. But they were alive for the moment. They were moving forward. It was enough.

Trudging slightly ahead of the others, the wind let up momentarily, so Theo stopped and looked around. There was no day or night here. Just the eternal dim twilight. It was beautiful, in a *nature-is-awesome-and-will-kill-you* kind of way.

Vin scooped up some ice and threw it at him. "Ah! Caught you actually liking something. Look at you."

Theo shook off the ice, looked Vin over. T-shirt and shorts. In this weather. "You think I like this, Vin? Look at my fingers. They're blue. This is awful. We're going to die. What do I do?"

Vin pouted. "Aww, little bro, I feel for you. But I'm coming up blank, I have no idea what you should do, other than keep walking. Maybe I'm here for something else."

"Huh. I think I just miss you. I want you to come home."

They began walking along in silence. After a moment or two, Vin snuck under the tarp with Theo to warm himself. "Home." Vin grinned. "There's a saying: home is where Pearl's farts are."

Theo laughed. "Oh my god, Pearl. She's probably furious right now, cleaning up after the thousand cats that have camped out in our flat. Ned smashed the door to pieces. I don't even know if it's fixed yet. I haven't been home since."

"Does Pearl miss me?"

"I'm guessing not. You were a royal pain in her ass."

"Yeah. Figured."

A few minutes later, Vin stopped him. Serious. "Theo. I don't want to be cold anymore."

Theo didn't know what to say. He took the tarp off and shrouded Vin with it. But it fell to the ice, for Vin was once again gone, and Theo lost his balance, and fell to the ice as well.

Kate rushed over. "Hey, Hoover, you okay? Because if you are, I can laugh. But if you're not, I'll have to get all concerned. Or in Luna's word, 'compassionate.' Don't make me do that." She reached out her hand, smiling, and he took it, and rose.

They returned to the march. He had begun to not mind the cold so much, but now it was biting. He was miserable.

"Is that your brother I keep hearing you talk to? Vin? Is he imaginary or something?"

Theo scoffed. "No. Of course not. It's just-"

She interrupted him. "Because if we ever get back, we can look him up in a second. Get in touch with him. The magic of the Central Clerk's Office. Like literally find anyone in five seconds. Look him up, easy peasy."

"No you can't."

"Why?"

"I just said you *can't!*"

She scowled. "Jeez, Hoover. Just trying to help. What's up with you? It's not like we're going to die in the middle of a frozen tundra or anything."

He laughed grimly. "Sorry. It's just not something I talk about."

"No kidding." A hesitation. "Hey, you know what I can't wait for?"

The hint of a smile lit Theo's face. "Let me guess. Personally kicking Hector Morgan's ass when we get back."

She laughed. "Bingo." And nearly tripped over the cat. "Woah. What's up with the cat, Skoop? It's pawing at the ice."

Skoop walked over, picked it up. "Cat is hungry. Not getting enough light for photosynthetic fur to provide nutrients. Wait until you see when we release it. Wonderful! Exciting! Astounding!" He put the cat back in the box. "But for now, stay in here you will for the duration. Sorry you're hungry, cat."

Luna called up from behind, "Hey, speaking of cats and

being hungry. We ran out of rations like an hour ago, and I'm starving. But I was thinking… we could always eat the cat."

Skoop immediately shouted, "No cannibalism! Luna Foster watch your language!"

And they laughed, and Skoop wondered why, and for a moment the horizon seemed a little brighter.

24. SHAGGY

Exhaustion overcame them, and they slept.

And some indeterminate time later, Theo opened his crusty eyes, aware in the darkness that there was no wind, and it was strangely warm. Skoop was inches from his face. He whispered, "Are we alive? I fell asleep."

Skoop nodded and whispered back, shaking his helmet. "Yes. I sleep too."

"You sleep?"

"Of course. Waking all the time will kill a species. Sleep we have found universal. And sorry, sleep overcame me. My heating element timed out. We could have expired. So very sorry."

Theo sniffed, looking around in the dark, squinting. "What is that *smell*?"

Skoop peered around, turning on his helmet lamp. "Yes. My sensors are detecting a very nutrient-rich gaseous cloud surrounding us."

Luna, also half asleep, actually held her nose shut with her fingers. "You can say that again."

"My sensors are detecting a very nutrient-rich gaseous cloud surrounding us."

They all tried to clear their heads of the obvious effects of exhaustion, sleep, and hypothermia, the confusion and complete disorientation. They must have been hallucinating. Because when a small lamp was turned on, what they saw and smelled before them couldn't be real.

They were surrounded by walls of ice about a meter high, in roughly a circle, perhaps five meters in diameter. Below them was bare earth. Above them was some kind of tarp flapping in the wind. It was quiet in this space, and warm.

And in the middle of the space, turning around and around, looking them all over, holding the lamp, poking and prodding them with a metal rod...

A man.

Well, Theo supposed it was a man. He couldn't exactly tell, as there was so much hair. Hair down to its knees, with a beard to match, and hairy arms, and hairy legs. This person seemed to be made of hair. And thin as a skeleton. A hairy skeleton. A smelly, hairy skeleton with an old polysuit nearly torn to rags.

Luna was the first to speak, in a hoarse whisper. "Hey. Shaggy. Mind telling us what the hell is going on?"

And the man, yes it was almost certainly a man now because he spoke in a man's voice, said this: "First, you're welcome. Do you have any idea how remote the possibility was of me being where I was and you being where you were?"

Skoop's speaker crackled. "Like a needle in a haystack!"

Shaggy looked puzzled at this robot – clearly a model he'd never seen before. "Um, precisely. Anyway, miracles aside, although you should never push aside a miracle, those are the moments of revelation after all, but, miracles aside, I saw the shuttle explode and the pod come down. You should've stayed there, you know. With the pod."

Kate jumped up, then fell, not ready for standing, and croaked, "I told you! I told all of you, dammit!"

Luna clapped weakly. "Bravo, Kate. You win."

"Thanks, Luna. Feels good. Gotta admit, even under the circumstances." And they bumped fists. And Kate realized: she wasn't shaking. She was calm. *Huh.* She had been thrown into the deepest of deep ends, and she was... swimming.

Shaggy continued. "Rule number one. Stay where you are. Help is on the way." And Kate nodded, and looked around squinting and accusing each of them. Shaggy nodded along. "Yes, yes, agreed, anyway, I found you, near to death I might add, all unconscious, you know that's right before the organs begin to fail, that part, another miracle. So that's two miracles. Although now that I think of it, seeing the pod might not've been a miracle, the odds being a bit less than astronomical. Okay, let's say one and a half miracles..."

Luna sat up straighter and winced, rubbing her bruised side. "Okay, Shaggy. One and a half miracles. Next."

"Well, then, sorry, it's just that I don't get to talk much. This is exciting! Anyway, I created this space around us, down through the ice, to the ground beneath. I'm not proud of that though, and I don't want anything in return, in fact I was happy just living out my days here alone thank you very much. Being a biologist on Sunnyside, well, that'll turn anyone's brain to mush, make one drift off into the wilderness, how long is it, twelve years ago..." and he trailed off, and they all waited for the rest of his soliloquy, but it never came.

The blood finally returning to his extremities, Theo reached out his hand to Shaggy. "Thank you sir. I'm Theo. What is your name?"

"Hmm. I..." Shaggy took Theo's hand and shook it and thought for a long moment. "Huh, I forgot. It's been a while. I guess I don't have a name anymore."

Skoop jumped up and down a little and jiggled in his fluid. "Ah! I don't have a name either! They call me Skoop though. Which feels right to me, very much. You like?"

Shaggy nodded, puzzled, then spun to Theo. "Hold on! That's not a robot! Is that...?"

"Yes. The first non-human intelligence humanity has ever encountered, floating in some kind of lubricant, encased in a fully articulating humanoid robotic enclosure."

"That's what I thought! And you decided to call him Skoop?"

Theo motioned with both hands to the blob that looked uncannily like a handful of everyone's favorite rice pudding. "I mean..."

And Shaggy suddenly understood. "Ah! Yes! Yes! TastySkoop! My, oh my. The likeness is uncanny. Ah, it's been forever." He shuffled over to Skoop and sat down, staring into the helmet. Eyes glassing over with tears, he extended his fingers and gingerly touched the faceplate. "I'm an astrobiologist, have I already told you that part? Not an engineer. This... this beautiful being... was the reason I came here. But Sunnyside, woe is me, while yes, it is teeming with microbes, primitive life, no offense to it, it is life after all, but I had lost the hope of finding something more complex... higher order...intelligent..." he tapped the helmet and Skoop turned around in his liquid, perhaps to face him more directly. "Like you... and here you are, you beautiful being...

thank you, oh dear Skoop, for answering the eternal question… we are not alone…" And he reverently kissed the glass.

Skoop's speaker crackled. "You're welcome? I guess. This is not weird, is it guys?"

And Shaggy eventually tore his lips and eyes away, rising and peering again at the other three. "Listen, all this talk about Skoop. Delicious stuff, as I vaguely remember. Did you happen to bring any? I'm famished."

Skoop tilted back a bit, as if to say *don't look at me*. Kate pretended to search her pockets. Luna uncorked her nose and nearly vomited. "Well, obviously you've been eating *something*."

Theo stood, a bit off balance, and put his hand on Shaggy's shoulder. "We are so very grateful to have found you. But speaking of eating, how are you possibly surviving out here?"

Shaggy sat once more, shifted his butt, entering a lotus position, clearly getting comfortable, and grinned.

He had an audience and he decided he liked it.

"Imagine yourself on the back of a turtle, on ancient Earth, swimming through the ocean, on the waves, in the currents, watching his journey, seemingly directionless, just moving and turning, moving and turning, but in the end, he reaches his destination. What is that destination, you ask? At the end of his life, he has lived a life. Swimming and turning, and eating and shitting, and copulating perhaps a few times, and swimming some more, and turning, and on and on and on for a hundred Old Time years. And it was enough for the turtle. It doesn't seem like much of a life to us humans, what with our minicomms and our WhatsFace and our life goals and our plans through next year, Tuesday the fourth of

March to be exact, I think I have an opening after that, let me check my WhatsFace." And he pretended to press buttons in the air. "But to the turtle, you see, it makes perfect sense. He is not happy about it, or sad, but exists only in a moment, a never-ending moment, and there is a sort of bliss in that. Living outside of time, all the time, accepting each moment without hesitation. That's how I survived, living in that state."

Theo said, "I wasn't asking about the meaning of life. I just wanted to know what you ate."

"Oh." And Shaggy pointed to the ice-free ground under them. "That."

"Dirt?"

"Wasn't pleasant at first. Body had to learn. It took a year, if I had to guess time, what is time though? There's an interesting parable I have about time-"

"Um, sorry. If we could get back to the dirt."

"Right. It took a long time, but time, what is time? See, the parable goes lik-"

"Ahem."

"Right. I eat dirt." He bent down, grabbed a fistful, and let it trickle out through his open fingers. "It's amazingly rich in microbial life that a human body can process, amino acids, minerals, et cetera, et cetera, not nearly enough fat, as you can see" he pointed to his skeleton, "but enough of all you need, you know. Nothing like it on the orbiters. I would venture a guess there was nothing like it back on Earth in the way, way back. A superfood, I tell you! Now... the engineers over on the ring are so concerned – or not concerned, really, they could care less about anything at all – they are only concerned with making the appearance of progress on terraforming in between cigarette breaks. They never looked under their feet!

In nearly ninety years! It's gold, no it's better than gold, gold is worthless of course, just a word we never forgot. For in the forgetting, we let little pieces of ourselves die off, now doesn't that sound sad? That's why we hold on to ridiculous words like 'gold.' But it isn't sad. No, it's the opposite of sad. It's a blessing. We should rejoice in the forgetting! Look here." He opened his mouth, showing off exactly five teeth, and somehow managed to speak while holding his mouth open with his fingers. The stench nearly knocked them over. "I've forgotten those old teeth, didn't need 'em anyways, they were a vestige, so I forgot them. Technically, I pried them out when they rotted, but philosophically, I forgot them."

Kate had had enough. "Good story, bro. I'm not eating dirt."

Shaggy, still a biologist at heart, shook his head. "No! You mustn't say it like that! Say it lovingly, for it brings life. Try it with me. Ddddiiiirrrrttt…"

Skooop alone tried to imitate him. "D-d-d-i-i-r-r-. I cannot do it."

Shaggy had already moved on. "That's fine. Anyway, the human body, in these environmental conditions, can last two or three days without the fuel. So do as you like. But you'll have to try it eventually. Billions of microbes in every mouthful! Gives it quite the twang on your tongue. But the water you'll need right away of course. And I mean, talk about gold!" And he pointed around and around at the walls of ice. "All you can drink. Keep you alive indefinitely. I melt it with this." Then he pulled out, astoundingly from within his tattered polysuit, a small metal cube. It had dials, and a short antenna, and… microphone… and a speaker!

Theo pumped his fists into the air and nearly tore the

fabric of the ice hole's covering. "Yes! A radio! Why didn't you tell us?"

Shaggy looked around, suddenly frantic, as if he were missing something. They all pointed to the cube.

"Oh. This. Right. No, the radio on this was busted before I even began this journey. A long journey it's been. Did I tell you about the turtle yet?"

"Yes. But you were telling us just now about your broken radio."

"Oh." He laughed. "No. It's a Tokomac 86 nano fusion reactor that happens to have a worthless radio receiver added on. The engineers use them to keep their feet warm. That's about all they're up to power-wise. I use it to melt the ice. This one's got, ah, let's see..." and he lifted it up and squinted at a small four-digit display on the bottom, "...three years left."

Luna barked, "Three years? What were you planning after it ran out three years from now?"

Shaggy shrugged. "If you'll remember my previous fable about the turtle."

Luna shook her head. "Yup. Heard it. Just living your life, moment to moment, perpetual bliss, got it."

"Ah. You're a fast learner!"

"Great. Hey, you think you can help us get back to the habitable ring? The engineers? You know – life? Before we have to start eating dirt?"

Walking around in a tight little circle, Shaggy mumbled and sniffed, and poked them again with his stick, each in turn, as if he were judging whether they were worth saving. "You could join me, you know, form a tiny commune together, like-minded thinkers and all... learn to eat nutrient-rich soil..." but he immediately sensed the despair, these people –

and their alien – did seem to truly need to get back, they stared at him with anxiety and only the faintest glimmer of hope. "...oh all right, yes, I believe I can help. I have wandered so long I'm not one hundred percent certain of the way, but I believe I can orient us correctly. It is long, will take much time, perhaps we will make it before you need to eat dirt, and of course walking is the only way, I have some tools and coverings and things I can bring, again it will be arduous and long, but as you know, time is a construct, what is time really-*hold on*... forgive me... did I just hear... a meow?"

25. THINGS WERE NOT GOING ANY BETTER BACK ON THE LUSITANIA.

Secret Service Agent Ned Weathers stormed into the courtroom.

"You can't do this!"

He marched past the empty rows of benches, fuming. He had just seen, on television, a *Breaking News* alert – something about the announcement of a new Grand Oversee, at Lusitania City Hall.

Right downstairs! Right under his nose! He had been in the top penthouse yawning through interview after interview of Tasty from all the major talk shows, then since the shuttle disaster waiting for news, waiting, waiting, distracting Tasty, whom he hadn't told anything – and down here these two were plotting a coup!

He charged to the front, between the judge's bench and Hector Morgan. It was just the three of them, aside from a bailiff standing in a far corner. Looking back and forth between Morgan and the judge, with disgust, he shouted again, "You can't do this!"

The judge peered down his reading glasses at Ned. "I've seen you before. Who are you again?"

"Agent Ned Weathers, Secret Service. Assigned to the Grand Oversee."

Morgan grinned. "Well, then you're just in time. To protect me."

Ned bristled. "Not you. I'm assigned to Theo Hoover."

Morgan frowned, but with a hidden smile. "You mean the *late* Theo Hoover."

Before Ned could strangle Morgan, the judge rapped his gavel. "That'll be enough out of you, mister Morgan. You think this is funny?"

Morgan tried hard to suppress his grin. "You're absolutely right, your honor. As Grand Oversee, I will ensure a solemn and dignified memorial. At my inaugural press conference."

Ned's hands took on a life of their own. They reached over and grabbed Morgan's collar. "No you won't."

"Yes I will."

"No you won't."

"Yes I will."

"No you won-" and Ned interrupted his own schoolboy retort, opting instead for schoolboy violence. He pushed Morgan to the floor and jumped on him with his massive frame.

The two wrestled for a few seconds, grabbing, punching, kicking, but just as Ned secured Morgan in his signature lethal chokehold, lifting him off the ground, the judge launched to his feet and banged the gavel down three times so hard it split the wooden plate beneath. "STOP IT! NOW! SHAME ON YOU TWO!"

And the two reluctantly separated, dusting themselves off

and glaring. Morgan wiped blood from his nose with a handkerchief.

The judge sat back down, glaring as well, and nodded to the bailiff, who approached, looking stern.

Ned raised his hands. "I'm sorry, Your Honor. But Mister Hoover, and the whole landing party... your honor, they're still alive. They're not dead. Just missing."

It was the judge's turn to apologize. "I'm sincerely sorry, Agent Weathers, but we've all seen the footage. The shuttle had a catastrophic malfunction and was torn apart on entry."

"But... there's a pod, an escape pod. And there are two shuttle teams scouring the surface from above. We need to give them time. Can't we just wait a couple of days? They'll be found. I know it. I have faith"

Morgan raised his hand politely, and the judge nodded for him to talk. "Your Honor, if I may be frank, we don't have the luxury of time and faith. We have no government, even our temporary Grand Oversee is dead, we have aliens with heaven-knows-what intentions, and *their* leader is dead-"

"They're not dead!" Ned's hands were slowly reaching for Hector's throat.

"I think we need to presume the worst, your honor," Morgan continued without even looking at Ned. "We need to avoid chaos. There can be no anarchy. Just stable, forward progress. The natives are getting restless."

Ned's desperation was rising. "Your Honor, what about... the constitution?"

The judge shook his head. "We are *way* out past the constitution now, Agent Weathers. The constitution can't include everything. Only I can make these kinds of decisions at the moment." He sighed. "And so, I take on the burden of declaring Hector Morgan as Provisional Acting Interim

Temporary Grand Oversee." He rapped his gavel again, with a sad little clunk.

Ned, defeated, mumbled, "But... why? Why him?"

The judge was getting tired of all this. "Look around, Weathers. Who's left? I have to pick *someone*. He's willing to step up. You have a better idea?"

Ned practically hurled himself at the bench, pleading. "Yes! Yes! I have a thousand better ideas than making *Hector Morgan* the Grand Oversee! Give me two days, that's all I ask..." but he was screaming now, and clutching the judge's robes in desperation, so the judge nodded again to the bailiff, and instantly Ned was in handcuffs and being led away. Ned noticed in the bailiff's belt one of those faux light sabers the Skywalkers cosplayed with. "Oh for crying out loud," he mumbled to himself.

The judge smoothed out his robe. "I'll let you cool off for a few days down in the basement holding cells."

Ned shouted across the courtroom, "You can't do this!" He looked up to the heavens. "And... what about Tasty?"

The judge looked to Hector Morgan, who confidently puffed out his chest. "Oh, don't worry, Weathers. You won't be alone down there. Your little rice pudding friend will be joining you." He turned to the judge. "Don't fret for a moment, Your Honor. I'll have my people take care of them. I'll also call off this unnecessarily long shuttle search. And now... you have my permission to table that chaotic election business until after we get some real order around here."

The judge raised an eyebrow. "Table...?"

Hector strode to the bench, took the gavel from the judge's hand. "I'm sorry if I'm not being clear. I think an emergency, indefinite suspension of elections is in order. Don't you?"

The judge looked down, averting Morgan's stare, and nodded.

"Good!" Morgan said, and smacked the gavel, sending the broken pieces of the base tumbling to the floor. "Let's get to work!"

An hour later, Hector Morgan strutted to the front steps of Lusitania City Hall for his inauguration (technically they were calling it a "press conference," but really, he thought, what was the difference). Beaming, flanked by a few of his robed acolytes and the judge, he bounded forward like he'd just won the lottery. Which he had. Morgan had his eye on political power for a long time now, but he'd been held back. It was torture. Until now. Through two terrible, random tragedies, he'd been elevated to the highest office in the land. He didn't know exactly *how* he'd deserved this change of fortune, but deserve it he did, and he liked the view from up here. As they stepped up to the podium, surrounded by news cameras and microphones, he turned to his companions and whispered, "On with the show."

And he turned back, and flashed a broad smile, and looked so thrilled he might start tap dancing at any moment. "Ahem. People of the Grand Orbiter Project. As your newly appointed Grand Oversee-"

The judge, who had insisted on accompanying the entourage, coughed.

Morgan scowled, but immediately flashed that smile again and continued. "Ah, yes. As your newly appointed *Provisional Acting Interim Temporary* Grand Oversee, which we will shorten and formalize shortly, rest assured, I am here to mourn with you. Our prior Temporary Grand Oversee

Hoover, whose noble works included planting some grass and allowing aliens to invade our orbiters-"

The judge coughed again.

Morgan covered the microphone, stared into the judge's eyes, and without a word, it was understood that another cough would mean the holding cells in the basement, right next to Agent Ned Weathers and Tasty the alien.

He turned back to the cameras. "Now, again, I mourn with you. Our grass-planting and invader-inviting heroes are gone." He took a moment to appear truly sad, and almost but not quite made a tear leave his eye. "But now we must clean up the mess. For we have one last uninvited guest with sinister motives." He paused, and squinted. "Yes, our little alien friend has something up his sleeve. I'm not sure what, but they arrive and suddenly a Sunnyside shuttle blows up? Could that possibly be a coincidence? I think not. It's just the tip of the iceberg if you ask me, and we don't want to see what's underneath!" He raised his arms, as if embracing the reporters and all the people beyond. "I will, as your humble servant, take on the responsibility of these invaders, and returning our home to the way it should be, keeping us on track for terraforming Sunnyside on a realistic schedule, not some crazy dream of photosynthetic cats. And once I'm done, you can join me in building an even better deterrent against future invasions. Forever!"

He bared his teeth in a manic grin, and couldn't help himself, winked at the cameras. As he sauntered away, surrounded by barking reporters with their lights and cameras and microphones, and a small herd of cats, and hearing the faint grumbles of the judge, he hummed an old tune to himself. He recalled the words to the tune, and was delighted at how perfect they were for this moment:

I'm gonna live forever,
They're gonna remember my name,
And build statues of me on Sunnyside
As a tribute to my fame.
They'll have parades all day and night,
Save every word that I write,
Name a holiday for me and put up the lights,
Yes, I'm gonna live forever...

26. HOW MANY OF THOSE CATS DOES IT TAKE TO CHANGE A LIGHT BULB?

The ice on this half of Sunnyside was endless. And so was Shaggy's verbal diarrhea. He continued to tell them all, Theo, Kate, Luna, and Skoop, at great length, at extremely great length, at unbearably great length, what he remembered of his story, and his thoughts on the universe. A single soul hadn't crossed his path in twelve years, so he was making up for lost time. He just couldn't stop. "So as I said, being an astrobiologist on Sunnyside can be a lost cause, as with all the microbial life, there should be more complex life, intelligent life, like your astounding catlike creature here..."

Kate swung around as she trudged across the barren landscape. "Heard it. A bunch of times. Can we just drag our asses along quietly for five minutes?"

"Oh, yes. Certainly." And so Shaggy closed his mouth, it took quite a bit of effort, and he replayed the story in his own mind, as if he were telling the group:

Once upon a time there was a young, brilliant astrobiologist named Henry Bokenham. *Wait.*

Shaggy stopped short and shouted, *"Henry!"*

Theo turned to him. "Are you all right? Henry what?"

"That's my name! Henry! Henry Bokenham!"

Luna, bringing up the rear, almost bumped into him. "Darn. Shaggy was growing on me. Are you sure?"

And Shaggy shrugged. "Yes. But it's just a name. Call me what you wish. A name, you'll know, is the thinnest gossamer wisp of self identification. If you blow on it with a single thought of the communal cosmic consciousness, it falls apar-"

Luna patted him on the back, a bit too hard. "Got it, Shaggy."

So they continued on their journey in silence, and Shaggy returned to his reverie:

Once upon a time there was a young, brilliant astrobiologist named Henry Bokenham – now known as Shaggy, he supposed – although names, really, were inconsequential, he had learned. Henry spent seven long years on Sunnyside, on that thinnest of habitable rings, in an above-ground mobile lab that could almost fit on the head of a pin, with two colleagues: one in chemical and pharmaceutical development, and one in mineralogy. They weren't engineers, thank goodness. No, the engineers lived across the landing field in an underground bunker system, housing about a hundred and fifty of them. Although calling them *engineers* was a stretch of highest stretchiness. Each and every one of the engineers was lazy, and unmotivated, and couldn't carry on a conversation about consciousness or the nature of reality if their lives depended on it. They were like groundhogs, popping their heads out only when necessary, scurrying about without a care in the world, not putting any pressure at all on their walnut-sized brains. Yes, Henry looked down on the engineers, but underneath that judgement was envy. For just like the turtle, these groundhogs, these engineers, didn't think about yesterday, or tomorrow. They lived only for the moment, for a can of Tsingtao and a cigarette, and the next game of blackjack. It was bliss, in a way, and Henry couldn't reach it. Because Henry thought and thought and thought, all the time, all day and night, and had no more answers to show for all that thinking than the groundhogs across the landing field.

One day, to clear his mind of all the thoughts and the envy of a thoughtless existence, he set out into the cold.

"Where are you going?" asked his friends, the mineralogist and pharmacologist. They knew each other well, seven years in a shoebox together will do that, and excursions to the dark side were *not* on Henry's daily to-do list.

"I'm getting a breath of fresh air, that's all."

"Don't stay out long. It's dangerous. And make sure you put on an extra polysuit, it's colder than usual. Are you sure you're all right?"

"Yes. I've just been thinking."

"Well, that's a surprise." And they laughed.

He took a short walk, from that perfect thirty-meter-wide zone of sunshine and temperateness, to the cold and the ice. The next day he took a slightly longer walk, he didn't know why. The following day it was a bit longer still, and again, he didn't know why, but the walks just kept getting longer, and longer, until one day, he simply didn't return. His mind had finally cleared. He was free from thought. He expected to mourn the loss of his life, his job, his two friends in the lab, but he found... he just didn't. The isolation suited him. But these new people, the ones he'd rescued from the crashed pod, his... friends? Yes, he decided. Friends. That felt right.

As he walked alongside Luna, he mused. "You know, Luna, I think you all were sent to me for a reason. Not in a *great-gods-above* way, no that's hogwash, there's no one looking out for us Luna, sorry to say, no bearded benevolent man from the beyond-"

"Hold on. *You're* a bearded benevolent man from the beyond..."

And they chuckled together. "What I mean to say, Luna, is that the universe is brimming with meaning, with purpose and order and will, and we only need to listen and watch, and sometimes, I believe, sometimes the meaning is right there in front of our face, a serendipity or synchronicity so obvious we can't look past it, or we shouldn't at least. So you all are to me: it seems I've been asked to return. To life." He pointed up ahead, to Theo and Kate, trudging along in lockstep. "And look at those two. They've been thrust together, couldn't be more opposite you know. But the universe has a way of mashing things together for some purpose we can't imagine..."

And Luna smiled, a little wistful smile, because she knew Shaggy was right, and she knew from the moment that damned call panel flashed red that she had lost Kate. Somehow the universe had other plans for her, and she knew that friendships, even the best, and ones that lasted twenty-three years, eventually would end. There was nothing permanent in this whole universe, she knew that, but it still made her sad. "Nah, Shaggy. She's just his chief of staff. It's nothing."

But Luna knew better.

She choked back an emotion. *No. You're not the crying type.*

Especially not now. Not with all this, their impending death, the bruise in her side that was getting bigger, not smaller, the pain getting deeper, the breaths getting shallower every step becoming a little harder. *Be tough, Luna. Think of something funny, Luna.* So she caught up with Skoop and pointed to the box. "Hey Skoop, how many of those cats does it take to change a light bulb?"

Skoop's speaker crackled. "Luna Foster I will need information much more. For example, what is the bulb of light size? Shape? Screw or plug in? How high is it? Or low? Is it under the ground more? In space? Why does it need to be change-"

"Forget it. It was a joke. You ruined it."

"What joke? What is that? Joke?"

"A joke. You know."

"No. I do not know. Luna Foster I would very much like to know. Definition will help me determine how many cats it takes for bulb to be changed."

Luna was losing patience. "A joke is something funny."

"Ah! Excellent. Progress. Now describe what means funny? Definition of funny."

Luna rolled her eyes and shouted up to Theo. "Your turn, dear leader."

So Theo slowed down to walk with Skoop, and as patiently as possible, took over. "Funny? Um. Let me think for a second. Let's see... funny is something that happens opposite to your expectations, or, ah, something surprising, or a clever use of words, or an action that's very inappropriate. Ah, yes, for example: do you remember the way I walked toward you at our first meeting? That strange lifting of my feet?"

Skoop's helmet nodded. "Yes. Of course. It was ceremonial type walk, very official I assume to be."

"No. I had something sticky we call chewing gum on the bottom of my shoe."

And Skoop hesitated, as was his way, but said nothing.

Then a small gurgling in the oil surrounding him. Then silence. Then more gurgling, stronger. Skoop stopped walking, and faltered.

Kate supported him as he fell. "Oh my god – is he okay? Is he dying?"

Skoop croaked, as afraid as a synthetic voice could. "Yes! I may be dying! This sensation never have I felt! Oh no!"

Together, they crouched around Skoop, as if that would accomplish anything. There was no chest to compress, no airway to force air into, they didn't have any medical instruments, and even if they did they wouldn't have had the faintest clue where to start, so they could only watch as the gurgling continued and poor Skoop's life drained away.

"But..." Skoop's speaker said.

Theo shouted, exasperated, "But? But what? Oh my god, Skoop, you can't die! But *what?*"

"But... the feeling is strangely pleasurable." And the gurgling stopped and then started again, in spasms.

Sudden realization dawned on Luna. "People. Relax. He's not dying. He's laughing."

Skoop lifted his robot enclosure to its elbows. "Luna Foster! I believe correct you are! That's my first funny! I understand funny! Luna, tell me another joke."

Luna grinned and scratched her chin, lifting Skoop back to his feet. "Hmm... give me a sec... okay. Why did the Skoop cross the galaxy?"

"Why, Luna? Why? Tell me, Luna Foster."

"To get to the other side."

Instantly, small bubbles appeared in Skoop's helmet goo, increasing to a low gurgle, and finally so intense he looked like rice pudding being boiled in oil. "You are extremely funny, Luna Foster! You should be funny for your work!"

"A comedian?"

"Is that the word? Then yes! A comedian! I would pay human credits for listening to Luna Foster jokes!"

And now they all were giggling, then laughing, then howling, and the release made them walk a bit faster, with less effort, and the thought went through each of them that maybe, just maybe, this wasn't a march to their deaths.

And Theo and Kate looked down, and were surprised to find they were holding hands.

27. CRYOCRYPT

ector Morgan walked briskly from his personal limo-pod, across the roof-park of the vast CryoCrypt warehouse an hour south from Lusitania City Hall, to the nearest elevator. It wasn't the tallest structure on the orbiters, only ten stories above ground. But with each floor covering 150,000 square feet, and an additional twenty stories *below* ground, it was by far the largest. The size of forty Costcos. However, it didn't house eight-dollar off-brand blue jeans, or twelve-packs of OxyClean, or giant tubs of TastySkoop. No, it housed something much, much more valuable.

Cryocapsules.

The very same capsules each human slept in for the 358-year journey from Earth to Sunnyside.

300,000 cryocapsules.

There were many more, of course, back in 2378OT, when the Great Star Orbiter Project launched. Back then – and it always boggled Hector's mind at the sheer number – there were *two hundred million* cryocapsules manufactured for the voyage. One for each man, woman and child alive on Earth.

No wonder his great-grandmother Daisy Morgan was so wealthy. Beyond wealthy. Not only had she devised the technology for cryogenic stasis, but also, in the spirit of Henry Ford, had perfected a manufacturing process that would allow the technology to be produced on an incredibly massive scale. Her genius didn't end there, either: she also had the business savvy to negotiate, single-handedly, the entire project – all by the tender age of twenty-seven.

He beamed with pride as the glass elevator rushed down, down, past floor after floor, each floor packed with over eleven thousand capsules. The remainder of the capsules, of course, were recycled into more important products after their one-time use was finished – another engineering feat also pre-planned and negotiated by his great grandmother. She personally decommissioned the entire fleet after their centuries-long trip, but kept these 300,000 intact, to preserve the technology. Then, tragically, only a year after reaching Sunnyside, she passed away giving birth to Hector's grandfather. The orbiters had lost a shining star. Their hero.

The technology and cryocapsules had remained strictly off limits since, illegal to even step on the property, until eighteen years ago, when Hector had the bright idea of using the unused capsules to scam dead people – *no, scratch that –* "give grieving families hope that their loved ones might be resuscitated at some point in the future." They wouldn't, of course, dead was dead, but hope was a valuable commodity, and Hector couldn't pass up an easy buck, even though he had all the money in the world.

He thought about that for a moment. Yes, technically, he had all the money in the world, as the sole heir of the Morgan fortune, but at his current age of forty-three (he wasn't a percentage kind of guy), the purse strings were still strangely pulled tight, and what he could and couldn't do with all that cash was dictated by a tangled web of trust lawyers and accountants and mysterious men in midnight-blue suits with no job titles. It irked him, but the money spigot, let's be honest, was still wide open enough that it made complaining about anything at all seem pretty damned petty. Still, "they" could be miserly tightwads.

And so Hector was amazed when they actually allowed him the use of 10,000 capsules to test his latest boondoggle, CryoCrypt. He was delighted, and it was an instant success. So the they allowed him 30,000 more.

Life was good. He hadn't been allowed to pursue politics, for whatever reason the tangled web had, but that had changed recently too. They had loosened the leash. He was on top. Life was good. Daisy Morgan would be proud.

"If she could only see me now," he said aloud as he stepped off the elevator at the bottom floor. He laughed at the thought – she'd have to be four hundred seventy-five years old to see him now.

He had never been on the bottom floor. Of all the off-limits places, this was the most off-limits. His ears popped from the depth as he peered around in the dimness. But he had been given instructions by one of the suits to come here, along with an access card, so here he was. There was a door at the end of the short hallway. Just one door. He inserted the card into the blinking slot, and the door slid open.

It was dark in this chamber. Directly in the center was a cryocapsule.

An *open* cryocapsule.

And a fine mist was rising from the interior: that special

combination of frost and chemicals that made cryogenic stasis possible. But that would mean... someone...

A hand, from behind, grabbed his shoulder.

He turned and screamed.

And a young woman, no older than thirty-five, let go of him and laughed.

"Hector, Hector, Hector. Is that how you greet your great grandmother?"

28. THE BONEYARD

"If you're thinking of hugging me, I wouldn't. I'm sweating like a pig."

The young woman in front of him – his actual, real-life great-grandmother, if what she claimed was true – was standing there, muscular and young, in yoga pants and a t-shirt, panting, clearly having just completed an exhausting workout.

Hector stammered, "..but... but... how...?"

In answer, she simply pointed to the cryocapsule. "It works. What can I say? This one is my personal unit since I was twenty-seven."

"But... you're... D-D-Daisy?"

"Don't call me Daisy. Too familiar. Call me Great-Grandmother."

Hector's knees were giving way. There were no chairs. So he knelt down on the floor, looking up at this ghost from the past. "But... you're four hundred seventy-five years old!"

"Four hundred seventy-three, but who's counting? Listen, Hector, time is the enemy. I don't mean to rush you through this, but every second I'm awake is one less second of life. So here's the good new-"

Hector held up a hand. "Wait!"

"What?"

"You're... dead!"

She slapped him. Hard. "Don't you *ever* say those words to me."

Hector's mind was racing. Did his great-grandmother just strike him? Was it really her? What was going on? "I'm sorry, Dais- Great Grandmother. But I thought... I thought... the fleet was decommissioned... I thought the tech was off-limits..."

"For everyone else. Of course."

"But what about... I don't know... hospitals? Or... emergencies?"

She stroked his face where she had hit him, comforting him. "Hector, Hector. I did my bit for the common good. Now it's my turn. I can't have anyone figuring the technology out, fighting over it, competing with me for immortality."

"...immortality...?"

And there it was, Daisy thought. The difference between herself and the rest of them.

No imagination.

Not enough brainpower to grasp the *true* power of cryogenic stasis. Yes, it saved humanity – oh, by the way you're all very welcome, humanity – but if used properly, it also granted a kind of immortality. One or two weeks a year, wake up, take care of business, crack some heads if necessary, and keep humanity in its own perfect stasis, too. That's the way she liked it. So that's the way it was. She pulled all the strings. And some day, as she dreamed for years, decades, even centuries, she would imagine true immortality, and make it real. For what was death? Death was a cruel joke played by God, who thought he was better than us. He filled the Earth, and now the orbiters, with the frail remains of humans who got to live a paltry eighty years or so. It was all a boneyard. Earth. Sunnyside. Everywhere she looked, the bones of the dead. It disgusted her. No, she was better than death. It was all just shared atoms, in a different arrangement. What were mere atoms pitted against her genius? Nothing. She just needed time. And once the time came, once she had decoded and mastered true immortality, she would reveal herself again to humanity, their resurrected messiah, and rule the roost – *forever*.

But that was a little much to share with Hector at the moment. Poor thing was practically defecating in his pants, trembling in fear. She didn't need him to be afraid. She needed him to get the job done.

"Never mind about immortality, my boy." She reached down and picked him off the floor. He marveled at the commanding strength of this four-hundred-seventy-three-year-old, and instinctively bowed. "Great-Grandmother. I'm sorry for my insolence. You are my blood. My family. It's an honor to meet you."

She waved off his fawning. It almost made her gag. "Yes, yes, fine. All right. I'm trying to keep this to the point. The good news, mister Grand Oversee-"

Hector interrupted. "Well, actually it's *Provisional Acting Interim Temporary* Grand Oversee."

She scoffed. "Tom-*ay*-to, tom-*ah*-to. Now stop interrupting me." She began peeling her sweaty workout clothes off, receding into an even darker corner, into what Hector assumed was a shower. She raised her voice over the sound of rushing water. "So that's the good news, boy. It took a bit more wrangling to get you there than I'd hoped, with the sushi, and the shuttle explosion-"

Hector interrupted once more, risking her scorn. "Excuse me...?"

She scowled. "What?"

"But... the sushi... the shuttle... they were accidents..."

Daisy peeked her head out from the steam and laughed. "Accidents?" But she saw that he had no idea. The poor thing. "Oh, yes. Accidents. Terrible, terrible, Hector. And so many, many accidents before that. Before you were even born. All those terraforming delays, too. Boo-hoo. Terrible, terrible, unfortunate and completely out of our control. Who would want to stall the terraforming of Sunnyside and keep humanity on the orbiters forever? *That would be insane!* But I digress. Now that all of that has happened, again unfortunately, and now that the propaganda campaign has begun to take root and grow within the general population – it's all put you in the position I needed you in right now: to rid ourselves completely of those meddling invaders. We didn't start their invasion, but we are damned well going to stop it. Hector, now that I've done all this for you, I called you here to ask you, in person, for a return favor. A little, itty-bitty, teeny-weeny favor for your great-grandmother."

Dramatically, she donned a silk robe, wrapped her long hair in a towel, and slowly approached him, leaving watery footprints behind her.

Hector was trembling. "A-a-a... favor...?"

"I need you to make a very public example of the alien."

"Example...?"

"Do I really have to say the words?"

Hector's blank stare was her answer.

She patted him on the head. "Ugh. All right then, my boy,

I'll make it crystal clear…" And she leaned down and whispered in his ear. "I've killed many in my long years. I killed Piper Montgomery. I killed a whole banquet hall of government officials. I killed Theo Hoover. I killed the first alien. *Now I need you to kill the other one. In front of everyone.*"

Then she walked over to her cryocapsule, let her robe and towel drop to the floor, and, naked, climbed in. As the lid closed, and the mist began to envelope her, Hector could hear her crooning to herself,

"I'm gonna live forever,
They're gonna remember my name…"

29. SHE'S GOING TO LIVE!

Luna fell.

She got back up, hoping the others assumed she'd only slipped on the ice. She walked on. Tried to smile.

But each step was torture now. She had stopped even looking at the bruise in her side. It wasn't going away. Of course it wasn't going away. She knew the moment that damned cat box jabbed into her side during the crash landing: *this was not going to end well.*

Her only hope, now fading, was that somehow they'd make it to the habitable ring, and a team of medics would rush out and carry her to some gleaming, futuristic operating room, and they'd declare a miracle, she was going to live, and that they could go home.

It wasn't to be.

She fell again, to her knees, and cried out, "Kate!"

Turning back and seeing Luna reach out, Kate rushed to kneel beside her. "What, Luna? What the hell?"

Words failed Luna, she couldn't breathe, so she just

looked into Kate's eyes, and twenty-three years went by in an instant, and for the first time, she let Kate see her cry.

Kate laid her down, her whole body shaking, and ripped at the fabric of her polysuit, revealing the dark bruise stretching from her hip to her shoulder on one side.

"oh my god..."

And then, "Luna! What the hell? Why didn't you say something?" She lightly touched the bruise and Luna groaned. Then Luna mustered the strength to whisper, "...I've seen worse..."

Kate wasn't in the mood for snark. "Luna, when we fix you up, I'm going to kill you." And she reached out her hand to Shaggy. "Give me a knife. And get down here. We're going to fix her. Get in there, find out what's bleeding, sew it up. Theo, give me the first aid kit. Skoop, you got anything to add?"

"I am not expert at human physiology. But estimate Luna Foster will expire shortly."

Tears sprung from Kate's eyes. "Goddammit, Skoop! Not now!"

She took the knife, and trembling like a leaf, aimed it towards Luna's abdomen.

Luna grabbed her hand.

"No. Kate." She coughed. A line of blood trickled down from the corner of he mouth. "...come on, I'm not stupid... there was nothing to be done... goddamned cat... funny, the cat that saved humanity, but killed Luna Foster... I'm dying, Kate..."

"Oh, you're a doctor now? Be quiet." She spoke to the others without taking her eyes off Luna's. "Okay, I'm going to make an incision, I don't know, I guess near the kidney... shit... Shaggy, you're a biologist, you know this better than me, right?" And she looked up, and Shaggy was shaking his head. It was obvious to anyone, no doctor needed, that massive internal bleeding wasn't going to be stopped by three people and an alien in the cold on the dark side of a barren planet with a knife and some thread and bandages. And Luna knew too, she'd known all along. She motioned for Theo to come closer, and whispered hoarsely, "...Theo, you're actually making a difference... well, you're trying to... keep it up... and take care of Kate..."

Kate began sobbing. "No! I don't need Hoover to take care of me! I need *you!*" And in that moment, she realized for the first time that Luna wasn't just a lifelong beer buddy. She wasn't just the casual friend from middle school she could share secrets with about crushes on boys. She wasn't just the knowing nod that hardly ever needed to be put into words. She wasn't just her constant co-conspirator, laughing together at the foibles of all the bureaucrats. She'd only known Hoover for ten days. She'd known Luna... forever.

"Luna, look at me!"

And Luna looked up, struggling to do so, her breathing so shallow now that Kate's couldn't see her chest move at all.

"No, no, no Luna... no Luna... please don't leave me... I... I love you...you know, not like that, but like... oh god, don't break my heart Luna..."

And Luna smiled, and mouthed the words *I love you too*, and closed her eyes forever.

Kate's body shuddered with sobs, her wailing filling the skies of Sunnyside. She pounded on Luna's chest, turning them into forceful compressions, which only made more blood trickle from Luna's mouth, and when she knelt closer to start mouth-to-mouth, Theo grabbed her shoulder. "No. She's gone, Kate."

"What do you know about gone, Hoover? Get your hand off me." And she swatted his hand away and whispered into Luna's ear. "I'm not letting you go. I'll figure something out." She looked around, frantic. "Hey, I know – we'll pack you in ice. We'll get you nice and frozen, and then when we get home, they'll figure it out, my mother knows all the doctors." She stood suddenly, tears gone. "Everyone. Start chiseling ice. We're going to pack her up good and Skoop can drag her along on a sled. Shaggy, you've got a few poles, and the tarp and bandages and stuff." They stood there, not knowing what to say. It was over.

"What the hell are you looking at? *Start putting her on ice! She's going to live!*"

The words pierced Theo's heart.

For seventeen years ago, almost to the day, he had shouted the very same thing.

Start putting him on ice! He's going to live!

It was the night Vin died – no, *almost* died – and they placed him in CryoCrypt.

Capsule number 903b87t.

Theo was transported to a memory: Vin painting. He loved to watch Vin paint, especially in their later teens, when Vin's skills really started to blossom. Theo would lay on Vin's bed, sneaking sips of Flint Special whiskey from their hidden stash, and marvel as the small blobs of oil paint would leave Vin's brush and become something on canvas, something from nothing. He felt like the luckiest person on the orbiters to see these little miracles appear. A sailboat. A small boy walking in a field of clover. An old-fashioned Earth car, gleaming in the light of the old Sun. Vin could paint for hours, only his arms moving, dabbing the oils, mixing the color, applying a stroke or two, and repeating that meditation over and over and over, occasionally glancing over at Theo and smiling the knowing smile that magic was happening right there, and that nothing else existed at that moment, or needed to exist, until Mom called them to dinner. "Vincent and Theo! For the last time, get in here, supper's getting cold!"

That was the only time she used his given name, *Vincent* – when he was in trouble or asking for trouble. Yes, their art-obsessed parents had named them Vincent and Theo, after the Van Gogh brothers, and pushed them both to draw and paint from their first years. Theo had none of the talent, he was the numbers kid, but Vin had enough for both of them and more. And unlike his namesake, Vin was a wild, very social creature, who eventually couldn't be contained. One day, at nineteen, halfway through a painting, he stood up, announced he was leaving for the Hindenburg, which seemed to Vin to have a burgeoning art scene, or at least a bohemian lifestyle. Mom and Dad laughed, until Vin walked out the door, with nothing but his brushes and tubes of paint.

Theo cried his eyes out for weeks. His other half had been torn from him – his better half. He was adrift on the sea of life, with no beam or cushion or door from the shipwreck to rest on. And that made Vin's return, after six months of whatever bohemians on Hindenburg did, even sweeter. Theo jumped up and down and hugged his parents and cried tears of joy. "He's coming home!"

When they met him at the shuttle bay, Theo could hardly contain himself, and he ran up to Vin and hugged him until Vin couldn't breathe. "Vin! Vin! I'm so glad it's over." And Vin grinned and whispered in his ear, "Oh, my boy, it's just *beginning*. Have I got plans for us."

And on the way home, zooming through the skies of the Lusitania, their pod was struck by a trailer pod and crashed into a parking lot below.

Mom and Dad were killed instantly.

Vin's left arm was crushed and left leg was paralyzed.

Theo escaped without even a bruise.

He did everything he could to manage the aftermath, the funerals and Vin's caretaking, and the fighting the bureaucracy for anything, anything at all to bring justice or at least fix the dangerous pod traffic problems. He pushed and pushed Vin to relearn to paint with his right hand, but something had broken, beyond repair, in Vin's heart. Vin had always survived on the energy of emotions, unlike Theo, and they had all abandoned him. Grief, joy, even rage, all gone. When Vin began to fill that emptiness with Vicodin, Theo wasn't surprised. He became the tough-love caregiver for a time, until that pushed them even further apart. Vin lost so much weight Theo would carry him to bed, though Vin fought that final indignity.

"I'm a burden, Theo. Stop."

"Stop? Stop carrying you? Leave you at your easel all day, staring at a blank canvas?"

Vin just nodded his head. "Okay. You're right. You're right."

But even their fights grew thinner and weaker, until the two simply coexisted, going through the motions of life, Theo working, Vin fading, slowly, slowly, until one day

Theo came home from work to find Vin unresponsive at his easel, with a tiny drop of wet paint still on the tip of his brush.

Before the doctors could call time of death, Theo screamed, "*Start putting him on ice! He's going to live!*" And reluctantly they did, and called CryoCrypt, and before Theo could have his better half torn from him again, Vin was rushed to their warehouse and placed in Capsule 903b87t. He remembered shaking the hand of the representative from CryoCrypt, asking, "He's alive, right? He's going to live?" and the representative looking blankly, seeming to be caught between a no and a yes, then asking Theo to sign on the dotted line.

Theo shuddered, stuffing the memories back where they were safe.

Vin was alive.

Luna was dead.

There was a difference.

He reached out and touched Kate's hand.

"Kate. I'm sorry. Luna is gone."

She glared at him. "What? Suddenly you're the expert on life and death?"

Theo knelt next to her. "It's over, Kate. I know what cryogenic stasis can and can't do. I know the difference between someone's who's clinging to life, and someone who's..."

She pushed him away and stood, furious. "Let me guess. Vin? Is this about Vin? Your little secret?"

Theo just looked at her.

"Wait. So Vin's in CryoCrypt? Hector Morgan's

resurrection scam? Ah, that's how Morgan knows your brother! You got scammed, Hoover."

"It's not a scam."

"Wow." She shook her head and actually laughed, tears rolling down her face again. "You know, I thought you were pretty smart. Extremely smart, if you want to know the truth. Moments of genius, I'm not kidding. But putting Vin into CryoCrypt? What's the *opposite* of genius? I mean Hoover, have you seen the stat? How many people they've brought back? Ever? Total?"

He didn't have to say the number. They both knew it was zero.

"So, Hoover. You say Luna's gone?" She pointed down to Luna's lifeless body, then into Theo's face. "I've got news for you. Vin's gone too."

"HOW DARE YOU!"

"How dare I what? Say it out loud? Your brother is dead."

"Vin is NOT dead! He's awaiting resuscitation. At some future date to be determined. He's alive. He's on ice. He's going to live..." and the words trailed off, because there stood Vin, right in front of him, a tear running down his cheek.

"Tell her the truth, Theo."

Theo closed his eyes and shook his head. "Go away." He was angry now, livid at Vin, and Kate, and the goddamned planet they were stuck on, and humanity for fucking it all up, in every way possible. He felt desperate and trapped. And this Kate Kingston had put it all into motion. Kate Kingston. It was her fault. So he said the worst thing to her he could think of. "I hate you. You did this to me. I didn't want this. Luna sure as hell didn't want this. Look what you've done."

The rage in Kate's eyes was like nothing Theo had ever seen – he was truly afraid of her for the first time. But she didn't scream, or slap him, or stab him with the knife. She only seethed, for a long minute, staring deep into Theo's soul and ripping it out and stomping on it with her eyes. She turned and grabbed the small shovel from their supplies and began chipping at the ice. "Don't talk to me. Ever again. Skoop, keep him away from me."

Skoop turned back and forth, almost comically, not having any clue what to do. "All right Kate Kingston. Will maintain distance between yourselves, although I am puzzled. May I ask several questions?"

Theo and Kate both shouted, "NO!"

So Skoop began helping Kate, and Shaggy bent down too, and started chipping ice.

Theo walked away.

30. LUXURIOUS ACCOMMODATIONS

n a dank, featureless Lusitania City Hall holding cell 5,632 kilometers from Sunnyside, three floors underground, Tasty the alien and Ned the secret service agent sat on a bench.

Tasty looked around, as he had been doing for hours, and his speaker crackled. "This is nice. Much nicer than the stateroom at the Lusitania Office and Residence of the Grand Oversee."

Ned let out a grim laugh. "We're going to have to agree to disagree on that one."

"No. Sincerely. Rarely hosts do they understand our preference for minimalism. Fewer distractions, no entertainment needed – or wanted actually. Refreshing. Less is more. And look," he pointed, "even has steel bars! Wow! Thank them, that's what would like to do."

And so he stood up and tapped the security camera mounted in the corner. He tapped and tapped – not aware that the human custom would be to tap maybe three or four times tops – he could've tapped for a thousand years, such was his enthusiasm for their luxurious accommodations, and Ned simply rolled his eyes and covered his ears. But the tapping was interrupted by the *stomp-stomp-stomp* of an approaching guard. "Hey! Stop tapping! It's annoying as hell! And you're going to break that!"

Tasty turned and faced the guard. "Oh dear. Sorry. Didn't mean to annoy or break." And he raised his hands and walked toward the guard to offer his repentance.

"NO! Stop right there, prisoner!" The guard paced, menacing, disgusted. "Look at you. Just look at you. I bet if I get any closer you'll eat my face off."

Tasty thought about this for a moment. "We don't eat faces off. Look." He pointed to Ned. "Secret Service Agent Ned Weathers' face intact." He was silent again for a few seconds. "Unless your desire is that. Do you want me to eat face?"

"No! You sick bastard. Stay back."

"Hmm. Not bastard, if that term understood correctly, as illegitimate offspring of unmarried humans. We, as you know, separate asexually from another, to have experiences for a time through a unique lens of consciousness. In fact, took us quite a while to understand concept of 'bastard.' Strange. Anyway, only wanted sincere thanks to give to you, our generous hosts. Felt in-person more appropriate it would be. Thank you!" The guard simply scowled, so he repeated, louder, "Thank you!"

Squinting at him suspiciously, the guard said, "You're welcome..." And he paced a bit more. "Now, no more tapping. Sit in silence and suffer your fate."

"Suffer? My oh my. No! Am *thanking* you for such gracious and opulent accommodations!"

In a huff, the guard turned to leave. Tasty called to him. "Oh. Gracious host. One more question?"

The guard turned back. "What."

"Not in a rush at all, could revel in this luxury for eons, however, curious become as to when other can join us? The one you call Skoop. Skoop is missing out on this! Calculated delivery of enhanced cat-like being to Keplar-4-Tidallock-G9 should be plenty over, no? While enjoying this super deluxe lodging, we have no access to transmission equipment aboard our primary vessel. In fact, primary vessel being empty, is essentially offline. No control. Also, short-range telepathy only works twenty meters perhaps. Therefore no contact at all. Do you have estimate of their time of return?"

The guard was done answering questions. He spit on the floor.

Agent Ned leapt to his feet and shouted, "Woah! Hey buddy! What the hell? How about a little respect?"

The guard turned on him. "Huh? You have a problem, you invader-loving freak? Are you not aware that the 'leader' alien sabotaged the Sunnyside shuttle trip and killed himself along with the Temporary Grand Oversee in a suicide mission meant to destabilize life on the orbiters, leading to chaos and a vacuum of authority, only to install themselves as our evil alien empire overlords for... *forever?*"

Ned shook his head. "What the actual fuck are you talking about?"

The guard continued, zealous, pointing at his cell mate. "Oh, they know. They know, all right. These crafty aliens are playing innocent, playing us for fools. *'Where is our poor leader?'* Well, we're not fools. We know what evil empires do, through malevolent emperors and wicked sith lords and such, using us naive worker bees to execute their designs on ruling the galaxy through planet-killing weapons and dark side tactics we can only imagine." He was disgusted by Ned's blank look. "Wake up, prisoner. It's all over the news. Everywhere. We were naive to embrace them. But the shows and the news, they've pulled the veil back, revealing the truth. It's not just us Skywalkers who know the truth now. People are protesting in the streets on all eight orbiters. They're scared. And you should be, too, unless you like having your face eaten off."

Ned's jaw went slack. He was speechless. He had lived his whole life thinking people had some baseline of common sense. That in the face of something truly outrageous, they'd stand up and say *Hey, what do you take us for, fools?* But now, in light of recent events, he had to reconsider. Was it possible... vast numbers of his fellow citizens were complete idiots?

Tasty clanked his mechanical finger on one of the bars. "Excuse me! Again, in case you not heard, we don't eat faces."

The guard grimaced. "Sure. Sure. Well, you can tell that to the Grand Oversee."

As if on cue, the guard received a beep in his minicomm. He listened and nodded. Then, reluctantly, as if he might get his face eaten off, he unlocked the cell, pulled them out, and prodded them along with a gun in his hand. "Go. No funny movements. You're wanted upstairs. By the man himself."

31. THE CAVE

Sitting in a cave to rest and ride out a sudden ice storm, Shaggy pondered his circumstance: He loved having people to talk to again, finally after twelve years, he was bursting with the urge to chat – but here he sat in silence. The Temporary Grand Oversee and Miss Kingston weren't talking at all, just exchanging seething glares. And Luna Foster, lain in ice on a makeshift sled, well, she had spoken her last words, the poor woman. The cat, obviously, didn't speak – or at least he presumed it didn't. Then there was Skoop, of course, but Shaggy hadn't found the courage to engage him in conversation. What do you say to an otherworldly mind? What could Shaggy possibly say that wouldn't be cringeworthy?

What he didn't know was that Skoop was thinking the same exact thing. Skoop found Shaggy endlessly fascinating, even intimidating. Yes, their own species had mastered faster-than-light travel (it was fairly simple, if one sat down and worked through the math), and had left war and suffering far behind, but there was something about the humans, and especially this Shaggy character, with his strange ways and words. It was impossible to categorize him or document exactly the way his brain worked. Humans, and very much so this particular one, were an enigma.

Then, in one of those strangest of synchronous moments, Shaggy and Skoop each decided to break the ice, and in perfect unison, said, "I had a dream."

They stopped, and marveled at the coincidence. Theo and Kate sat at opposite ends of the cave, deep in their own reflections, oblivious.

Skoop broke the silence and pointed to Shaggy. "You first."

"No, I think as our guest, you should."

"No. You first."

Shaggy acquiesced. "Well, all right. I've been having a recurring dream, for perhaps three years now. It's exactly the same every time, so exact I have it memorized. I'm walking in a field, and I meet a stranger. I ask her to tell me the history of man, and this is what she says: 'There was a day filled with blue sky and rainbows, and the sky was overflowing with life, birds of all shapes and sizes, and insects and bats. And on the land trees grew, too numerous to count, and covered the land, and it was home to innumerable animals, living their lives, whether foraging for a tasty leaf, or hunting on weaker prey. And rivers flowed through the land, and in that water more life, fish upon fish, so great in number a land dweller could stick its hand or paw or claw in and pull one out every time. And on this land grew man and woman, the humans, and they lived and loved and died just like the rest. Of course we know something happened, the brains of the humans evolved, and their reasoning skills advanced beyond all the other life of the planet, and this evolution brought miracles like agriculture, and medicine, and tools for building towns, and philosophy and art and commerce. And somewhere along the way, their brains evolved beyond the limits of what the planet could offer them. It wasn't their fault they were smart. They were both too smart, and yet not smart enough, and neither was their fault. It just was. And so the world was shaped in their image, their perfect-yet-imperfect image, and miracles flowed everywhere, but also scarcity and famine and war, because the humans were afraid.

'Then the humans took to the sky, to find another home, to become smart in the right ways, to start over, to learn from the past but not repeat the past. And they found their new home, and after a time, it became resplendent with all the miracles the humans had known before, but there was a difference this time. They had grown. And the world was rich and plentiful and peaceful for eons beyond counting, and the humans dispersed outward, spreading peace, helping other worlds along the way, worlds that were also too smart but not smart enough. Because that's the way it was meant to unfold.

'And in the end, the universe let out a great contented sigh, for it was done, and it turned out the lights. But it knew that tomorrow, it would begin again.'" Shaggy scratched his beard. "Now, isn't that the strangest dream?"

Skoop was rapt. "No. You see your species' future."

"You think?"

"I know. Free will exists of course, and can change, but if current trajectory holds, yes. We see it time after time. Our own species has stories like this. We await the "great contented sigh" you speak of. You have prophecy. Henry Bokenham you are a prophet. It happens."

Shaggy didn't know what to say. A higher intelligence from another galaxy calling him a prophet! It might just have been the high water mark of Shaggy's life. He blushed, trying to wave away the compliment, but also basking in the glow. And then he remembered. "Oh! Please, mister Skoop, tell me. What did *you* dream of?"

"Pizza."

"Excuse me?"

"Pizza. We sample human food on Lusitania. One was pizza. Can't stop fantasy about it. Came into my dream. Bread, cheese, tomato, herbs. Delicious."

Shaggy couldn't help himself. He laughed out loud, trying to catch himself. "Oh dear. I'm sorry."

But Skoop was gurgling too. "No. It is good. We make the thing you call friendship."

And so they continued talking, and in the next silence, Shaggy again couldn't help himself, and shouted to Theo and Kate. "If you didn't hear all the way over there, it seems I'm something of a prophet. Available for hire, as it were, should you have the need. At your service. Ask away."

So Theo rose, crossing over to Shaggy, and sat opposite him. He had a question. Without a sound, Shaggy knew the question that anyone with eyes would know if they saw the look on Theo's face.

Shaggy thought for a moment. No vision of the future appeared to him, but he opened his mind, and a certainty filled him, and he reached out and held Theo's hands. "I don't know what's going to happen to your brother, Mister Hoover. But... if you'll allow me... I have a fable to tell you instead of a prophecy. Would that be all right?"

Theo groaned, and from across the cave Kate did too, but for some reason Shaggy took this as a *yes* and launched into another of his stories. "This one is a fable, yes, but also a true story. There was a man, over on Chernobyl, who had a dog.

The dog wouldn't leave his side, but the dog wasn't allowed in the man's work office, so you see, a conundrum! The man thought and thought, and spoke to the dog, his best friend, about it, and they agreed – and yes, I understand that dogs and men can't converse – anyway, they agreed that the man would bring the dog as far as the exit to the trainpod station, one block from his office. The dog wagged his tail, and for the next three years, every day, he would wait at the exit for the man, all day, and the passersby got to know the dog, and petted him, and gave him treats, you know how dogs love being petted and getting treats, and everything was working just fine.

"Until one day, the man didn't come to the trainpod exit at the end of the workday. And so the dog waited, thinking the man must have been delayed by a meeting, or to help some other dog in need, surely. The dog was still waiting the next day. And the next. And the passersby began to ask, 'was the dog here all night?' and 'what has happened to his master?' But nothing changed. The dog remained at his post, being fed here and there, and petted, but over time, you'll know, he began to waste away. Three weeks to the day, as a dog catcher approached him with a leash, a lonely old woman, well let's just pretend it's a woman for our purposes-"

Theo interrupted him. "Wait. I thought you said this was a true story?"

Shaggy looked annoyed. "It is! And who's telling it, you or me? Now hush, and learn something!" He stood, and brushed the pebbles off his ragged polysuit, and pulled Theo up, and addressed all of them together. "Where was I before you interrupted me...? Ah, yes. Listen, here's the meaty part, Theo, and the rest of you: Moments before the dog was to be taken, a lonely old woman stepped in front of the dog. 'He's mine,' she announced, and she looked down at the dog, and the dog wagged his tail. And he did become hers, and she became his, and they lived the remainder of their days in each other's care."

After a minute of silence, Skoop raised his hand. "A question. What happened to the man? The office man?"

Shaggy opened his mouth to explain, but Theo put his hand on Shaggy's shoulder and spoke first:

"That's not the point."

For Theo knew now that he was the dog, waiting, and Vin was the office man, and for the first time, he knew that the answer to what happened to the office man wasn't the point. The point was what happens next. He looked into another far corner of the cave, knowing what he would see.

Vin was there, sitting cross-legged, with a wide grin, beaming up at him.

"*Now* you're getting it."

And Theo smiled, and tears welled up in his eyes, and he didn't care if anyone thought he was crazy anymore, he spoke aloud to his brother. "Don't go, Vin. Who's going to carry me?"

Vin laughed. "Carry you? Theo. You literally carried me in those last days." He rose and approached Theo. "I never told you this, little bro, but you were *always* the one carrying me." And now, grinning again, Vin embraced him. "It's time. Time to go home."

And he turned and walked out of the cave. As Theo looked after him, quietly sobbing, Vin disappeared into the white.

Theo turned back to the others. "Um. Sorry about that."

But he felt – no, he *knew* – that they each understood,

without a word or a nod, even Kate in her lingering rage and hurt.

The storm passed.

Theo took a deep breath and said, "It's time to go. We have a cat to deliver."

They emerged from the cave.

As they walked, in the distance, it was subtle but discernible, the horizon grew brighter.

They were headed in the right direction.

And Theo was probably imagining it, but he thought he saw, along with the rising sun in the distance, a tiny figure approaching them.

32. HE WAS GOING TO THROW UP.

Hector Morgan couldn't stop shaking.

He was going to throw up.

He swallowed hard.

You are not going to throw up. You are not going to throw up.

He couldn't understand. He'd been here many times, at the entrance to Lusitania City Hall, standing on the steps, in front of throngs of people and surrounded by reporters. He loved this.

But of course, he did understand: this time was different.

He had just found out his four-hundred-seventy-three-year-old great-grandmother was still alive.

He looked around, at every person, every building, every detail, and thought, *she's still alive, and pulling every string. Every single one. Including mine.*

Without a will of his own, he plastered a grin on his face, and spoke into the cameras, millions of people watching at home, stammering. "P-p-p-people of the O-o-o-orbiters…" He took a deep breath. *Calm down, Hector. You have a job to do.*

He began again. "People of the Orbiters, we're gathered here to welcome Tasty, the alien."

Behind him, the guard pushed Tasty and Ned to the front, right next to Hector.

Tasty was confused. He expected the cheers he'd grown accustomed to, the welcoming spirit of the humans. But these humans were jeering and booing, holding signs that said "Go Home!" and "Not Welcome Here!" What Tasty didn't know was that, for the past several days, the TV-watching and news-reading population of the orbiters had gone from watching friendly interviews with Tasty, to being fed a constant diet of conspiracy theories and motivations and fear and rage, until even the most moderate didn't know what to think. And so the aliens they danced with just a few days ago had somehow been reduced to an enemy, an enemy of unseen evils, but if you listened to the news, those evils were hiding in there somewhere, just under the skin, trust them, they were ready to pounce at any moment and rip your throat out.

A large cup of Coke sailed through the air and hit Tasty on the helmet, splattering soda over him. Tasty turned to Hector. "Don't understand…"

Hector Morgan felt another wave of nausea. Swallowed hard again. Cleared his throat. "And… and now, people, we must deal with the cancer that has entered our body. The uninvited illness that threatens to infect us. Their leader, if you can call it that, in… intentionally sabotaged a mission in order to kill our dear departed Temporary Grand Oversee and multiple crew members! Who knows what calamity and cruelty the aliens had planned for us next! Now… what do you, the people of the orbiters, want? For these creatures to continue to live among us, as equals – wait, no… as *betters*?"

Boos resounded from the crowd.

"I didn't think so."

And now, with hands trembling like leaves, Hector reached into his pocket and pulled out a small pistol.

The crowed gasped. When was the last time they had seen a gun?

In the silence that followed, each person, there and at home, realized that a line had somehow been crossed. Yes, they wanted these invaders gone. But… did they want them dead? And did they want to… see them be killed? Live on television? Hadn't humanity left public executions far, far in the rear view mirror? The guillotine at the French Revolution? Lynchings in the American South? The Nazis? Saddam Hussein? ISIS? *What was happening?*

Hector, too, was lost in thought in that moment. Of course he had done bad things. Stolen people's money. Exerted inappropriate pressure here and there. Made gobs of money the wrong way. But he had never killed anyone. It had never even crossed his mind.

Slowly, he lifted the gun and pointed it at Tasty's helmet.

Without a human face, no eyes, nose, or mouth, Tasty somehow still looked deep into Hector's eyes, and what Hector felt from it was… compassion. Tasty's speaker crackled. "Do what you must do. Peace we bring, that is all. Here to facilitate the unfolding, nothing more. No aggression will change that. Not the first to misunderstand are you, and not the last."

And then Hector dropped the gun.

"I… I can't."

And he turned back to the cameras and spoke before he could stop himself. "I'm sorry. This isn't right. This whole thing is wrong! It's insane! The aliens are here in peace! *We* are the ones stoking fear and violence. It was… it was… my great-gran-"

A shot rang out.

Hector looked down. Blood was gushing from his abdomen. He fell to the ground.

The nearby Skywalker – the guard that had been watching Tasty and Ned – held Hector's pistol. He turned it from Hector to Tasty, and pulled the trigger before Ned could lunge.

A bullet tore a hole through Tasty's helmet, and yellowish liquid began to drain out. Tasty fell backward.

The crowd screamed as one, and they and most of the reporters and crew ran in all directions, away, away from the chaos and danger on the steps of Lusitania City Hall, into the streets beyond. The remaining Skywalkers and police surrounded Hector, Tasty, and Ned, who had the guard in a chokehold. The guard passed out and went limp on the ground, and Ned screamed to the rest, "Secret Service! Back off!"

And in the confusion of the moment, there was enough uncertainty, where even the police and the Skywalkers had to ask themselves, "Who's in charge?" And they looked up at Ned's extremely large frame, and they stepped back.

Ned knelt down and cradled Hector's head. "What have you done, Morgan?"

Hector coughed blood, but said nothing. He reached into his pocket one last time, with all his strength, and lifted out an old fashioned, ornate iron key. He looked at it with his dimming eyes, proud, for even though he had lived a life of privilege and vice, underneath he had some kind of integrity, even if it was the sick, ailing integrity of a mildly sociopathic narcissist. He thought of his great-grandmother Daisy in his last moment, how she might actually be proud of him, that he wasn't just her elite playboy idiot great-grandson after all. *Take that, Daisy.*

And with that thought, he handed the key to Ned. He could see Ned was baffled, that he needed instruction, but words failed Hector, unable to make it past the blood flooding his esophagus. Finally, with a great heave, he emptied his throat and croaked weakly, "...hoover... spotted... approaching habitable ring... alive... coming... give this to him... he'll know..."

Ned slapped him. "Stay with me, Morgan! What do you mean, Hoover's alive? They're alive?"

Hector nodded, and wheezed, and died.

Ned pocketed the key, frantic now with this new knowledge: *his friends were alive!* And maybe they could fix this mess! He'd have to get Tasty moving immedia- and then he remembered, and swung around, hovering on his knees over Tasty's robotic enclosure. "Oh no. Tasty! No, no, no. What do I do for you? Are you dead? Please don't be dead."

And he watched in amazement as the hole in Tasty's helmet shrank, as if tiny nanobots were repairing it molecule by molecule, and the hole disappeared, and his helmet filled again with yellowish liquid, and Ned sighed with relief when he heard Tasty's speaker: "What happened, Secret Service Agent Ned Weathers?"

"No time to explain. Gotta go." And he stood, lifting Tasty along with him, grabbing Hector's gun, shouting to the remaining Skywalkers to step aside, he had the prisoner under control, back off, he was taking the prisoner back down to the holding cell, step aside. Official business. Step aside.

And incredibly, it worked. In fact, as the reporters tried to follow them into City Hall, the Skywalkers held them back, still confused and leaderless, looking for anyone to tell them what to believe, what to do.

When they reached the elevators, Tasty remarked, "Will be happy to see the holding cell again. Very nice."

Ned pushed him inside. "We're not going down to the holding cells. We're going to Sunnyside. To save our friends. They're alive."

Tasty did a little jig. "An adventure? I can't wait! Tell me more, Secret Service Agent Ned Weathers!"

He pressed the top floor button, and in another stroke of luck it worked – apparently they hadn't revoked his thumbchip privileges. They shot up to the roof, scrambled into the nearest pod, and took off into the skies, toward the airlock and the shuttle bay.

When they arrived, the shuttle bay was swarming with police and Skywalkers.

"Shit. I don't think the *you're-my-prisoner* thing is going to work again. You got any tricks up your sleeve?"

Tasty thought about this for a moment, looking at his own mechanical arms. "Don't have sleeves."

"Ugh. I meant any diversion you can think of? So we can get to a shuttle?"

Another dramatic pause. "What if you were MY prisoner?"

And Ned smiled.

Walking confidently into the shuttle bay terminal, Tasty cranked his speaker up to eleven and shouted. "Attention humans. Secret Service Agent Ned Weathers will be expired by this weapon if you approach." With one arm he held Ned tight against his chest – even though Ned stood at least a half-meter taller than Tasty – and with the other he pointed the gun up to Ned's head. Tasty was enjoying this adventure immensely.

Police and Skywalkers circled the duo, afraid for Ned's life, their fellow human, this sick, twisted alien threatening his life. They kept their distance, and one shouted, "What do you want, creature?"

Tasty stopped, first to remark silently to himself that he liked the word *creature*, it had an interesting sound to it, *creature*. Then he spoke the lines he and Ned had quickly rehearsed in the pod. "I am afraid of humans. Will leave humanity forever. You are so so very strong and powerful! Scary powerful! All I demand is that leave you let me, never to return, safe for all time humanity will be, oh powerful humans, our kind again never to be heard from. Oh we quake at vision of your mighty power."

The authorities, such as they were, looked at each other, and it must have seemed reasonable, as several of them nodded. One said, "Fine. But leave the human."

Oh no. Tasty and Ned hadn't rehearsed this part. Why would Tasty need Ned to come with him if he was leaving forever? Ned sensed Tasty's paralysis, and blurted out the first thing that popped into his mind: "I'm ah, I'm going to, um, yes, I'm going to go with him on his alien shuttle cloud thing, to the main ship, and ah, make sure he has his coordinates set to somewhere very far away, and make sure he, ah, erases, yes, erases all records of visiting us. Then I'll take the cloud shuttle back here. Sounds good, right?"

The crowd of police and Skywalkers stared, trying to

process what they'd just heard. Ned saw their hesitance, and shouted, "FOR HUMANITY! I'M DOING THIS FOR US! FOR HUMANITY! I LOVE YOU GUYS!"

And they cheered him, Ned had guessed right, that they just needed a little push, and they parted, creating a path for the dangerous alien and his poor, poor captive human, straight to the alien's cloud-shaped shuttle.

Ned hadn't remembered how small their shuttle actually was, now that he was standing right next to it. It barely held Tasty and Skoop when they had first arrived. Ned was a big man. He wasn't going to fit.

Tasty pushed him along. "Get in."

Ned whispered back, sharply, "Get in? Look at me."

"Trust Tasty."

Ned sighed and grumbled, as he crouched to climb in the microscopic vessel, "So much for higher intelligence."

"Excuse me?"

"Nothing." And Ned curled up his knees and sat at one side, and sucked in his gut, praying that he wouldn't have relieve himself in the next half hour.

Tasty let the gun drop to the ground outside the shuttle, and hurried in next to Ned. Whoops. It was tight, just like Ned said. Extremely tight. Whoops.

The cloud closed around them, and within moments they were off, out the airlock, zooming into space.

Inside the cloud shuttle, Ned marveled that there were no windows, no control surfaces he could see, no obvious propulsion source. Just a single thin microfiber connecting the cloud wall directly into Tasty's helmet.

Tasty tilted this way and that, apparently controlling their direction and speed. "Systems working, Secret Service Agent Net Weathers. Will be on Sunnyside surface in nineteen of your human minutes. Wait. Detecting gaseous anomaly. Now running diagnostics to determine source and danger level."

He turned his helmet toward Ned, waiting.

"Okay, okay. I farted. You happy?"

"Yes, Secret Service Agent Ned Weathers. Only danger to yourself." And Tasty tilted, and the shuttle made a full barrel roll, and shot even faster down to the planet below. Tasty was having the time of his life.

33. WHAT A MESS.

n a darkened chamber of the Lusitania, a thumbchip was tapped, and Daisy Morgan turned off her security-modulated voice – she didn't need to hide anymore – and she began recording:

"What a mess.

"Oh, my dear people, what a mess.

"These aliens keep screwing with my plans. They simply won't die.

"And Hoover is still alive? How in hell did that happen? He's a nothing. A bug crushed underfoot. But perhaps more like a cockroach, that resists extermination even when you stomp on it with your boot.

"I've also lost at bit of control over the authorities, and those silly Skywalkers.

"Oh, and one last minor annoyance: I had to have my great-grandson Hector killed. My bloodline is finished.

"Boo-hoo. Whatever.

"If I'm being honest, I never really worried much about the bloodline thing. Who needs a line of heirs when you'll be alive to succeed all of them? They were all good foot soldiers. Useful idiots. But their time is over.

"And that brings us to today, my dear people.

"It's premature, *very* premature, but I have to come out of my cocoon early. For you, of course, for *your* sake. I haven't cracked the nut on true immortality, it hasn't yet left the realm of the theoretical, so I'm still a bit vulnerable. But... you're worth it. This is a time of crisis for humanity, with a real vacuum of order, a bit of anarchy going on, and aliens, aliens, aliens.

"Enough already.

"Your messiah has come. She withdrew as a caterpillar, four-hundred-some-odd years ago, young and naive, but a hero nonetheless, and as far as you know, she died – heroically, I might add – in childbirth of all things. But then, tomorrow, after her incompetent-but-loyal terraforming engineers have done away with Hoover and his band of misfits for good, she will make her grand entrance, as a butterfly, risen from the dead, not the Daisy you knew from ancient Earth, but the new Daisy, and hallelujah choruses will announce her arrival, and the sun will shine down and illuminate her gown, and it will hurt your eyes, the brightness of her, and you will bow down and genuflect, and sing praise to the One who has saved you once and for all from danger and death.

"Then I'll blow that goddamned alien ship out of the sky.

"And then you'll see, in terrified wonder, what I can do, and you'll learn once and for all:

"Don't fuck with the queen."

34. THE HABITABLE RING

Theo finally confirmed that he was in fact seeing a figure, no wait, *two figures*, like ants, across the limitless ice. At first he thought it was a mirage, for why would anyone be crazy enough to trek across the cold featureless landscape on purpose? Other than Shaggy of course, who was, in fact, crazy. Theo shook his head. Cleared the frost from his brow. Squinted. Yes, they were still there. He pointed. "Hey. Guys. Look."

And they all saw the two figures now, lit from behind by the ever-rising sun just beyond the horizon of Sunnyside. Theo thought he had never seen anything more beautiful, this permanent sunrise, with a line of puffy clouds at the habitable ring, and for the very first time, a word popped into his head, unbidden, that he had never associated with Sunnyside: *home*.

Now he saw low buildings in the distance as the sun, thirty degrees up from the horizon, peeked through those clouds as it would stay all day, and all the next day, and forever. Theo thought about the artificial day and night schedules on the orbiters, modeled after Earth's daily rotation on its axis. He would miss that, the fabricated circadian rhythms. It was familiar, and connected him to the past, and the home he never had but felt was his. And it helped the ancient earthlings survive the transition way back when the Great Orbiter Project was launched. But eventually day and night would no longer be needed. They would have to adapt to this ever-present sunlight.

Would they be able to? He was hopeful. It seemed to him that humans, and maybe even himself, were endlessly adaptable.

Wow. He caught himself thinking all these positive thoughts, and remarked silently that it was quite a change from three-weeks-ago Theo. He thought Vin would like that, and then looked around, half-expecting Vin to appear. But Vin was gone.

As the two figures got a bit larger on the horizon, Theo wanted to run to them, they all did, to run and shout, and jump up and down, for they were not going to die after all, but they were all so very cold and tired, more tired than they'd ever been, from trudging and shuffling and laboring and staggering and slogging and every other word for tortured walking that lasted an eternity. Even Skoop, whose reactor was fine, had never been through such an ordeal, and was exhausted. He was thankful, at least, he was among new friends, even if they hated each other at the moment, but he was drained, and desperately needed to see his own... *friend?* Is that what he should call the one they named Tasty? He had never called him that before, things weren't like that for his species, where your *other* is simply a literal extension of yourself. Individualism was an illusion, he knew that, knew it at the very core, but still... this thought excited him, this idea that he would soon reunite with a *friend*. What a wonderful word.

He didn't have a mouth, not in the human sense, but he smiled anyway.

They marched, onward, until the ice became bare ground, then small rows of crops like tomatoes and squash, then the concrete of the airfield. Theo grinned and announced, "Ahh... Everything's going to be all right."

Shaggy pointed ahead. "Hold that thought, Theo. Something is amiss."

The two figures were near enough now to see that they were engineers, with bright orange coveralls and hard hats. One man and one woman, both with hair down to their waists.

Kate couldn't help herself. "What's with all the hair on Sunnyside? Is it a thing?"

The woman engineer, the one holding the flamethrower, took her hard hat off and swung her hair back dramatically as they got closer. "You like it? I'm growing it out, but the split ends, ohmygod, and with the wind it's a wild untamable beast, sticks to my lip gloss. Honestly I'm not sure it's worth it. But what's your opinion?"

"Janey! Shush!" It was the other engineer, the man holding a baseball bat. "We're not supposed to talk friendly to them!" He swung his own hair semi-dramatically in protest. His hard hat fell off.

Janey pouted. "But... but Jimmy, it's been soooo long since we've met someone new, and they're... they're celebrities! Well, the guy and the robot alien are. I'm not sure who she is."

The other engineer hissed, "Janey, listen, why am I the

one that has to be serious? I don't want to do this either. You're so selfish."

"Whatever. Can't we just be a *little* friendly?"

"No! I mean whatever, I don't care. But they told us not to be. The bosswoman herself up on Lusitania said stuff about treason and jail time and executions and stuff. Don't you ever listen?"

Janey rolled her eyes. "Whatever. You're contemptible."

Kate pointed at her. "Wait. Did you just say contemptible? The word *contemptible?*"

"Uh, yeah. It's a word. I use it sometimes. What's your problem?"

"I don't know, it's just, I literally never hear that word... wait. Janey. *Jane.* Jane Ewald? From sixth grade? Westside Middle School? The spelling bee?"

Janey's eyes widened with recognition. "HOLD ON... YOU... you're... I know you... huh. Nope. Almost there, but not clicking."

Kate waved her arms at herself. "Kate! Kate Kingston!"

"OH MY GOD!" Janey dropped the flamethrower and leapt into her arms, wrapping her legs around Kate. "Ohmygod you look good! Your hair could be longer, but otherwise, wow. I am sooo happy right now! Hey Jimmy, look! I know her! Like *really* know her!"

Jimmy was not impressed. "Janey. Get down off her now. I'm not going to get upset. But you do this all the time. Try to get me upset. Listen, get down, we were told to put these nice folks in the cage until the bosswoman tells us what to do next." He turned to Theo. "Hey. A little help here?"

Theo actually laughed. "You want me to help you detain us? And put ourselves in whatever the cage is?"

Jimmy shrugged. "It was worth a shot." He dropped his baseball bat and picked up Janey's flamethrower. "We don't have weapons, you know, for obvious reasons, just terraforming, that's all we do, day in and day out. That there baseball bat's for, well, you know, baseball, and this here flamethrower is for clearing ice. So I know how it looks. Pretty lame. But they said, 'you burn 'em to a crisp if they don't cooperate,' so I'm sorry, mister celebrity, I'm gonna have to ask you nicely to cooperate or I have to burn you all to a crisp."

Oh, okay, this is actually kind of serious, Theo thought. He wasn't one for physical violence, and didn't think he could wrestle away a flamethrower from Jimmy without getting someone hurt. He was more of a negotiator.

"Jimmy. Hi. I'm Theo Hoover, Temporary Grand Oversee. If you'll just give me the flamethrower, and we can call Lusitania City Hall and clear all this up…"

Kate wasn't waiting for a negotiation. She grabbed Janey and pulled Shaggy's knife from her pocket, holding it across Janey's neck. "We are calling City Hall. Now. Or Janey here gets more than a haircut."

Janey wriggled, to no avail. "But… I know you!"

"Yeah. And you beat me at the spelling bee. I don't forget stuff like that, Jane Ewald. *You're* contemptible."

Janey began to cry, but through her tears admitted, "I'm so disappointed in you, but mad credit for holding a grudge that long. I'm impressed."

Jimmy was not crying. He was freaking out. "Hey! You Kingston woman! You let Janey go! Or I swear to God, I'm gonna have to fry your ass!"

The situation was spiraling fast now. Jimmy's finger put

pressure on the trigger, and a short lick of flame jumped out at them.

After all this, Theo thought, *we're going to die at the hands of Jimmy Longhair with a flamethrower. I knew my luck would run out.*

But then, as a second, longer lick of flame shot out of the flamethrower, threatening to reach Kate and her captive, something rose in Theo. A combination of feelings he'd never had:

Rage.

Courage.

Love.

"DON'T YOU TOUCH HER!" he screamed, and lunged at Jimmy, crossing the space between them in moments. He smacked the flamethrower down, hard, and in doing so pinned Jimmy's finger onto the trigger, releasing the full power of the weapon, and flames surrounded the two of them.

Theo, jacked with adrenalin, instead of feeling terror, welcomed the flames as a distraction, and – instinctively drawing on his thousands of hours playing *Suburban Curmudgeon* with Vin – roundhouse kicked Jimmy in the head, knocking him down. Theo's insulated tarp was on fire now, like a flaming cape, like the flaming cape of a superhero in a video game, so Theo tore it off, his shirt with it, and wrestled Jimmy into submission, pinning his arms behind his back, like one of the punks in the game. The flames subsided, leaving the two with minor burns. Theo shouted to Shaggy, "A little help over here!" And Shaggy ran over, stamping out the last bits of flaming fabric, and tied Jimmy to a post.

Theo, shirtless, burned, and sweating, rushed to Kate. "Are you okay?"

Kate let Janey go, and stood there, dumbfounded. "Was that... you? I mean, no offense, but... shirtless hunky Theo Hoover?"

Theo was trembling. "I have literally never done anything like that in my life."

And they stood there for a long moment, just looking at each other, until Theo mouthed the words *I'm sorry*.

Kate mouthed back the words *you better be*. And after a pregnant pause, *I'm sorry too*.

And they laughed, and Kate's eyes lit up, for the first time since Luna fell, this time with something she never expected to feel with Theo: desire. She wanted to touch him. On the lips. Now.

They stepped closer to each other.

Skoop, of course, ruined the moment. "Keep you two apart. Was my instruction. Please move back three steps at least Theo Hoover. Kate Kingston never talking to Theo Hoover again."

Kate sighed, patting Skoop on the shoulder. "It's over, Skoop." She took his robotic hand, and with her other hand reached out to Theo, who held it in his, and Theo completed the circle by grasping Skoop's.

Theo, feeling like a true Grand Oversee for the first time, beamed and announced:

"Friends. It's time to release the cat."

Janey wiped the last of her tears and pointed across the airfield. "Um, hate to ruin your little joy circle or whatever that is, but I think somebody made another call."

They turned in the direction of her finger, and saw dozens of engineers crossing toward them, with several flamethrowers, baseball bats, tire irons and the like.

Theo gulped. "Uh oh. Hey, Skoop. You have any miracles you've been holding back?"

'I am sorry, Theo Hoover. Miracle's don't exis-"

And at that exact moment, like a bolt of lightning, something shot down through the sky.

A cloud.

Looking up in awe, a profound silence came upon every engineer, Temporary Grand Oversee, Central Office Clerk, and astrobiologist, as it seemed God himself was intervening in the coming battle.

But it wasn't God.

It was, of course, Tasty and Skoop's cloud-shaped shuttle, lighting up the heavens, zooming to the ground, opening with a dramatic mist, and revealing...

"Ned?" Theo did a double-take.

Yes, it was Secret Service Agent Ned Weathers, extricating himself from the shuttle, with much effort, his middle-aged knees aching from the cramped confines of the little cloud.

As he unfolded and stood, slowly, the mist left a fine white powder on him, covering him completely.

He shouted, *"Put your weapons down!"*

And perhaps because he really did look like God, snow white from head to toe, taller than everyone there by at least a half-meter, the engineers dropped whatever makeshift weapons they held, and raised their hands in surrender.

Tasty exited the tiny shuttle behind Ned and patted him on the shoulder. "Well. That was easy."

And so Kate and Skoop and Tasty and Ned corralled the bewildered engineers into the supply cage and locked them in, while Shaggy tended to Theo's burns, wrapping them up in gauze and applying ointment, and giving him badly needed food and drink. Ned looked over at Theo, he needed to tell him they had to get back to the Lusitania pronto, that the shit was really hitting the fan there, and on all the orbiters, that Hector Morgan was dead, and that meant that something even more diabolical was going on behind the scenes, and that there was chaos everywhere.

But he stopped short, knowing Theo had just had the week of his life, enough danger and drama for a lifetime already, and he decided that the extra chaos could wait another hour or so. Theo was exhausted, and would need strength. He should rest. Ned turned to Tasty and whispered, "Listen, do me a favor and don't say anything about what's going on back home just yet. It can wait an hour."

Tasty nodded, and now that things had calmed down, addressed his fellow alien. He spoke to Skoop, not in the stilted language the humans heard, for they had no mouths or vocal chords, or even need for language, but by using their short-range telepathy:

It is good to see you again. Something is different. I can tell.

Skoop peered closely at Tasty. *I was going to say the same. You have a small metal object swishing around in your helmet.*

Tasty replied, *It's something called a bullet. Yes. Long story. But the thing I notice about you is not physical. It is deeper. Psychological. Philosophical.*

Skoop nodded. *You are very astute. I have experienced two profound things with the humans. The first: this thing they call funny. Wait until you experience funny! It does not make sense as a concept, but that makes it all the more enjoyable.*

Tasty asked, *And the second thing?*

The second thing is harder to explain, but at its core, extremely simple. You know how we are cleaved from the same source, all of our kind, sharing the same chromosomal structure, and therefore considered just one being in many forms?

Tasty telepathically nodded.

Skoop continued. *The humans do not see it this way. They are birthed differently, so have a strong sense of this thing called "self" which separates them from others. While this separation leads to alienation and isolation and conflict, it also draws them together, for safety, and shared experience, and something called love. For one another. It is sweet and warm.*

Tasty asked, *And what is the second thing called?*

Friendship. Skoop reached out his mechanical hand. *I know you are my other, but we have shared many experiences together, had many adventures, you and I. I would like to call you my friend. Will you be my friend?*

In answer, Tasty took his hand, leaned forward, and clinked Skoop's helmet with his own. *Yes. I would like that. Friend.*

Meanwhile, Kate was looking around, surveying their future home. "You know what this place needs, Hoover? Grass."

Theo chuckled. "Wow. Yes. And a In-N-Out Burger drive-thru."

"Oh my God yes. And cats. Lots of cats. Herds of migrating cats. Hey, remember your complaint? I mean proposal? The one about the cats?"

Theo nodded. "*Twenty-three Steps to Eliminate the Escalating Problem of Feral Feline Overpopulation. By Theo R. Hoover, member of the S.O.L. Concerned Citizens Committee.*"

Kate patted his back. "As genius as it was, you didn't foretell the possibility of aliens using all the feral cats to terraform Sunnyside. Losing your edge, Hoover. I expected more."

Theo smiled. "Shame on me. And it was so obvious. It was bound to happen. When we get back I'll add it as Step Twenty-four, after *Incineration*."

"You mean In*carc*eration."

"Oh. Right. Just wishful thinking, I guess."

And then suddenly, out of nowhere, she stopped, grabbing his arm, serious, whispering. "Theo? What do you think happens when we die?" She looked back at Skoop, tending to the sled with Luna and the cat.

Theo shrugged. "I don't know. Maybe ask Shaggy. He's got all the answers."

"No. I want to know what *you* think. I mean, we've both lost…"

"Okay. Yes. I've thought about it a lot. You sure you want to hear this?"

She looked up into his eyes. "I need to. I want to understand."

"Well, there was this turtle, swimming and turning, swimming and turning, see…"

She punched him in the shoulder. "No. Come on, I'm not kidding."

"Ouch. Okay. Until a few days ago, I thought we were just insignificant little specks of dust, utterly inconsequential to the universe, living our speck-of-dust lives as if they meant something, and then we simply ceased to exist. Poof. Oblivion. Our only existence after that would be memory, our historical existence, and even that, over time, would fade, and people's memories and even the digital records would eventually corrupt and disappear."

She whispered, "The second death."

"Exactly! How did you know that?"

"Come on. I've read all your masterworks, Theo. Including *Thirteen Steps to Ensure Proper Archiving of Digital Records. By Theo R. Hoover, member of the S.O.L. Concerned Citizens Committee.*" She nudged him with a finger. "So, what's changed *after* the past few days?"

Theo gazed up, into the blue and purple, cloud-filled sky. "Now? After the Skoops, and the crash, and Luna, and Shaggy? I still think we cease to exist, the body and brain anyway, but the memories? Now I don't believe they're these external things that evaporate... I think they're part of who we are in a real way. I don't know, somehow written into our DNA, and then our children's DNA, and their children's DNA and on and on. And I don't think it's just heredity. I think something like... let's say Luna... every moment you shared with her has been literally written into your brain, hardcoded in there, and the next person you share time with will inherit some of that, more hardcoding, some of that atomic or quantum memory or whatever it is, and in that very real way, Luna will live forever."

Kate put a finger to his lips. "Stop." And she leaned into his chest, sobbing, and he put his arms around her awkwardly, and then they relaxed into each other, their bodies rising and falling with the tears and the release.

After a while, Skoop finally spoke. "That was all very exciting."

They laughed, and Theo pointed to the sled, remembering. "Hey! Speaking of herds of migrating cats! Skoop, aren't we supposed to...?"

"Ah! Yes! Forgot! Whoops! Release the cat we will! Of

course! And start right this moment the process accelerated terraforming! Very wise you are, Theo Hoover, Temporary Grand Oversee!" He reached down and reverently brought the box directly to the center of their little huddle, and placed it on the ground.

Together with Tasty, they slid open the cover.

The cat was dead.

35. DEAD CAT JOKES

They were silent. Only the warm breeze made a sound. For a long time.

Kate broke the silence. "Listen, I know this is the worst possible timing, I mean, our terraforming dream is over, but a dead cat joke just popped into my head. You guys mind?"

Ned knelt down to take a closer look at the cat's body. It was the grayest gray he had ever seen, and its tongue was hanging out, almost comically. "Might as well."

Skoop raised his hand. "Yes. Very inappropriate, but tell us the funny joke, Kate Kingston. I would like Tasty to experience funny for the first time."

"Okay, what do you call a dead cat?" She waited a moment. "It doesn't matter what you call it. It's not coming."

Skoop gurgled a little. He looked to Tasty, and noticed the beginnings of a gurgle there, too. "Hurry! Tell another funny dead cat joke for Tasty, Kate Kingston."

"Sorry, Skoop, that's my entire inventory of dead cat jokes."

Finally shaking his head free from the shock of their profound failure, Theo spoke. "I have one. So Schrodinger's pod gets pulled over by the police, and they search the trunk. The officer says, 'Did you know you have a dead cat back there?' and Schrodinger says, 'Thanks, asshole, I do *now*.'"

Silence.

"I guess you have to know the whole Schrodinger's Cat thought experiment to get that one. See, it's about quantum mechanics, so the cat isn't dead or alive until it's observ-"

Skoop patted him on the back. "No further explanation. Not Funny. But good try. Secret Service Agent Ned Weathers?"

Ned cleared his throat. "Okay. Let me think.... Oh, here's one... Where does a cat go when it dies?... *Purrrgatory.* Get it? Cats purr. *Purrr... purrrgatory.*"

The joke was both so bad and so good that they all groaned, even Tasty, though he found himself gurgling in spite of himself, and couldn't stop. And that made Kate and Theo laugh, Skoop gurgle even more, and Ned joined in, and before long, they were all sitting on the ground, howling and gurgling like mad, looking at the symbol of their grand plan in ruins, a dead cat.

Once they'd calmed down, they sat in silence again, waiting for something miraculous to happen, though they each knew it wouldn't.

Theo poked the box. "Skoop and Tasty, did your engineers not anticipate this? It was designed for this planet, right?"

"Cat was designed and manufactured by us two locally on our vessel, designed for regular migration from light side to dark side, to facilitate heat transfer and ice melt. Not good, too much time on either side. She is like one of your human batteries, drained beyond ability to recharge. Photosynthetic fur is very much like plant life. Go too long without sunlight and heat as fuel means expiration. Like plant life."

Kate asked, "Can we get another one?"

Skoop shook his helmet. "I am sorry Kate Kingston. As stated, designed and manufactured locally by us. Much time, since we received your transmissions, have we been developing her. Many unique and likely unrepeatable conditions met. Many scarce resources gathered during journey of ours that cannot replicated. Many trials failed. She is our only success. Unique. Crafted. What you would call a 'work of art.' SkoopCat is a work of art. Our gift to humanity. One of a kind."

Damn. I was just starting to like this place, Theo thought. But now, he knew, beyond any doubt, that the terraforming of Sunnyside would continue to be a lost cause, and the aliens' microprobe sent to Earth would probably return with a big "NO" in its results, so that bet was off as well. So here they were, indeed stuck without a home, neither here nor there. Not in his lifetime anyway. Maybe in the distant future, after this whole disaster, maybe, just maybe, humanity will rise from the ashes of these experiences, like a phoenix, and make a home. A thousand years from now. Probably not.

Wait.

Phoenix... Rising from the ashes... Like plant life... Phoenix... Fire... Rising from the ashes...

Something was tickling his brain, a historical tidbit from the archives, something that couldn't be proven, a small, inconsequential item, he and his colleagues in History Repair would pick it up from time to time, to noodle with it, a little side project, see if they could find the Objective Truth, an inconsequential puzzle of sorts, they all wanted to believe it, hmmm, what was it…?

Yes. The Phoenix Plant. There were several entries in hacked scientific journals recounting a cycad plant that, after complete desiccation, when exposed to extreme light and heat – for example, a forest fire – would bloom. The chemical reaction of the fire would stimulate the core of the plant, like an intense burst of photosynthesis, reviving it. And it would bloom from the ashes. He had even seen photos, beautiful photos, of the floor of a forest after a fire, covered in ash, with little yellow blossoms pushing through everywhere. But there weren't enough data points to ever confirm its truth. It was one of those things – and Theo hated to admit it – that you simply had to believe on faith.

Suddenly he stood.

It was time for a leap of faith.

He wasn't going to make humanity wait a thousand years.

He was going to make change *right now*.

He reached for a flamethrower and threw the tank over his shoulder.

Kate scrambled to her feet and approached him. "Um, Theo. Are you aware that you just picked up a flamethrower?"

Theo nodded. "Kate. Everyone. Stand back. A lot." He aimed the tip of the flamethrower directly at the cat.

Skoop and Tasty politely raised their robotic hands and said together for emphasis, "Theo Hoover, this scenario never tested. Not impossible, but facts predict following outcome: dead cat becomes charred dead cat."

And for the very first time in his life, Theo said, "Screw the facts."

And with the faith of an insane man at the end of his rope, without a home, he pulled the trigger.

A stream of flame engulfed the cat. He squeezed the trigger harder, until the light and heat coming from the cat was nearly unbearable. They all had to step back further.

Theo held the trigger for one second, two seconds, three, five, a thousand, forever. He wouldn't stop. He thought for a moment how absurd it was that the defining moment of his life was throwing fire on a dead cat. He laughed, and shed a tear.

Suddenly a hand touched his forearm. "Theo. It's over." It was Kate.

Utterly spent, Theo dropped the flamethrower. They all stood there, resigned. Before them lay a large, vaguely cat-shaped pile of ash.

It truly was over. The hope of terraforming Sunnyside had just literally gone up in flames.

So would begin the first day of the next thousand years. Or never.

But then.

Something.

Something moved.

The ash pile stirred.

And in the next moment *the cat bounded from the ash.*

Ned fell to his knees, astonished. "Holy shit!"

None of them could believe their eyes.

But there it was, right in front of them, real: the cat, shaking its fur of the rest of the ash, and casually sauntering up to Shaggy, purring.

Kate laughed. "He likes you."

And Shaggy picked up the cat, and held it above his head, like something from the ancient Earth movie *The Lion King*, and they marveled at its fur, glowing, in infinite different colors, like the teeny ends of fiber optic threads, the colors moving in mesmerizing patterns. Shaggy, in a reverent tone, christened the cat. "Henceforth, you shall be known as Phoenix." And the cat purred its approval. And in that moment Shaggy had another prophetic vision: he with a wooden staff in hand, shepherding herds of these magnificent beasts, year upon year, until their numbers were abundant, and the planet flourished under them, and the humans came and lived and flourished too, and one day far in the future a small child looked up at a bronze statue near the airfield and asked her father, "Who's that?" and her father said, "The Shepherd of Sunnyside." He liked this vision, so much so that he repeated the last line aloud. "And I, friends, will do my part as Shaggy, the Shepherd of Sunnyside."

Skoop reached out and patted Theo's shoulder. "Congratulations. That certainly better worked than we thought it would." And Tasty added, "You are a brave human. Or insane. Not sure which word more appropriate would be in this scenario."

Kate took Theo's hand. "He's insane." Then she looked up at him. "But in a good way. I'm glad *the guy* got his shot."

Theo grinned. "You don't mean got shot?"

"Nah. You're growing on me. Like grass."

They all now joined hands, their faces beaming with wide smiles, even Skoop and Tasty if they had faces, for hope had sprung from death, and they wouldn't have to wait a thousand years or more, they could start today, and see the flowering of Sunnyside within their own lifetimes. They began to shout, no words, just shouts into the void like cavemen might have shouted when they discovered fire. And they danced to some primal music in their heads, for joy and for the future, and to welcome themselves to their new home.

36. THE KEY

After Ned had briefed Theo and the others about the developments on the orbiters and the urgency to get back, and Theo had a private moment to freak out and wish again to be anything *other* than Temporary Grand Oversee, Kate asked them all to stay near the supply cage, and she walked over to the sled Skoop had been pulling, and knelt down alone beside it. She removed the cloth that had been covering Luna's face.

"Luna Foster. I know you'd want me to be real, so I'm just going to say it: you're dead. You know it. I know it. I just got crazy back there, I don't know, the thought of ever being without you honestly never crossed my mind. Even after I retired, I kind of assumed, though I'd never asked you, that you would retire too, and come with me to Oyster Cove, and we'd be like two drinking buddies, taking the boat out fishing every morning and throwing back Tsingtaos by the fire on the beach at night."

She stroked Luna's hair and chuckled a little. "Hey, you remember that time we took a field trip to Fukushima, I think it was to review some land tax issue or whatever, and we took a second day for fishing, put our poles in the river, and didn't catch a single thing? Then we spotted a gaggle of people over at the mansion across the shore, and we rowed that old decrepit dinghy over and snuck in to the most over-the-top wedding we'd ever seen. God, I don't think I've ever had such a good time, dancing to ancient Earth disco and getting completely obliterated, until they found out we were crashers and kicked us out, and we could barely find our way back to the boat in the dark, and the next day the bay constable found us downstream on some rocks, laughing and throwing up into the river. Holy cow, Luna, that was a humdinger."

She waited for Luna to respond, knowing that the sound of the sand getting kicked up around them would be the only answer. "Well, anyway, for a second, you'll love this, for a second I thought about engulfing you in flames with that flamethrower too, like maybe it'd bring you back like it brought the cat back..." and now she was full-on crying, but forcing herself to see this through. "...but we both know that's not how it works with us regular humans, only super-phoenix cats, fucking super-phoenix cats, Luna, of course it's cats, isn't that a kick in the crotch..." She rose, and patted Luna's cheek, and laid a tomato on her chest. "Sorry, they don't have any flowers for some stupid reason, a tomato is the best I can do. Anyway, goodbye Luna Foster. You were my best friend. I really did love you – *do* love you. I'll always love you." And she replaced the cloth, and stood there for a long time, remembering, the wind twisting into little tornadoes around her.

.   .   .

Eventually, she returned to the others, and tugged Shaggy's ragged sleeve. "Hey. Bury her somewhere nice and plant a tree there, I think she liked weeping willows, and make sure nobody eats the dirt near her, okay?"

"No cannibalism!" Skoop shouted, and Kate laughed despite her grief.

"Yeah, no cannibalism, okay Shaggy?"

Shaggy smiled a sad little smile and nodded, and escorted the group down the airfield to the nearest shuttle.

Theo smiled confidently. "Okay, who knows how to fly this thing?"

They all looked to each other. No one. Shaggy shrugged. "Oh."

So Kate marched back to the supply cage, yelling. "Hey! Ewald! Any chance you know how to fly a shuttle?"

Janey nodded meekly. "I mean, it's like one button, so yeah."

"Okay, as Chief of Staff to the Temporary Grand Oversee, you're officially pardoned. Let's go. Now!"

Janey jumped up, wrestling her hair away from the parts container it was stuck in, and rushed to join them, giddy to get off this rock for a while. "So that means I'm forgiven too, right? For the *contemptible* thing? And for potentially killing you with a flamethrower? Good. Anyway, we've got like so much to catch up on. Do you remember that kid Mark Capi-"

Kate put her hand up. "Less talk. More fly."

Janey instinctively saluted her, and skulked in silence to the rest of the group.

Next to the shuttle, Janey noticed the little cloud. "Hey! Can I fly that one?"

Agent Ned looked down at her petite frame. "Be my guest. At least you'll fit."

"No," Theo said, "We'll all take this shuttle, the regular human shuttle, with Jane Ewald flying, and Tasty and Skoop will take their cloud shuttle. Let's move out."

As they ascended the shuttle's ramp, Theo motioned Shaggy over close, and whispered, "Before we leave you, there is something I'm still wrestling with... The cat returned to life. But Luna did not return. And you returned to life, in a way, after many years of a quest. But Vin... well, I don't know... so who gets to return? And who has to move on?"

Shaggy rested both hands on Theo's shoulders. "Theo Hoover, my friend, I have a story..."

"Oh, jeez. I wasn't asking for a full story."

Shaggy raised his eyebrows, and Theo sighed. "Okay, I guess I walked into that one."

"Yes you did. Anyway, way back on ancient Earth, there were turtles called leatherbacks – yes, another turtle story, you'll have to bear with it – and each year, these leatherbacks would return to the beach of their birth to mate and dig nests in the sand and lay eggs. And on the same exact day, all the eggs would hatch, and hundreds of thousands of tiny turtles would make like hell for the ocean. And many of them would make it, and return to the sea, and many of them would not make it, and be devoured by predators or burn up in the sun or simply run out of steam. But the ones that made it and *moved on* would *return* the following year, and continue the cycle. Moving on. Returning. Moving on. Returning." He paused to let his point linger in the air, as usual. "Do you see?"

"So... returning is a form of moving on... and moving on is a form of returning...?"

"Bingo. Chew on that for a while." And he patted Theo on the knee, and said his goodbyes to everyone, and walked down the ramp with Phoenix the cat strutting by his side, off to become Shaggy the Shepherd of Sunnyside for the remainder of his days.

And Theo, satisfied, looked around for Vin to share this little nugget, but knew he had moved on. Or returned. And now it was Theo's turn.

The shuttle lifted off, banking and nearly crashing into the control tower before heading for the Lusitania. Janey blushed. "Whoops. It's been a while." Then she pointed to the big button labeled AUTOPILOT and said, "See, Kate?" And Kate rolled her eyes, and Janey pressed the big button and they zoomed upward toward the Lusitania.

Ned felt something in his pocket. "Oh, jeez. Theo. Memory's not the best. With everything going on, I totally forgot to give you this." He handed Theo the strange key. "Hector Morgan told me to give you this. Sorry about the blood."

Theo wiped the red smears off. "How did Hector Morgan get his hands on the Bastille Key?"

"The what?"

"The Bastille Key. The Bastille was the state prison in France, until it was raided in 1789OT, starting the French Revolution. The key became a symbol of tyranny and oppression of the Bourbon monarchy. This is it. The exact key."

Ned scratched his head. "How could you possibly know that?"

"History repair, Ned."

"Whoops. Right. Anyway, Morgan said you'd know what to do with it."

"I have absolutely no idea what to do with it." He turned it around in his palm. Could it possibly be the original? No. It had to be a replica. But why? Did it open something special? A prison? Was there a revolution going on and he was the key? Was Hector Morgan trying to tell him something about tyranny and oppression? Was he warning Theo? All of the above? None of the above?

"Wait." Something tickled the memory banks in Theo's brain. "Hmmm. It's extremely obscure, not fact, we couldn't verify it at the office, it's just a legend..."

Ned and Janey and Kate all leaned in. This was getting juicy.

Theo continued, "...the legend goes that many made copies of the key, for their own corrupt purposes, but none were ever successful. Because the *shape* of the key wasn't the secret, but the *way it was used*." He demonstrated in the air with the key as he spoke, the others rapt. "First, you insert the key, like this, turning it clockwise, then counterclockwise. Then you take the key out... *turn it around*... and insert the *head* of the key, like this, into the keyhole and turn it again clockwise and counterclockwi-"

And as he said it, the key vibrated.

He instinctively let it go, afraid it might blow up, or kill them, but it simply floated there, in gravity-free space, vibrating.

Then... it projected an image.

Of Hector Morgan. A tiny hologram of Hector Morgan.

And it played this message:

"Congratulations. Hector Morgan here. Insurance recording. I am not sure what I'm going to do. I'm conflicted, to put it lightly. On the one hand, it's family. I have a job to do. For loyalty to the family. On the other hand, *are you fucking kidding me?* But in any case, if this winds up in someone else's hands, things have likely gone sideways. Oh, and forgive the obvious *Star Wars*/Obi Wan/R2D2 reference, but... *'you're our only hope.'*" He laughed to himself. "I'm a clever one, aren't I? Well, you're not here for my blatherings are you? If you've figured out how the key works, you're here for this..."

And as the recording continued, Theo's eyes widened, as did Ned's and Kate's. A wave of shock ran through them all.

Janey whispered, "O-M-G..."

37. THE CORONATION

This is going to be good.

Just the coronation I deserve. I love a nighttime crowning.

Daisy Morgan twirled in the mirror once more, admiring her billowing white gown, with its three-meter-long train, then strode into the shuttle bay, thousands of eyes on her, surrounded by guards and police and Skywalkers, all in awe, bowing to her, most still unable to fathom that this ghost, this hero from the distant past, had returned from the grave, to lead them all to safety. Many shed zealous tears.

She loved that part the most. The zealous tears. Bring 'em on.

"Have you prepared my throne?"

She admitted to herself that an actual throne was a bit much. But how often is a hero who saved humanity four hundred years ago brought back from the dead, to save humanity – again? *Never!* Yes, she deserved this. Deserved it very much, thank you.

The throne had been built, hastily but with cult-like care,

perfect down to the tufted velvet fabric and real brass accents. It sat atop a ten-step platform, two meters high, to ensure that Daisy could look down – far down – on her people, the people she saved, the people she loved. She loved them so much, she even had a little surprise planned.

She climbed up to the throne now, each step met with fanatical cheers. The sound was deafening.

The best kind of deafening.

She couldn't contain her smile, she had promised herself she'd portray seriousness and solemnity, but damn, this moment had been a long time coming, and it was better than sex.

It was so good, she didn't even mind the damned cats pawing at her gown's train.

Waving down the cacophony of her adoring mob, Daisy Morgan spoke softly into her microphone, as the television networks watched their ratings skyrocket. "Ahem. Can I just cut to the chase and say I love you?"

The crowd went wild.

"Now, I'm sure you've all seen the news. Yes, I did not in fact die. Death will never take me, but that's another story for another day." Her voice rose as the adrenalin hit. "Today I am back, for I could sleep in the shadows no longer, knowing that my people were in danger. I rose from my slumber – *for you!*"

The assembly grew into a fevered chanting. "DAI-SY! DAI-SY! DAI-SY!"

She hushed them again. "Now, now. Listen to your great-grandmother. I am back to comfort you. I am back to care for you. I am back to protect you. And I am back to prepare the path. For the future of man rests in my – I mean *our* – hands!"

"DAI-SY! DAI-SY! DAI-SY!"

She put on her stern face now, forcing the giddy grin back down, come on Daisy, get serious, and she shouted, "Now... the main event!"

They all watched as two tiny objects, blinking lights against the darkness, approached the shuttle bay. A shuttle and a tiny cloud. Both descended into the airlock. The outer set of airlock doors closed behind them, the chamber filled with breathable air, and the inner set of doors opened slowly.

Emerging warily, Theo and his group, and the two aliens, slowly approached the gathering, and looked up at the woman in the gown. It was a surreal scene.

Daisy called down calmly, "Oh, there you are. You're probably wondering why I let you land safely. It's not because I'm compassionate, though I'm *supremely* compassionate, as all my people of the orbiters can attest. No, it's because I wanted you, and everyone, from all corners, to see... *this. SURPRISE!*"

And she waved her arms and pointed to the alien's ship floating far off in the nighttime sky, her hands poised like a wizard about to cast a spell or throw a bolt of lightning. All eyes were fixed on the ship.

There was a flash, a flash so bright it blinded, becoming daytime for a blistering moment, and the ground shook. No human alive now had ever seen or felt a nuclear device detonate.

Daisy Morgan shouted into the microphone, "WITNESS MY POWER AND TREMBLE, FOR I AM THE DESTROYER!"

But when the eyes of the assembly had adjusted again, and the debris cloud dissipated, and the darkness returned, the alien ship remained. Unscathed. The crowd hushed, and if one really listened, they could hear a small gasp from Daisy Morgan.

Skoop raised his hand to speak (he was always very polite), and turned up his speaker. "Pacifists we are. That you have correctly assumed. But idiots we are not. It's called a shield."

Tasty stepped forward and added, "Do what you must do. Peace we bring, that is all. Like you, we prepare the path."

Daisy was unimpressed. "Whatever." She looked to one side, then the other, at her cowed minions. "Take them to the penitentiary. For treason. All of them!"

And some of the Skywalkers, and the police, and the mysterious men in suits, advanced on Theo and his friends.

But Theo knew something they didn't. Theo knew he had a weapon much more powerful than a gun, or a posse of underlings, or even a nuclear device.

He had the truth.

Retrieving the Bastille Key replica from his pocket, he thrust his hand in the air, turning and twisting the key in its arcane pattern. In the space above, for all to see, appeared a hologram of Daisy Morgan. And the hologram said, "I've killed many in my long years. I killed Piper Montgomery. I killed a whole banquet hall of government officials. I killed Theo Hoover. I killed the first alien. Now I need you to kill the other one. In front of everyone."

The silence that fell now was absolute. Not even a single meow from the cats who had stopped to listen. Every soul there turned to Daisy Morgan, in unison, confused, looking for an explanation.

She looked down at them all. "Well. It's a fake, obviously. Misinformation. History is riddled with it. That's all." She peered around. "What are you staring at, you fools? Get them!"

But no one moved. Something had happened to the trance. A crack had formed.

So Daisy hiked up her gown, and began running down the steps of her queen's dais. "Fine. I'll do it myself!" But on the third step, her shoe landed in a fresh wad of gum, and she tripped, and tumbled down the final seven steps to the ground, breaking her right collarbone and left ankle.

Crying out in pain, pain she hadn't felt in over four hundred years, pain she had forgotten, a thought, unbidden, entered her mind:

I am mortal after all.

"No!" She screamed, at the top of her lungs, pushing that horrid thought away, and rose slowly. Almost fainting, she somehow remained standing, and limped to Theo, groaning in agony. "You!" She spat at him. "A cog in the machine. No, you're less. You're *nothing!*"

And she raised her good arm, preparing to strike him.

In that small moment, Theo felt many things: *Fear*, at her crazed clinging to power; *rage*, at all the things she'd done, and the people she'd killed, and the purposeful delaying of the terraforming of Sunnyside; *sadness*, for humanity being this frail; *pity*, for the broken woman he saw before him, succumbing so completely to her delusions; *doubt*, for they had come so far these past days, but was it enough?

However, in that smallest of moments, he also had a practical thought: is it okay to hit a woman? Under the circumstances? I mean, she's clearly unhinged and dangerous, and if she were a man he wouldn't hesitate...

Kate had been having all the same thoughts, and knew that Theo was a good man – no, not good, a *great* man, now –

and that he would pause in a moment like this, wanting to do the right thing. He was always trying to do the right thing.

So when Daisy Morgan's hand came down hard to strike Theo, Kate didn't pause – her hand rose to grab Morgan's wrist.

"Sorry, Daisy. He's not nothing. He's everything. He's all of us. He's the *best* of us."

And it did't take much effort, just a little pull to Daisy's left side, to put all her weight on that broken ankle, and Daisy Morgan crumbled and fell, trying to wriggle her arm free from Kate's grip, cursing. "You fucking imbeciles! Ignorant rubes! You wouldn't know a savior if she punched you in the nose! I gave you everything, you ungrateful fucks! Now let go of me! Restrain these criminals! Do it now! I command you!"

No one moved. It was clear now to Theo's eyes: the spell had been broken. He saw eyes fluttering, as if waking from sleep, looking around, each trying to understand how they got to be standing here, cheering for a complete maniac.

Theo stepped into that moment. He looked into the eyes of one of the bewildered Skywalkers. "You. It's over. Take her, gently, to City Hall, down to a holding cell. Ned, go with him."

And so he watched Secret Service Agent Ned Weathers, his protector and now friend, lead Daisy Morgan away, putting his sunglasses back on. In the middle of the night.

To the rest of the crowd, Theo spoke. "I won't say much, but I will say this: *without* Daisy Morgan's intentional delay of the terraforming efforts, and *with* the help of our two new friends Skoop and Tasty, and their amazing cat, we have calculated that the terraforming will be sufficiently complete in fifteen years. In fifteen years, we can move to our new home."

For the crowd assembled, it had been a day. It began with

the celebration of a risen savior, the shock of a nuclear explosion, then a brutal betrayal, and now the promise of *home*, within their lifetimes. Many fell to their knees, and hugged and kissed each other, crying, utterly exhausted.

Someone in the back shouted, "*You* are our savior!"

And Theo shook his head. "No. No, I'm not your savior." He looked at Kate. "We are each other's saviors. We will be having an election in forty days, and you will choose your own saviors." He smiled and shook the hands of several people approaching him. "Now, I'd invite you to all go back to your homes, and give thanks to all who've come before us, all they've sacrificed to get us here, and sleep tight, morning is almost here. For tomorrow, we prepare the path!"

There was a cheer now, an exhausted cheer, the release of all the anxiety and fear and rage of the past days, and in a semi-orderly fashion, the throngs of people left the shuttle bay and went home, with cats walking beside them, purring their approval.

Theo and Kate plopped down on the first step of the ridiculous throne platform.

Kate grinned. "I know we're tired. But..." she looked up, "can we take turns?"

So Theo and Kate and Skoop and Tasty, and even Janey, took turns bounding up the ten steps and sitting on the throne, dramatically acting as kingly and queenly as possible. Even Skoop and Tasty learned to pretend they were royalty. The laughs and the gurgling filled the bay with joy.

Suddenly, a red light flashed on Skoop's chest. He looked down and said, "Oh."

Theo ran to him. "Oh my God. Skoop! Are you okay? We can't have another crisis today! Are you dying?"

A small gurgle from Skoop's helmet. "No, no. I am fine, friend." He looked up to see Kate and Janey sharing the throne high above, laughing, out of earshot. But just in case, he lowered his speaker to its lowest whisper. "Mister Theo Hoover – our microprobe has just returned. *From Earth*. We have the results-"

Theo held up his hand. For at that moment, the sun had begun to rise over the silhouette of Sunnyside, filling the shuttle bay with sunlight and warmth, and turning the surface of the planet into an inviting crescent of light. And he looked close, and he could see little clouds on the habitable ring, and he imagined that ring growing wider and wider and wider, soon enough, sooner than they had dared dream, and he imagined Shaggy down there, leading his cats, and he imagined laying on the grass down there, looking up at the permanent sunrise, and wondering with Kate what the shapes of the clouds reminded them of. He smiled, wider than he had in a long time, and said:

"No, Skoop. I don't want to know. Because we're already home."

Skoop didn't tell him the results, but if he could have winked, he would have. He said simply, "You are a wise man." He rose, and with Tasty, called to Janey, and the three of them headed in the direction of the Office and Residence of the Grand Oversee.

Now just Theo and Kate in the vast space, she wearily descended the steps one last time, stood in front of Theo, and took his hands. "Well. You ready to call it a night? Or morning?"

Theo looked off into the rising sun. "There's still one thing left to do."

38. GOODBYE

The limo-pod zoomed through the morning light, and landed gently on the roof of the CryoCrypt warehouse.

"Well. This is it." Theo tried to sound calm, but his heart was pounding out of his chest. Kate saw this, and took his hand. "If you don't want to…"

"Don't tempt me." He reached for the door. "Let's do this before I change my mind."

Helpfully, Ned had called ahead – a wild, cursing Daisy Morgan on the minicomm with him – so a staff member was waiting for them. "Grand Oversee. Miss Kingston. Here's your access key. It's on the eighth floor below ground."

As they descended in the glass elevator, Theo admitted, "I've never been here," and he realized now that the secrecy of CryoCrypt was part of its draw. The fact that you weren't ever allowed here somehow added to the idea that doctors and researchers and experts were working feverishly behind the scenes, helping people come back from the edge of death, and in the meantime you could keep your loved one in your mind, imagining them however you want, rather than seeing them in a casket with a window, frozen and gray.

Thousands and thousands of cryocapsules whizzed by as they dropped to the eighth floor. *All these people,* Theo thought. *It's like a boneyard.*

The elevator slowed to a stop, and the doors opened. They walked on an elevated pathway toward a single door. "Don't look down," Kate suggested, after taking a peek through the iron grating, down god-knows how many more stories. It was endless.

Finally, they reached the door. "We're here." Hand shaking, he inserted the card into the blinking slot, and the door slid open. They entered.

Inside, there was no furniture, no desks or chairs, only a small podium at the far end of the small room.

At the podium, the screen showed three buttons: *Retrieve From Assigned Bay*, *Return to Assigned Bay*, and *Goodbye*. He pressed *Retrieve From Assigned Bay*. The screen prompted him to insert the access card.

Bleep.

Immediately, in the warehouse beyond, a hanging articulated robot arm went to work, speeding down the rows, out of sight. An endless minute later, it returned, carrying a cryocapsule. It pushed the capsule through a small opening in the room's wall, as a stand rose from the floor to support it.

Theo looked at the label on the side.

Capsule number 903b87t.

Vin.

He ran his hand across the small window framing Vin's face. It was cold, with a thin sheen of frost.

Vin looked like hell.

Theo turned back to Kate, searching. "Maybe... isn't there some small, infinitesimal hope? Isn't there always?"

Kate put her hand on his shoulder. "Yes. For the living. It's time to let go."

Tears began to run down Theo's cheeks. "I don't... I can't... let go. It's so hard. This is all that's left of him."

Kate smiled a knowing smile. "A wise man once told me that every encounter is hardwired into us. That our memories are real things, passed on for eternity. That we live forever. That there's way more to Vin than this. That Vin will live forever."

And Theo knew she was right, and knew what he had to do, he knew that he was keeping Vin in this prison between life and death, but his heart screamed *NO!* He hesitated.

"I'm sending him back."

He turned and hovered his finger over the second button: *Return to Assigned Stasis Bay.*

Kate whispered, "You know I want to lunge and stop you from doing that. And you know that I won't. Because I know that you love your brother, and you're struggling like crazy right now. But I also know that Vin would want to go. To move on. And you're ready to move on too, whether you realize it or not. Vin has already said his last goodbye, hasn't he?"

And Theo looked around, searching, hoping, desperate, for one last grin or smart-ass remark, or one last word of encouragement, or one last hug. But the only Vin here was the one frozen in the capsule.

The one that was ready to go home.

Theo could hardly see through his tears now, and leaned over the small window. "Vin. Are you ready?" There was no answer, of course, and Theo cried harder. "Vin, I'm sorry. I tried. And I know if you were awake, you'd say not to be sorry, you know I tried, I tried like hell, but we're done carrying each other now, and you're ready for the next thing, and just shut the hell up already and press the button." He kissed the frosty window, and looked for the last time at his brother.

"Goodbye, Vincent Hoover. I wish you could've seen Sunnyside. The sun is always rising."

He retreated back to the podium, and tapped the third option: *Goodbye.*

The display was filled with a message:

Are you sure you want to cancel your CryoCrypt subscription?

Theo winced and tapped *Yes.*

Nothing happened. Then the display actually spoke: *"Your loved one will be thawed, cremated, and shot into interstellar space. Are you sure you want to do this to them?"*

Theo wiped his tears. *"Dammit."* And he pressed *Yes* again.

"TODAY ONLY! Five years for the price of two! Would you like to take advantage of this exclusive offer?"

"Oh for God's sake!" He jabbed at the *No Thanks* button, over and over, until all the special offers were exhausted, and the capsule finally retreated and disappeared, and there was silence.

Theo wept.

And Kate reached out to him, and for the first time, opened completely, like a flower, like those little yellow blossoms from the ashes of a fire, spreading her arms out wide and embracing him. She was warm, and Theo couldn't remember how long it had been since he'd felt this warm. And then he did remember: sitting on the bed in Vin's bedroom, in their early teens, playing *Suburban Curmudgeon* together for endless hours, the light of Sunnyside's sun streaming through their window, how it warmed him all over and made him feel invincible, like nothing could stop him, as if the warmth was life itself, pouring into him. And he looked over, and instead of seeing Vin's face, he now saw Kate's. He smiled.

It was over.

He was home.

39. HELLO

The punks were back. With reinforcements.

But that was okay. Because the Old Man had a new friend: The Guy Next Door. They shared a driveway, they both had mint 1984 Buick Regals, and both their lawns were impeccably kept: green and lush, cut to just the right height, with the curbs perfectly edged. And they were ready to defend their turf.

They had agreed, upon seeing the marauding teens approach from the shadows, not to use guns. For now they knew death was not the answer. (And also, hand-to-hand combat was much more fun.)

The Guy Next Door, tense, fidgeting, looked to the Old Man. The Old Man only sneered. "Not yet. We're peaceful folk. We don't attack. We defend. We wait."

They didn't have to wait long. Bad Haircut strode directly up to them, smoking his reefer cigarette like the punk he was, his fellow punks ready to rumble behind him. "Hello. Who's the new chump?"

The Old Man laughed. "The Guy Next Door. Interesting backstory, if you want to stick around to hear it, Smiley."

Bad Haircut didn't wait for the backstory. He lunged at The Guy Next Door, and the two tangled, wrestling to the ground. The Old Man watched, not because he was afraid, or sadistic, but to gauge The Guy Next Door's skills. He was impressed. The Guy Next Door jammed his first knuckle into Bad Haircut's throat, causing him to freeze, allowing The Guy Next Door to scramble to his feet. An elbow strike to the ear followed by a roundhouse kick to the back completed the job. Bad Haircut, barely able to breathe, croaked, "Get 'em!"

The Old Man and The Guy Next Door grinned at each other and stood back-to-back. All those classes at the CobraKai Karate dojo up at the strip mall in downtown Ridgewood New Jersey would pay off tonight.

With quick, efficient strikes, they punched, kicked, blocked, and swept the legs of the eight suburban lowlifes who had nothing better to do on a summer Tuesday evening than terrorize two helpless old suburbanites. *Shame!*

The neighbors began to congregate.

The beating continued, until, accidentally, the Old Man let his confidence get the best of him, and left his friend momentarily to enjoy a side battle with Punk Number Seven. The punks saw this vulnerability and immediately took advantage, leading the two old codgers further and further apart.

Incredibly, even more punks emerged from the darkness. The Old Man and The Guy Next Door were pummeled with punches and kicks themselves, blood spurting from their mouths, teeth being knocked out. Finally, Bad Haircut, back on his feet, placed his knee on the Old Man's shin, ready to break it in two, and his hand on The Guy Next Door's neck, ready to crush his larynx. The two men looked desperately at each other, for they feared this truly was game over.

But a sound emerged from the darkness and everyone froze.

It was like the sound of a thousand vacuum cleaners.

And with it came a vision, running down the street at full speed, housecoat flapping in her wake: The Lady At The End of The Block. In a blur of fists and feet and housecoat and hair curlers, she dispatched each punk, threw them into a pile, and berated them for their poor behavior.

"You go home now, bad boys!"

And somehow, against all logic, they did. They stood, shamed, licking their wounds, and skulked one by one off back toward the train underpass and the QuickMart dumpster.

And The Lady At The End of The Block picked up the Old Man and The Guy Next Door, and patted the grass off their robes. "Well just look at you two."

"I said, well just look at you two!"

Theo swiped off his VR helmet, laughing, and Skoop detached the helmet mod he had rigged to play *Suburban Curmudgeon* with his new friend. The liquid in his faceplate was gurgling like crazy. "Very good at this game you are!"

Pearl pulled her own VR helmet off, tossing it onto the couch. "Stupid game." But she grinned at the two of them, these children, maybe even a bit like her own children, and she winked. "Now, pick up your feet, I have to vacuum there."

Bzzzzzzz. Bzzzzzzzz. Bzzzzzzzzzzz.

Pearl rolled her eyes, the damned vacuuming would never get done at this rate, and answered the door. Kate bounded in, shooing away five cats in the hallway, and closed the door. She looked at the game console, then to Theo and Skoop, and tutted.

"Theo. Come on. You have to get ready. The shuttle for Oyster Cove is boarding in four hours, and freaking security, you know." She turned to Pearl. "And yes Pearl, I did remember the ring, and yes, I picked it out and took care of the whole thing myself, because as genius as your boy Theo over there is, he's still got a lot to learn about the whole engagement process." She popped open a Tsingtao and gulped. "Oh, and you, Skoop. Shouldn't you be getting your lazy, game-playing ass back to your own galaxy?"

Skoop gurgled, and whispered through his speaker, "Sorry, Kate Kingston." He got off the couch – finally – and looked down at Theo. "Goodbye friend. Perhaps see each other again."

Theo said, "Of course," but they both knew that Skoop and Tasty were nomadic folk, and wouldn't be around this corner of the galaxy any time soon. They were needed in some other desperate situation, to help with the unfolding. He rose and escorted Skoop through the kitchen to the front door of the flat. On the way, he snuck a sip of Kate's beer. "Hey, you know what would go good with this?"

Kate protested. "No. No. We don't have time. No."

But it was too late. Theo had already opened the fridge, and taken out the cheese, and they all sat around the little kitchen table for a while, laughing, and eating cheese, and drinking beer.

Skoop raised his beer in a toast. "Here is to Theo and

Kate, good friends, on Theo's election to post of Grand Oversee."

Theo groaned. Yes, somehow the people of the orbiters, the last of humanity, the little bud that was waiting to grow again, had elected him Grand Oversee, only reinforcing in his mind that most people didn't know what was good for them. Then he smiled, thinking maybe he was wrong, maybe the people were smart and right, because by electing him, they got what they *really* needed: Kate Kingston, the kick-ass, take-no-prisoners Chief of Staff. Or maybe they were just a great team, and that was obvious enough to any random orbiter-dweller. In any case, he reached out and tapped her bottle. "Here's to one term."

Kate clinked with enthusiasm. She wasn't going to lose her down payment after all. They were finally going to visit the flat on the beach that she'd only seen in pictures. They were both absolutely certain that in four short years, they were going to disappear from the landscape, never to be heard from again, and enjoy their life together, to the end of their days. Let someone else take the reigns for a while.

Theo's minicomm buzzed. He sighed. "Hello?"

"I need more cats!"

It was Shaggy. His little hologram looked as ragged as ever. Though he had achieved notoriety now, and a bump in income, he didn't spend any on new clothing. "Theo, look. I know you can only fit so many on a shuttle, but it's mating season, and-"

Theo interrupted. "Wait. They have a mating season?"

"Well, it's always mating season, of course, can't keep 'em off each other, the herds are growing like crazy, like a sea full of turtles. Have I told you-"

"No. I have to go, Shaggy. I'll see if we can schedule some extra cat delivery shuttles. Goodbye."

Secret Service Agent Ned Weathers barged through the front door next, followed by Tasty. "Kate. You told me to wait on the roof. It's getting late. I mean, Tasty could sit in the limo-pod for a thousand years, but I can't. Kate. Theo. Let's go."

And so they wrapped up their impromptu picnic.

On the way out the door, Ned turned to Theo. "Oh. Always forgetting stuff. Forgot to tell you. As soon as you get back, big meeting. They want to get a jump on it before it's too late."

"Who?"

"The re-election committee."

Theo turned white as a sheet. "Oh no..."

But Kate was there in an instant, reaching up, kissing him, reassuring. And she didn't even have to say the words, because Theo knew that everything was going to be all right.

YOU'VE FINISHED.

PLEASE REVIEW THIS BOOK!

One of the best ways for independent authors and small publishers to get exposure for their books is to receive as many honest, thoughtful reviews as possible.

It's simple: go to **rob.cm/sun** for links to this book's page on Amazon, Audible, Goodreads, Barnes & Noble, and more.

You can also include that URL or tag the author in your social media posts. His tags are:
Twitter/X: @robdircks
Instagram: @rob.dircks
TikTok: @robdircks
Facebook: @robdircksauthor

Oh, and if you're ever curious why it took me five plus years to finish this novel, email me from the contact page at **robdircks.com** and I'll tell you the long and winding tale.

Sincerely, thank you for reading, I hope you enjoyed this crazy story, and thank you in advance for your review.

– Rob

GOLDFINCH PUBLISHING

ALSO BY ROB DIRCKS

WHERE THE HELL IS TESLA?

The #8 Audible Bestseller!

SCI-FI ODYSSEY. COMEDY. LOVE STORY. AND OF COURSE... NIKOLA TESLA. I'll let Chip, the main character tell you more: "I found the journal at work. Well, I don't know if you'd call it work, but that's where I found it. It's the lost journal of Nikola Tesla, one of the greatest inventors and visionaries ever. Before he died in 1943, he kept a notebook filled with spectacular claims and outrageous plans. One of these plans was for an "Interdimensional Transfer Apparatus" – that allowed someone (in this case me and my friend Pete) to travel to other versions of the infinite possibilities around us. Crazy, right? But that's just where the crazy starts."

"Hilarious time-travel odyssey" -- *Kirkus Reviews Magazine, June 2017*

"★★★★★ Without a doubt the funniest and craziest syfy adventure I've ever read... I made the mistake of reading this book in public and was laughing like a crazied mad man with tears in my eyes. NO BS. I had people glaring at me and hiding their children like I was some kind of lunatic. Great book. I can't wait to read more from Rob Dircks."

"★★★★★ LOVED IT! I loved this book! Hysterical, interesting, cool, just awesome. I flew through it in a few days and laughed the whole way through. I love sci-fi, I love humor and this is the perfect mix of both. Loved!!"

"★★★★★ We need more Bobo! Where The Hell Is Tesla? is one of the funniest books I've read in quite some time."

"★★★★★ Best comedy sci fi in a decade... a fun and hilarious romp through the multiverse with a group of very likable characters, witty and addictive writing."

"★★★★★ Rob Dircks' narrative style and his characters' surprising wit are a breath of fresh air for a genre that I have a great deal of love for but is all too often hit or miss."

"★★★★★ By far the most amusing, funniest and laugh-out-loud audiobook I have ever listened to!"

ALSO BY ROB DIRCKS

DON'T TOUCH THE BLUE STUFF! (WHERE THE HELL IS TESLA? BOOK TWO)

The sequel to Where the Hell is Tesla? is HERE!

SOMETHING CALLED THE "BLUE JUICE" IS COMING. FOR ALL OF US. Luckily, me (Chip Collins), Pete, Nikola Tesla, Bobo, and FBI Agent Gina Phillips are here to kick its ass, and send it back to last Tuesday. Maybe. Or maybe we'll fail, and everyone in the multiverse is doomed. (Seriously, you might want to get that underground bunker ready.) Either way, I've got to get home to Julie and find out... woah, I'm not about to tell you that right here in the book description! TMI.

WARNING: If you haven't read *Where the Hell is Tesla?*, I apologize in advance, as you might get completely freaking lost. If you do, just call my apartment, I'm usually around, and I'll fill you in. (If I'm not stuck in the ITA.) – Chip

"★★★★★ **An amusing and unexpectedly crazy ride** - a perfect and hilarious follow-up to *Where the Hell is Tesla?*" - *AudiobookReviewer.com*

"★★★★★ **An incredible, madcap adventure that only Dircks could deliver.** The "Tesla" books are living proof that original stories are still out there waiting to be discovered."

"★★★★★ **I love this series!** It gets better and better. Love wins! If you haven't read *Where the Hell is a Tesla?*, you must. You'll love both. I promise. Thank you Mr. Dircks!"

"★★★★★ **So damn funny and insanely entertaining!** Loved the first one and this was just as fun."

"★★★★★ **You never know with sequels... Fortunately, you don't have to worry about this one.** Dircks' second in the *Tesla* series delivers every bit as well as the first - in the same balls-to-the-wall writing style that made the first book so entertaining."

"★★★★★ There isn't another writer like Rob Dircks in the entire multiverse."

"★★★★★ **The CHIP MASTER IS BACK.** My second favorite of all audiobooks I've ever listened to... only because *Where the Hell is Tesla?* is number one."

GIGI MAKE PARADOX (WHERE THE HELL IS TESLA? BOOK 3)

The Audible Bestselling trilogy comes to a close! (Or does it?)

Listen, having kids is great, my little Gigi Collins and Pete's daughter Hannah are sweet little fluffs of cotton candy, spun from the silk of fairy spiders who live in the clouds. But MAN, can they cause trouble. Seriously, you'd think a two-year-old couldn't possibly threaten the very existence of our physical reality, but, well, you know where this is going.

So join me and Pete, and Bobo, and of course the man himself, Nikola Tesla, on another spine-tingling, bowel-loosening thrill ride, and remember: bring your adult diapers.

WARNING: If you haven't read Where the Hell is Tesla? and Don't Touch the Blue Stuff! (Where the Hell is Tesla? Book 2), I apologize in advance, as you might get completely freaking lost. If you do, just call my apartment, if I'm not watching Gigi I'll try to pick up the phone, and I'll fill you in. (Assuming our physical reality still exists.) – Chip

"★ ★ ★ ★ ★ Head into the ITA for one last grand adventure! "Gigi Make Paradox" writen and read by Rob Dircks is the third and final installment in the 'Where The Hell Is Tesla' Trilogy. I stumbled upon this series by accident as a daily deal on Audible, and I'm so glad I did. The first 2 books were amazing, and the 3rd lives up and perhaps even passes its predecessors. Right from the get go I'm pulled back into the world by Chip Collins and we are ready to go on another adventure in the ITA. For this final installment the author pulled out all the stops, the stakes are much higher (multiverse time ending high) , the action amazing (pow bang smash), the comedy brought me to tears with laughter, and the character development was perfect and brought me to tears for a whole different reason (Im not crying. You're crying). Rob Dircks trilogy (and his other books) prove there are still original ideas out there that make life wonderful and full of delicious possibilities. The only bad thing about this book is that it is the end, no more ITA and no more amazing cast of unforgettable characters. I hope you give this tale a chance and enjoy it as much as I did. I leave you with the books motto and true words to live by dude, "Sh**'s Crazy. Don't ask."

"★ ★ ★ ★ ★ Lovable characters & bizarre worlds woven together with a fast-paced, natural voice. What a friggin' blast! I couldn't put down this epic final installation in Rob Dircks' Tesla trilogy. Hilarious and endearing, it starts with a fart joke and ends with a poop joke—and takes the reader through an extraordinary adventure in between. Lovable characters and bizarre worlds are woven together with a fast-paced, natural voice that goes down smoooooth. This book in particular (and this series in general) deserve a permanent spot on the shelf of outrageously fun, thoughtful science fiction."

"★ ★ ★ ★ ★ What a great Trilogy! I'm actually kind of sad that the trilogy ended. I'm certainly going to miss Chip, Pete, Nikola, the kids, Julie, Meg, Gina and of course Bobo! They actually read way too fast and I found myself laughing on almost every single page. It was a fabulous series and a must-read in my opinion!"

"★ ★ ★ ★ ★ Absolutely brilliant book. Just as entertaining as the other 2 parts. I was laughing and crying reading the book. Great job Rob!

YOU'RE GOING TO MARS!

The #1 Audible Bestseller!

Living and slaving in Fill City One, you get used to the smell. We call it the Everpresent Stink. But every once in a while, on a spring day with a breeze, it clears away enough to remind us that there is something more out there. Most Fillers' wildest dreams would be just to get past the walls and live in the mainland. But my dream? It's a little bigger.

I'm going to Mars.

Well, I'm only going to Mars if I can find a winning Red Scarab to get on Zach Larson's crazy reality show. And then I'll have to figure out how to escape this hellhole. And then compete on live television for three months. And somehow win a spot on the crew of the very first manned mission to Mars. Oh, and one more slight obstacle? There might be a reason that by 2085 a human still hasn't set foot on the Red Planet. A dangerous reason. A reason worth killing for.

———

In *You're Going to Mars!* Rob Dircks, Audible best-selling author of *Where the Hell Is Tesla?*, creates a near-future filled with family (the good kind and the insufferable kind), pop divas, mobsters, and the world's first trillionaire - and sends them all on a science fiction odyssey/comedy/love story/adventure that will change their world forever.

———

"★★★★★ Reviewers' Choice Award – it's THAT good. Captivating, interesting and creative. I could not put it down. I would love to see it filmed!" — *AudioBookReviewer.com*

"★★★★★ One of my favorites of the year! This book was a pure joy to listen to. One fist-bump moment after another. I enjoyed every minute of it." — *DabOfDarkness Book Reviews*

"★★★★★ A remarkable book. *You're Going to Mars!* was one of the most interesting, entertaining stories I've listened to in quite a while. A fabulously written book with a unique plot, endearing characters, and a richly crafted world, You're Going to Mars is one of those books I just didn't want to put down until I finished it." — *BriansBookBlog.com*

"★ ★ ★ ★ ★ **Mr. Dircks once again hits a home run!** I have been a fan of Mr. Dircks' works from his premiere release... you cannot go wrong giving this book a listen if you like science fiction and great writing." — *Quella Book Reviews*

"★ ★ ★ ★ ★ **Fun, Fast-Moving, and Genuinely Funny Sci-Fi.** This audiobook was a blast! A comedic sci-fi take on the Charlie and the Chocolate Factory story with a female protagonist. Even though *Ready Player One* was similarly-themed, this book is about as different as you can get, and in many ways a better book." — *Wynne McLaughlin, Author of* The Bone Feud

"★ ★ ★ ★ ★ **Hits it out of the park again!** Dircks' unflagging ability to imbue plot-crackling science fiction with a deep vein of humor, heart, and hope reminds me of Ray Bradbury with curses. An incredibly inventive plot of a young woman's journey in a world both similar and very different from ours. Wow, just wow." — *Wendy Mass,* New York Times *bestselling author of* Pi in the Sky *and* The Candymakers

ALSO BY ROB DIRCKS

THE WRONG UNIT: A NOVEL

I DON'T KNOW WHAT THE HUMANS ARE SO CRANKY ABOUT. Their enclosures are large, they ingest over a thousand calories per day, and they're allowed to mate. Plus, they have me: an Autonomous Servile Unit, housed in a mobile/bipedal chassis. I do my job well: keep the humans healthy and happy.

"Hey you."

Heyoo. That's my name, I suppose. It's easier for the humans to remember than 413s98-itr8. I guess I've gotten used to it.

———

Rob Dircks, bestselling author of *Where the Hell is Tesla?*, has a "unit" with a problem: how to deliver his package, out in the middle of nowhere, with nothing to guide him. Oh, and with the fate of humanity hanging in the balance. It's a science fiction tale of technology gone haywire, unlikely heroes, and the nature of humanity. (Woah. That last part sounds deep. Don't worry, it's not.).

———

"Rob Dircks manages to bridge the tricky divide between science-fiction and humor so effortlessly that a comparison to Vonnegut is not a hyperbolic stretch." - *Ruth Sinanian, Literature Reviewer*

"★★★★★ **The Wrong Unit is the right story for today...** it reacquaints us with our human ingenuity and shortcomings, our deepest longings, and, most notably, our great capacity to love."

"★★★★★ **FUNNY. HUMAN. A GREAT RIDE!** The Wrong Unit is a fun and twist-turning journey that keeps you on the edge of your seat."

"★★★★★ **I'm such a fan of this book** that I'm going to recommend it for next month's Book Club pick!"

"★★★★★ **OUTSTANDING!!** With The Wrong Unit, Rob Dircks has established himself with this potentially prophetic view into humanity's future and the consequences of our growing reliability on and appetite for technology."

"★ ★ ★ ★ ★ **The Wrong Unit is such a great ride!!** The pace is fast, the dialogue is smart and sarcastic and witty. The sci-fi world created by Dircks is new, imaginative, and so original. No easy feat! I loved the main characters Heyoo and Wah. Laugh out loud funny and sure, I'll admit, I got a little weepy at some spots. Highly recommended!"

ALSO BY ROB DIRCKS

LISTEN TO THE SIGNAL: SHORT STORIES VOLUME 1

Like episodes of *The Twilight Zone* or *The Outer Limits*, the sixteen stories contained in *Listen To The Signal, Short Stories Volume 1* ask questions like, "What would happen if an iPhone game was addictive - to everyone?" and "Are we all living inside a simulation? And if so, who's running it?" and "When a pilot has to emergency land in a remote town near Area 51 what does he find?"

Hi, Rob Dircks here. I'm the Audible bestselling author of *Where the Hell is Tesla?*, and I've been writing and narrating these stories since 2016 on my podcast, *Listen To The Signal*. But now I've made them available ONLY here in this book. They include: Dakō • Today I Invented Time Travel • End Game • November 8, 2016 • Quick Fix • Horatio Breathed His Last • Purgatory • Out of the Blue • Tick Tick Tick • Rose • Red Parka • Bloop • Their DNA Was No Longer the Same • The Last One • Mister Personality • Christmas in Silver Peak.

"★ ★ ★ ★ ★ There is no one writing scifi as well as Rob Dircks right now, and this short story collection proves it.

I listened to all of these stories when they originally came out on his podcast, and was blown away every time by the quality of his writing and his mastery of the short story form. He knows the tropes and how to subvert them. He can build a world in a few paragraphs so that you understand it intuitively. He creates characters that are uniquely relatable and gosh darn it, he's funny to boot.

That is when he is not making me tear up. Add to all that the fact that he does a terrific job narrating his own stories and you have a very appealing package.

But now that I have been able to re-listen to all the stories again via this collection, hearing them all together rather than strung out over a series of months, I perceived something I had not noticed before. Something that unites not only these stories but also his novels. Something special that only Rob Dircks can deliver.

It's a sweetness, a love of life and humanity, that shines through all of his characters and all of his imaginary worlds. I feel instantly better when I finish something he has written, I feel uplifted and hopeful. What a wonderful gift Rob has to allow us to see the good in one another, and how lucky we are that he is sharing it with us through his art.

Can't wait for the next collection."

ABOUT THE AUTHOR

Rob Dircks is the #1 Audible bestselling author and narrator of *You're Going to Mars!*, the *Where the Hell is Tesla?* trilogy, *The Wrong Unit*, and more (including the anti-self-help book *Unleash the Sloth! 75 Ways to Reach Your Maximum Potential By Doing Less*). He's also got a drawerful short stories, some of which appear on his original audio sci-fi short story podcast *Listen To The Signal*, (which he also narrates).

He's a member of SFWA (Science Fiction & Fantasy Writers of America), and a big fan of classic science fiction. When not writing, he's helping other authors publish their own work with Goldfinch Publishing, writing and designing for the award-winning ad agency he owns with his brother (aptly titled Dircks Associates). He lives in New York with his wife and two kids.

facebook.com/robdircksauthor

x.com/RobDircks

instagram.com/Rob.Dircks

goodreads.com/robdircks

amazon.com/author/robdircks